To God, who constantly shields and protects me from all manner of harm. Thanks for the 'God Winks', too.

To my wife, Sandy, who provides a constant source of love, affection, friendship and honesty which I've cherished for thirty-two years.

To my father, Jerry, who earned a Combat Infantryman Badge and Bronze star while serving as an infantry lieutenant during the Korean War. Looking back on his life now, I believe he struggled with PTSD for thirty years after that war before he died of cancer in 1982.

To the twenty-plus veterans suffering with wounds of war who commit suicide each day.

FOREWORD

I first met Kelly Galvin back in 1980. At that time, he was introduced to me as Sgt. Galvin, one of three outstanding noncommissioned officers who would be working with me at my new unit. Almost forty years later I am honored Kelly remains a close friend and brother in arms. I am even more honored he asked me to write this foreword.

Our connection started when we learned we both served in Germany during the conclusion of the Vietnam War, and shared the same training grounds in Grafenwoehr. He served there as an infantry private, and I served as a Chemical Corps lieutenant who later branch transferred to Medical Service Corps. With limited field grade positions in the Chemical Corps, I transitioned from the motto of "Bugs and gas, up your ass!" to "Care with Compassion."

It was my honor to have served the country twenty-five years in uniform until retirement in 1998 from the Western Regional Medical Command, and the I Corps Surgeon's Office, Fort Lewis, Washington. After military retirement I served a four-year stint as a fisheries biologist for Washington State, and subsequently as a general manager for water and wastewater utilities in both Washington and California an additional sixteen years. In these forty-five years of public service, every job was in a leadership position. I have been fortunate to work with some great leaders, and others who never got it.

The Army has always been the model for integration and diversity. Soldiers come from all walks of life, and every corner of the country. The ability to coalesce individuals from different backgrounds, customs, cultures, and skills into a unified team that accomplishes the mission requires quality leadership. The effective leader exhibits exemplary values, always doing the right thing even when nobody is looking. Kelly Galvin is that leader.

Duty, honor, and country are easier said than done. One doesn't have to look past the current political landscape to experience polarized words and dishonorable actions. Narcissism trumps country, and honor is forgotten in the age of reality television and social media dysfunction. Even "friendship" is defined by social media. Relationships are often superficial, built on a persona created by their authors with little regard to truth. Capt. Kelly Galvin transcends these societal norms. Strong values and ethics are not just traits; they are who Kelly is.

Imagine being retired from the military for thirteen years, enjoying life with family and friends, only to be told your country needs you to return to service. A selfless leader answers the call to serve the country.

Kelly tells the gripping tale of Capt. Jerome, a fictional character who returns to duty from retirement as Kelly did.

During the late 1990s under the Clinton administration, the number of soldiers in the Army was reduced by half. Peace through strength was realized during the Reagan administration, but was this lesson lost in later administrations? If his skills were in such short supply, requiring Capt. Jerome to return out of retirement, why did the Army assign him outside his specialties? Or was military staffing so depleted, any warm body that didn't require training funds would do?

Downsizing of the military has contributed to the use of joint services working together. Joint operations provide many benefits and efficiencies. Redundant support positions are eliminated, reducing personnel and associated expenses. Learning to work with all the services provides a deeper comprehension of the big picture. Joint operations provide opportunities to leverage all branches of the military to bring decisive action at strategic levels.

But like my professor taught me at the University of Delaware in quoting Barry Commoner's fourth law of ecology, "There is no such thing as a free lunch."

Capt. Jerome goes from peaceful life in an Arizona woodshop to working a stressful Joint Operations Center (JOC) in a war zone with Gen Xers and Millennials. The working conditions are tough everywhere in the military, but preparing briefings in Iraq about the details of fallen heroes day in and out requires attentive leadership to prevent further stress casualties. Individuals from multiple services thrown into a meat grinder operations center do not have the luxury of training together, getting to know each other, and finding common ground in a way the military excels at as a melting pot. Leaders responsible for the product of JOCs have little opportunity to overcome the challenges faced. Perhaps more hands to share the work and frequent changeout of personnel dealing with the ugly parts of war is not a bad strategy. Post-traumatic stress disorder and suicide of returning soldiers is real, and understanding our invincible soldiers can be vulnerable and in need of professional help is an underlying theme in *PowerPoint Ranger: My Iraq War Logs.*

Another theme is the military's increasing difficulty in controlling classified material. Technology allows near-instant communication of important battlefield details. But this too falls prey to the "no free lunch" law. Julian Assange and Wikileaks are in the news, and striking parallels in *PowerPoint Ranger* could explain how breaches in security could occur due to casual attitudes and failure to do the right thing, even when nobody is looking.

No matter if you are a PowerPoint Ranger or working in everyday life at a private business, this book provides valuable lessons. Water district board members fight for hours over which lawnmower to buy to save money, yet they spend scant minutes approving a $3 million reservoir. They dwell on what they know, rather than the difficult issues that need their attention. Capt. Jerome's JOC was no different. Rather than work to solve the challenging issues, leadership nitpicked the font color of a single period that wasn't black.

Team building and caring leadership builds professionalism and prevents the dysfunction commonly found in committees absent an effective chain of command. Reading *PowerPoint Ranger: My Iraq War Logs* provides valuable insight into this and many other rewarding lessons.

Lt. Col. "Marc" Marcantonio, USA, Retired

AUTHOR'S NOTE

The foundation of this book rests on my experience with being recalled to active duty by the Army at age fifty-two after thirteen years of retirement. I overcame the difficulties of age, weight, physical fitness and knowledge deficit to be recalled and deployed. I describe the "retiree recall" and training process, but I focus on illustrating the deployment challenges of arriving, living, serving and departing the combat zone at Camp Victory in Baghdad, Iraq.

Military acronyms, slang terms, and abbreviations are described in the text or defined in a footnote on the page where it's first used. At the end of the book you will also find a full glossary of all these terms. Where possible, I try to describe or explain the unique term within the text without resorting to a footnote, but this is not always possible in dialogue. You will see this in the next paragraph for the acronyms, MNC-I, JOC, SIGACT, and EOD.

The book highlights the job of a PowerPoint Ranger[1] serving in the Al Faw Palace, Multi-National Corps – Iraq (MNC-I), Joint Operations Center (JOC). PowerPoint Rangers worked tirelessly during twelve-hour shifts to create classified presentations from the raw, battlefield in-the-shit reports known as SIGACTs (significant activity reports), along with forensic photos and reports from responding explosive ordnance disposal (EOD) units.

The JOC acted as the eyes and ears of the commanding general

---

1   PowerPoint Ranger: A person whose sole duty is to create graphic presentations and briefing slides using the Microsoft PowerPoint program.

in Iraq. It functioned as a chokepoint through which everything that happened in Iraq flowed. PowerPoint Rangers sifted through myriad SIGACT reports and other data coming into the JOC to find the important nuggets of information that provided the most accurate situational awareness (SA) of operations. Operational planners outside the JOC used this work product to guide their work.

The book exposes the stressful and emotional environment inside the JOC, where immersion is required in the never-ending quagmire of SIGACTs detailing horrific battlefield attacks and the inhumanity of war. Every assassination, suicide bombing, improvised explosive device (IED) attack, Coalition Forces KIA, and rocket and mortar firing that occurred ended up as a SIGACT funneled to the JOC for review.

Imagine toiling for several days reviewing and learning in great detail how a suicide bomber in a vehicle attacked a convoy and how, tragically, five US soldiers died, and then standing at attention during those same soldiers' fallen hero salutes to learn how they *had lived* before the attack. If you can imagine binge-watching the scariest horror movies available on Netflix, but knowing *this* horror was all real, you'll begin to appreciate the difficulty of working the JOC for twelve hours a day, seven days a week.

I weave the JOC story into the background fabric of foibles, idiosyncrasies, and challenges of Army life in general, but specifically the difficulties associated with deploying overseas and living in a combat zone inside the wire. The book also merges the background plot with the thriving military-industrial complex of well-paid government contractors where "the business of war" is a business enterprise.

This is a book of fiction based on those experiences, incidents and situations—with fictional characters, names and duty positions.

Anyone who has ever served in the military will have war stories to tell. Some tales may be true, but many begin with a little bit of truth and then morph into mere fantasies, which get more elaborate with each telling. This storytelling sometimes helps to pass the time with others while sitting in a Humvee,[2] a Rhino bus,[3] or the back of an MRAP[4] while waiting for a move order, LD[5] time, or the convoy start time. It's very similar to how a fisherman, lawyer, politician, or some other fancy liar will tell you a story.

I would like to think this is generally not true for combat veteran war stories—if you can coax them into telling them. Theirs are the truer stories because they have no reason to embellish. It's just the facts—the way it was—my own personal after-action report (AAR) tales offered up as a testament to train someone or to learn lessons, things to not repeat, or things to do *this way!*

However, to the uninitiated, there is a simple way to tell the difference between a fairytale and a true and accurate war story. A fairytale usually starts out with the words "Once upon a time," whereas a combat veteran with an honest to goodness war story will say with a wink, "Now this is no bullshit!"

---

2   HUMVEE: High Mobility Multipurpose Wheeled Vehicle or Humvee (pronounced "Hum Vee")
3   Rhino Bus: An armored bus for transportation to the Green Zone (The most common name for the International Zone of Baghdad.)
4   MRAP: Mine-Resistant Ambush Protected vehicle (pronounced "Em Rap")
5   LD: Line of Departure is a point on the battlefield where forces cross/leave friendly lines into a possible line of contact with the enemy (pronounced "El Dee").

CHAPTER 1

Fat, Dumb and Happy

Early April 2008

"Honey," my wife, Sara, called as I entered the house after another grueling but productive day at the woodshop. "A Major Pendleton at Human Resources Command St. Louis called for you while you were gone. He said he'd call back, but left his number."

Human Resources Command (HRC) St. Louis, formerly known as Army Reserve-Personnel Command (AR-PERSCOM), managed all records for the Individual Ready Reserve (IRR), the Standby Reserve and the Retired Reserve—emphasis on *Reserve*.

"You're kidding," I blurted out incredulously. I had no clue of the reason for such a call and wanted to ignore it. "What the heck is HRC calling me about?" I said to Sara.

"He didn't tell me. He said he had to talk to you first," she responded with some annoyance. "Call him," she added with a hint of command.

"No, thank you," I abruptly replied. "I guess they'll call back if it's important."

I joined the Army in 1975 at the age of eighteen, and cut my teeth serving as an infantryman in Germany to help deter the infamous

Warsaw Pact nations from crossing the Iron Curtain. I honed my fieldcraft skills with the 46th Infantry Regiment in the 2nd Brigade of 1st Armored Division for three "asshole-deep in snow" Bavarian winters. I later taught those infantry skills of map reading, terrain association, land navigation and patrolling as an instructor at the 9th Division and Fort Lewis NCO Academy, and in my other units.

Being born under the sign of Gemini, the *Remus* side of me had a love for the medical field. Consequently, I became a 91B combat medic, but halfway through my military career I graduated Officer Candidate School (OCS) as the distinguished honor graduate. My *Romulus* side walked across that OCS stage, where I garnered myself a neat-looking saber, a loving cup trophy and appointment as a Signal Corp second lieutenant.

The Signal Corps suited my technical side, and I once again graduated at the top of my Officer Basic Course (OBC) and Officer Advanced Course (OAC) at Fort Gordon, Georgia as a company-grade[6] officer. I served the Signal Corps as an assistant operations officer in my home unit, where I helped plan and manage elaborate multichannel communications systems for a mechanized infantry division in the field. I held a security clearance commensurate with my position for managing frequencies, code books, encryption keys and equipment.

The path forward to being promoted to field-grade[7] officer involved graduating the Combined Arms Services and Staff School (CAS3), where I was enrolled in the initial, non-resident phase of the course. Later I was able to transfer from the Signal Corps branch to the Medical Service Corps (MSC), where I could be closer to my wife's career where she served as a captain in the Army Nurse Corps. I kept working on my CAS3 non-resident courses.

I attended California State University at Long Beach at night to

---

6   Company Grade: Army officer pay grades O-1 thru O-3 (second lieutenant thru captain.)

7   Field Grade: Army officer pay grades O-4 thru O-6 (major thru colonel)

work on a master's degree in health care administration. The degree would complement my MSC branch status, increase my eligibility for promotion, and provide needed credentials for a second, post-retirement career. It all seemed destined for success and longevity.

Unfortunately, the tide for continued military service began receding rapidly in late 1992 when the man who loathed the military, Bill Clinton, became president. It was the same year that the USSR became defunct. *Uh-oh! Military no longer needed.*

Upon taking office, Clinton seized upon this political opportunity to rein in the Defense Department by declaring a peace dividend. He then downsized US military forces as fast as he could manage. Suddenly my path forward to a lengthy MSC officer career became cloudy. My wife, Sara, and I decided to pull the plug on my military life, forgo the resident phase of CAS3, and retire when I finished my twenty years in late 1995. I was only thirty-nine and ready to take on a new mission.

We moved to Georgia, where my master's certificate in health care administration and background as an MSC officer landed me a job with the Georgia Department of Veterans Service. I served in one of the department's nursing homes for veterans, and using my old signal officer skills I took on additional responsibilities for information technology upgrades for client management.

The Georgia phase of life lasted about nine years; then we decided to downsize from the multi-level home we'd built on the lake. We both experienced creeping orthopedic issues hampered by the stairs in the house, but we also needed to escape the humidity and undercurrent of racial tension present in Georgia at the time. Both our daughters lived on the West Coast, so retiring to Arizona seemed like the right fit.

Between twenty years of running in the military and nine years of walking up and down stairs at both the nursing home and the lake home, I needed to get my hip fixed. A resurfacing procedure provided me with a new ball and socket as well as a pain-free life. Thank you, Tucson Orthopedic Institute!

I lived fat, dumb, and happy, volunteered at the Department of Veterans Affairs and my woodworking club, and played daily for four years in my Arizona community woodshop. I created items on the lathe by turning bowls, pens and peppermills from mesquite and other hardwoods. I once made a four-foot-long peppermill, which I sold to a local restaurant owner who displayed it until they retired too. Unfortunately, the woodshop would have to wait until I got back from Iraq.

So that is where I, Matt Jerome, Capt., US Army Retired, found myself in early 2008, when I got the call from HRC St. Louis asking me to be a retiree recall for the Global War on Terror.

CHAPTER 2

The Call

I hesitated to return Pendleton's call, not wanting to be shuffled around in a god-awful voice menu hell and back, but also because I suspected nothing good would come out of a call to Human Resources Command (HRC). I decided he could call me back, but the message had left me intrigued and a little vexed.

Why are they calling me?

I'd been receiving my retired pay each month with no issue for over thirteen years. I received 40 percent service-connected disability compensation from the VA for several maladies I obtained during military service, too.

After 9/11, while living and working in Georgia, I had volunteered to return to active duty but received a very polite "no thank you" from the secretary of the Army along with a computer-generated letter of appreciation for my "eagerness" to serve.

Sara had been finishing her career with the Georgia Army National Guard during 2001, and we both believed her duty demands might increase after the Twin Towers fell. The Guard relied on her and other Army nurses to serve extra weekends and a full week here and there, providing the medical processing portion of guard units under the Soldier Readiness Processing (SRP) mission. SRP ensured that soldiers and units would be ready in case of activation for war. It proved its worth when Operation Iraqi Freedom was launched in early 2003.

Perhaps HRC had reconsidered my offer? No way. I was too old, way too old. Fifty-two years way too old, and my knowledge, skills and abilities were thirteen years out of date. Not to mention I had gained about thirty pounds and had other health issues, too.

President Bush had announced the Iraq War Surge in January 2007, and it took another twelve months to achieve the force levels intended, with the majority sent into the Baghdad area. It was now April 2008 with 150,000 US forces in Iraq, but the jury was still out on the success of the surge. *Is that why HRC called me? No, it couldn't be!*

The phone rang early the next day. The caller ID read, *HRC St. Louis.*

"Hey, honey, HRC calling me back. Now we'll see what's going on," I remarked casually as I lifted the cordless phone from the cradle and pushed the talk button.

"Good morning. This is Major John Pendleton from Officer Records Branch at Human Resources Command, St. Louis. Is this Captain Matthew Jerome?"

"It is," I heartily chimed back. "What can I do for you this fine morning?" He sounded like a pleasant enough fellow, so far, so I thought I would be pleasant, too.

"Well, Captain Jerome, it's nice to talk with you finally. I had a brief but nice chat with your wife the other day, and I didn't spill the beans either. The Army needs your help." Pendleton let that sink in for a moment, then continued. "My mission for the next several months is to find and place retired Reserve officers identified as candidates for recall to active duty into appropriate assignments commensurate with their specialties, knowledge, abilities and grade. There's a SecDef[8] memo of March 2007 that gives us implementing guidance on the use of military retiree *volunteers*, paragraph four to be exact. Anyway, they thrust a WIAS[9] list of vacancies on me and told me to fill 'em up as fast as I can."

---

8   SecDef: Secretary of Defense
9   WIAS: Worldwide Individual Augmentee Systems (pronounced "Why As")

He took a breath, so I took the opportunity and jumped in. "Seriously, Sir? But what is WIAS?" I asked with a heavy dose of skepticism.

"Yes, really, Captain Jerome. WIAS stands for the Forces Command[10] system called Worldwide Individual Augmentee System. It's an Army *help wanted* list. Listen, Matthew. May I call you Matthew?" He waited for my response.

"Sure, sir, it's always a senior officer's prerogative, but call me Matt," I said while wondering why he was going *"personal."*

"Good," Maj. Pendleton continued. "Here's the thing, Matt. A little over a year ago in January 2007, the SecDef issued new principles for mobilization/demobilization of reserve component members under the 200K mobilization order which has been in effect since the 9/11 attacks. That January '07 memo facilitates the personnel surge in Iraq. The under secretary memo of March 2007 now makes it clear that we should *strongly support and encourage retiree volunteers.* Your name popped up on a list of retirees who had volunteered earlier for service after the 9/11 attacks. We didn't need you then, but now we do. The surge in Iraq is taking hold, but not without creating shortages in other places.

"Right now, we're looking for retiree volunteers to give us a hand. We can and do involuntarily activate IRR people, but we hope to find willing volunteers before that. We are only one step away from the authority to involuntarily activate retirees, also. We aren't there, yet, but it could happen. Will you consider volunteering your service. . . once again?"

Maj. Pendleton let that sink in.

"Maybe," I said.

He pushed on. "You would be recalled to active duty under the Department of Defense Mobilization authority for reserve components. The surge in Iraq, which President Bush authorized, is placing stress on the personnel needs of all the services. More

---

10   FORSCOM: United States Forces Command (pronounced "Force Com")

units are being alerted for deployment to the Middle East, but some of those units have internal vacancies they can't fill. Some people are being diverted from schools and other assignments to fill these, but that leaves vacancies in other positions around the world. We're trying to fill these vacancies with reserves from the Individual Mobilization Augmentees (IMA), Individual Ready Reserve (IRR), and the Retired Reserve, anywhere we can get our hands on up to two hundred thousand able-bodied reserves. So, there you are."

He continued. "Just so we're clear, the reserve component of the armed forces of the United States comprises several different lists of pre-trained individuals who, in the event of war or conflict, can be called to active duty via a mobilization order or a presidential reserve call-up order. One of those lists is the IMA list, which is composed of individual reservists who are assigned to active-component units and government agencies. IMAs work with their unit on a very flexible schedule and will deploy with the unit—if and when needed.

"The IRR members list forms a category of the Ready Reserve members who haven't fulfilled their military service obligation or MSO.[11] Every person, on initial entry into US military service, incurs an MSO of eight years. The MSO can be fulfilled on active duty, reserve duty, National Guard duty, inactive reserve duty, or a combination thereof. Most IRR members complete an initial active duty stint of three to four years, then transfer to the IRR list for the remainder of their MSO, and are subject to recall if needed. We're trying to get as many IRR members to volunteer as we can, without resorting to involuntary call-up."

He finished his explanation with, "The Retired Reserve list is just that, members who've served long enough in the military to earn a retirement pension."

"Sir, with all due respect," I said gingerly, "I think you must be dyslexic because certainly you must be looking for a twenty-five-year-

---

11   MSO: Military Service Obligation

old captain, not a fifty-two-year-old captain. And most certainly not one who has been retired for thirteen years. When I first volunteered after 9/11 as a retiree, I had only been retired about six years. A lot of water has flowed under that bridge since then."

With a slight chuckle, the major said, "One would think so, wouldn't one? However, that's not the case right now, I'm afraid. We're hoping to get enough volunteers to avoid recalling people involuntarily. Involuntary recall screws up a lot of lives of people who are still working. Hence, the retiree recall."

His pause was palpable. I asked with some incredulity, "Could I be recalled involuntarily?"

"Yeah, it's possible, but I'll admit very highly unlikely. Right now, that is not an option at our disposal. However, if you volunteer for the retiree recall, then you and I can work together on one of those worldwide vacancies I talked about earlier. The choice would be in your hands. If we ever have to resort to an involuntary recall of retirees, the shit would really hit the fan. Assignments would be for the good of the service . . . whatever and wherever that might be."

"If I volunteer, then who decides on the assignment?"

"Well, Matt, you do mostly," he responded cheerily. "Most of the Medical Service Corp (MSC) officers I've called so far are still working after they left the service. You're the first MSC I've called who is fully retired."

The major let that last tidbit sink in.

"Frankly, Matt, I just started calling people a week ago and around one-third of the people decided to volunteer. You are number twelve on my call list, so you are one of the first to be asked. We are nowhere near meeting our quota, so I would say involuntary recall is a real possibility for those in IRR status. The other real possibility is that if and when we get to the involuntary selection process, the *good* jobs will already be snapped up by the volunteers. Only the shit vacancies will be left. I don't think anyone wants that. If you want to go back on active duty, my advice is to volunteer."

"Okay, sir," I said. "Is the surge in Iraq really going that badly that the Army has to scrape the bottom of the barrel by recalling retirees? I had heard that the surge is working," I added with a hint of suspicion.

"It does appear the surge is working, but it's still tenuous in Iraq, especially in and around Baghdad. The fact remains that Operation Iraqi Freedom (OIF) and Operation Enduring Freedom (OEF) have been sucking up a lot of forces at the expense of other missions. We are trying to use as many volunteers from the Reserves as possible without recalling people involuntarily."

I hesitated then offered, "Well. I need to think this over a bit and talk with my wife before I decide. So, just for grins and giggles, what kinds of duty assignments are available that you could offer me if I chose to volunteer?" I felt like a fish looking over the bait. Was it bait? "And what timeframe are we talking about for a start date?"

Maj. Pendleton sounded pleased. "It just so happens that I've got a list, our worldwide help wanted list, if you will. There are pages and pages, but it contains vacancies in units and commands that cannot be filled organically. In some cases, you'll be sent to that unit, train with them and then deploy with them. In some of the other vacancies you'll be an individual replacement for a unit already in place."

Without skipping a beat and as if he already knew I would ask, the major added, "For someone like you, Matt, who is qualified in two different branches, Signal Corps and Medical Service Corps, there are more opportunities available. The one I'd like you to consider is located at Guantanamo Bay Naval Base or GITMO[12] in Cuba."

I interrupted. "Doesn't the Navy run GITMO? Why would they need an Army guy?"

"Good question," he responded. "Actually, Joint Task Force (JTF) GITMO[13] needs an Army officer to serve as an intelligence analyst, branch-immaterial, in the grade of O-4. One rank lower should be

---

12   GITMO: Slang for Guantanamo Bay Naval Base (pronounced "Git Mo")
13   JTF-GITMO: Joint Task Force Guantanamo

OK and with your Signal background, I'm pretty sure you'd meet the security clearance requirement. You must have a secret clearance with the ability to get a top secret. I see you once had a TS/SCI[14] when you worked Signal. It should be no problem to get an interim top secret. The process to get your clearance is all online via EPSQ.[15] The fact that you've held a higher clearance makes you a little more valuable."

"OK, I give. What is EPSQ?" I quipped while wondering how many other acronyms I wouldn't know after being out of uniform for so long.

"Oh. Sorry 'bout that. EPSQ is the Electronic Personnel Security Questionnaire. The Standard Form 86 questionnaire is now electronic. It becomes the basis for granting your secret clearance as well as a starting point for the FBI if you need a top secret clearance," Maj. Pendleton explained.

"And the time frame we're looking at for boots on the ground in Cuba is mid-September. That means you'll have to go to regreening in August. Regreening is three weeks of training and mobilization processing at Fort Jackson, South Carolina. You'll receive training and be evaluated for deployment medical standards. If you fail medical, you will go back home, do not pass go and do not collect two hundred dollars. If you pass training and medical, then you'll ship out to arrive no later than the reporting date."

Uh-oh! My mind flashed to the term *deployment medical standards*. When I said I was fat, dumb, and happy, I meant it! I was about thirty pounds too fat, dumb, and happy to be perfectly honest. Not to mention that I had my right hip repaired only a year previous. The hip was perfect in my mind, having taken only about three weeks of physical training and exercises to get right. But I'd also have to complete the APFT,[16] consisting of push-ups, sit-ups and a two-mile run. *Ha!* I hadn't done that in years.

---

14   TS/SCI: Acronym for Top Secret - Sensitive Compartmented Information security clearance
15   EPSQ: Electronic Personnel Security Questionnaire
16   APFT: Advanced Physical Fitness Test

"All right, sir. Can I assume meeting deployment medical standards includes the height-weight standard and completing the APFT?"

"You know, Matt, I can only assume that's the case. It's all part of being a soldier."

"Well, of course I'm leaning toward volunteering. If I'm truly needed, how can I say no? Is there any other training I've got to do?"

"It all depends on the deployment location. There can be various training requirements specific to a particular region or area of responsibility [AOR] for combatant commanders. It really depends on the assignment.

"I might add that generally the intention is to try and keep retiree recalls in CONUS assignments to free up active component personnel for deployment. They figure you've done your time," Maj. Pendleton remarked with a hint of optimism, "but once again it all depends on availability and choices."

"If it will help you find reasonable vacancies, I worked in a veterans' nursing home for almost nine years after I retired. About half that time was in health care management and the other half was in health care information systems management," I offered. "You already know that I had extensive service in signal operations engineering and management, so I would be comfortable doing that, too. Computers, database, telecommunications planning, you name it."

Maj. Pendleton paused and then chuckled. "OK, Matt. I'm not surprised. After I reviewed your CV,[17] I guessed you would probably volunteer. Why don't you just take a few days to run this up the flagpole with your own chief of staff . . . Sara, right? I'm going to be out of pocket until next Monday anyway. Meanwhile, I'll look through the projected assignment vacancies and highlight a few where I think you'd be interested in serving. I'll call you next Monday and we can review where it all stands. K?"

---

17   CV: Curriculum Vitae

"Sure, sir. That's reasonable enough, and I'm sure I'll generate some more questions by then, too," I said with a sense of relief.

"Very good then. I've got more of these phonecons to make, so I might as well get to it. Take care. You know, everything will be fine. Tell your wife that. Out here."

I gently placed the cordless phone back in the charger base.

"Honey, life as we know it is going to change," I blurted. Sara looked up from her book with a mixture of surprise and bewilderment. Then she quietly and pathetically asked, "Can it wait until I finish this chapter?"

CHAPTER 3

The Decision

For the rest of that week, Sara and I talked through the implications of a recall to active duty. We had both been victim to Murphy's Law while serving in the military—"Anything that can go wrong will go wrong"—and usually at the worst possible moment.

"If the Army says it needs me, why not?"

Sara agreed. "Might as well jump in with both feet as soon as you can and submit for something of your choosing."

It was hard not to see the wisdom in volunteering. In the past, we had both bet against the Army on various occasions—and usually lost those bets. Things like "should we take leave now or later" to take advantage of a special occasion or event, hoping that the Army would not change its plans for us, often did not pan out. The Army has a perverse way of cropping up just when you think things are settled, only to totally scuttle your plans with a mission or duty change. Hence Murphy's Law.

We mulled the consequences, both the real and the unimaginable, of being recalled to active duty. Of course, there was the age factor and physical condition, which bothered me, but mostly I felt a bit guilty leaving Sara alone at home. *What if I don't come home? How will she ever set the clocks on the VCR and stove without me?*

Sara was fully supportive. Being retired military herself, she understood completely. I'm sure she didn't like it, but she knew everyone had to suck it up.

"You gotta do whatcha gotta do, don't you?" she said. It's hard to say no when you get a personal request to add your skills to the fight. The only way to do this was to be all in, and Sara and I did just that.

I got the call back from Maj. Pendleton on Monday as he promised. He began, "Hello, Matt. I hope you and Sara have had time to think this over."

"We have," I answered with a touch of finality. "I intend to volunteer for one of those plumb, hopefully REMF, jobs in the good ole USA," referring to the age-old term for "rear echelon mother fuckers."

"Not sure we've got any REMF jobs available," Maj. Pendleton said. "But what I do have is a branch-immaterial position at GITMO authorized up to the rank of major that I told you about last week. Once again, the position title is intelligence analyst, and it doesn't require a branch-qualified Intel officer. I think we can fill the position one rank below; otherwise the position description would say *required rank* rather than just *authorized rank*."

"Sara and I talked about the GITMO assignment," I responded. "It would be a relatively safe assignment, but getting home to visit would be complicated. If we could find a position in the US, hypothetically I could visit home much easier on leave. Any kind of OCONUS[18] deployment would mean a lot of stricter controls on taking leave."

"You got that right, Matt," Maj. Pendleton said. "Everything in and out of GITMO is military transport, but I really think this fits you. However, I recently saw a position in Djibouti for an MSC major, but I think the position requires an O-4. I would have to sell you to them to accept you as a captain. Between you and me, you *don't* want to go to Djibouti if you can avoid it, and because of your rank, you *can* avoid it. I pity the poor guy that gets that job. Very Spartan living conditions there. On the other hand, JTF-GTMO provides first-rate lodging since the Navy runs it. Four officers share a two-bedroom cottage. To be very clear, the position is with the Joint Task Force,

---

18   OCONUS: Outside Continental United States (pronounced "Oh Cone Us")

which is commanded by a flag officer. The current commander is a Rear Admiral Donald L. Thompson, Jr."

"Well, I used to scuba dive in a previous life, so maybe I'd have the opportunity to do that again down in Cuba," I thought out loud.

"Are you kidding? The diving at GITMO is totally awesome," said the major, sensing he was closing the deal.

"So, volunteering for the GITMO gig is your recommendation?"

"Yes. It's the best thing going from the list I'm working from," he said.

"Ah. That brings up a question. The *list* you are working from. Does that imply that other people have lists with different assignments?"

"Good question. I'm working off a filtered list for which company-grade officers might be eligible, which means it includes *branch-immaterial* assignments."

"OK. I'm retired as MSC, but I'm also branch-qualified in Signal Corps," I offered. "Does your list include signal positions?"

"Another great question, Matt. Yes, it does. However, this is pretty much your best choice in MSC. In fact, most of the company-grade offerings for MSC that you are qualified to serve in are all branch-immaterial slots."

"You mean you don't have any positions for a Patient Admin Division [PAD] officer, S-1, logistics, etc.?"

"No. There *are* some positions, but just a few really. We have some MASH[19] units getting ready to rotate to Afghanistan. I didn't think you'd want to go into that kind of unit as an augmentee without some recent branch train-up. Besides, there are lots of younger guys on the IRR list who we can activate and send to the unit almost immediately to train up with them. However, there are some MSC position vacancies on this list right now—and I emphasize *right now*—that require additional qualification such as completion of CAS CUBE[20]

---

19   MASH: Mobile Army Surgical Hospital
20   CAS CUBE: Acronym pronunciation for Combined Arms Services Staff School or CAS3

or other schooling certifications like medical supply management for those assignments. You've got to hold that additional skill identifier with your area of concentration [AOC]. You only completed Phase I of CAS CUBE, which doesn't help much. I will add this: things could change in the future if we can't get fully qualified people to fill the positions. Suddenly things like specialty qualifications or CAS CUBE completion might not be as important. Better to have a body in the assignment that is at least advance-course qualified with no certifications, than to have nobody to fill the assignment at all."

I pondered his wisdom aloud. "So if I hold off for a position that I'm rank, branch and specialty qualified for, it may be for an assignment in an undesirable location."

"Yes, but actually it could be worse than that," he suggested. "If you wait, you could get activated for a branch-immaterial slot in an undesirable location. This Cuba slot is the best thing on the list. Everything else is in Afghanistan, Iraq, Africa, Indonesia and other locations best suited for those who have not yet retired. There are also a few good MSC officer positions for field-grade officers, but the rank of major or higher is required. My advice is to let me lock down this GITMO slot for you, which I can do."

I guess I just needed to trust him. It's not like he was a recruiter or something and spinning me a tale to get me to join up—or was he? I relented. "OK. Go ahead and put me down for the intelligence analyst position at GITMO. I may as well get this show on the road. Waiting for something else and not knowing would be a major headache."

The rest of the phone call with Maj. Pendleton was a basic outline of things to come, forms to complete and a tentative time schedule. He announced, "You should be in Cuba by the end of August or early September."

Oh goodie, I thought. *I've only got four months to get my butt back in shape.*

CHAPTER 4

The Regreening

Late July 2008

Those four months getting back in shape were pretty tough in Arizona's heat. Well, at least it's a *dry heat*—yeah right! This was phase one of my personal *regreening* mission. I marched with a pack for hours at a time and logged about twenty-plus miles per week, with a total of over 350 miles on my Garmin GPS device. Fortunately, I could hike the state land trust to the west of my subdivision, complete with its many trails up and downhill, for my training mission. I pretty much abandoned playing in the club woodshop to concentrate on physical fitness and weight control.

Besides my long marches on desert trails, I practiced for the Army APFT by doing push-ups, sit-ups and two-mile runs. I found a flat, straight one-mile trail leading to the backside of a Catholic church. I'd run to the church, then return to find my two-mile run times. Back in the day I could do this run in sixteen or so minutes. I got my time down to eighteen minutes, but I was also thirteen years older and fifteen pounds heavier. Still, it was qualifying by Army standards.

Maj. Pendleton sent me the required forms to complete: a DA Form 160-R Application for Active Duty, a DA Form 7349 Annual Medical Certificate, and a Volunteer Selection Form. On the medical certificate I made sure the Army knew about my resurfaced right hip, too. As my former commander Col. Sanford used to say, "No surprises for the old man."

The months of April through July flew by without me hearing from Maj. Pendleton or receiving paperwork. Certainly, I would get some orders soon if they expected me to report in August or September.

"Darling," I said to my wife, "I'm going to make some minor changes to banking stuff so it'll be easier for you. I'm going to put everything on autopay and have notices sent to your email address. All you'll have to do is enter those in the checkbook."

We sat together and went over the household management stuff I normally handled. We sorted out the car payment, trash pick-up, gas, electricity, cable, etc.

It was the first week of August when Maj. Pendleton finally called. "Captain Jerome—*Matt*—we need to talk."

His voice sounded ominous. "Hello, sir," I answered. "What's happening? I expected some orders by now."

Maj. Pendleton replied rather sheepishly. "I've got some bad news and some good news. The bad news is that JTF-GTMO changed the Intel position description to *rank required* Major/O-4 from what they posted and announced online, which said *rank authorized*. Your application for that got kicked back. I did everything I could. I even called them to reconsider. In fact, it was your application that got them to look at their announcement. It seems someone made a mistake when they sent it out. I am really sorry about that. That was a good job. I even told them you had completed Phase I of CAS CUBE, but it didn't seem to matter. They want a field-grade officer . . . period, end of story."

"Nothing ventured, nothing gained," I said. "Have any of those REMF jobs at military entrance processing stations [MEPS] come online?" I half-heartedly joked.

"No, sorry to say. But here's the good news. I found another position on the WIAS which you might like. 1st Corps at Fort Lewis needs an electronics warfare officer [EWO]. You'll help plan frequency management, electronic warfare [EW], and CREW efforts for convoys. CREW is a new acronym for counter remote-controlled explosive device electronic warfare planning. With your Signal Corps background and clearance, this is a perfect fit. You'll deploy to MNC-I in Baghdad on or about January 2009 with 1st Corps."

"*Iraq?* But I had my heart set on scuba diving in the Caribbean. That changes the recall dynamic. Sara and I have been focusing on Cuba, not Iraq. I'll need to talk with her again."

"Hey, I completely understand," Maj. Pendleton offered. "If it's any consolation, you now have three or four more months to prepare and your billet is with the Corps HQ. Regreening training at Fort Jackson and forward deployment through the CRC[21] at Fort Benning will probably occur in December. Sorry about Christmas."

"What else can you tell me about train-up?" I asked.

The major was ready for my question. "1st Corps published a staff training memo which has all the particulars. It's pretty lengthy, but you'll have time, and a lot can be done over the internet. Since you have a paragraph and line number assignment, I can give you a point of contact at 1st Corps you can call to coordinate. This isn't a bad job, other than being in a combat zone. You'll probably be stationed in the Al Faw Palace or in the Green Zone.[22] Eighteenth Airborne Corps currently acts as MNC-I and will hand off that mission to 1st Corps next year. Pretty heady stuff, if you ask me. Right in the middle of history being made."

"But it's in Iraq . . . with lots of sand . . . sir," I hesitatingly joked. "I already live in the desert. And that job is *really* close to the flagpole!"

---

21   CRC: CONUS Replacement Center
22   Green Zone: The most common name for the International Zone of Baghdad.

A long silence passed between us. "Are you still there?" the major asked.

"Yes, sir," I chimed. "Just thinking. I'll double-check with the wife, but pretty sure she'll be OK with it. We said we'd be all in on this deal, whatever came of it. Put me down for the electronic warfare officer slot at 1st Corps. I'll call you back in twenty-four hours only if my wife vetoes the decision."

He spoke with an air of reassurance. "Will do, Matt. Make the most of it and. . . thank you for your service."

———————

For the next two or so months, I kept walking the desert with a pack during the morning and working on correspondence courses in the afternoon. Essentially, I added personal and professional development training to my regreening phase one list of things to complete.

I even spoke with the schoolhouse at the Army Intelligence Center in nearby Fort Huachuca, AZ, and tentatively worked out a plan to take their four-week electronic warfare course. Fort Huachuca was only an hour and a half away from the house, and the course would bring me up to snuff on current skills needed for my projected assignment. When I told the EW instructor about my recall assignment to MNC-I, he said he'd do everything in his power to get me into a class. However, after speaking with my future first-line supervisor at 1st Corps, he told me the training course wasn't necessary. I'd get everything I needed with on-the-job training in Iraq.

"Spend that time at home with your family. You'll be glad you did."

So, I scrapped the Fort Huachuca idea.

I called Maj. Pendleton in early November and asked, "Sir, I don't have any orders yet. What gives?"

I could hear the frustration in his voice. "Things have been kind of fluid with 1st Corps, to say the least. I hesitated to call until we got something more solid. I've got three others in the same boat as you for recall to 1st Corps. It appears the deployment of 1st Corps to the Iraq theater has been pushed off. They've got a major Corps COIN[23] CPX[24] scheduled for January 2009 and decided to delay augmentee deployment until February or March to arrive with the main body elements in theater. Looks like you'll have a couple more months to train. We'll get orders to you soon enough based on this."

"Honey," I said with some relief. "The Army just saved our holidays. 1st Corps wants to delay my deployment until February or March! Isn't that good news?"

"Small mercies, indeed," Sara remarked.

My regreening regimen continued unabated through the New Year. Besides my road marches and physical fitness events, I endured hours of individual training directed by the Department of Defense (DoD), Forces Command, Central Command, Multi-National Force – Iraq (MNF-I) and, lastly, 1st Corps. I also obtained the electronic warfare training modules from Fort Huachuca and got familiar with these. Every echelon of command imposed its own knowledge or training requirement before I headed off to war.

Of course, someone deemed all these topics as vitally necessary, but I couldn't help thinking these constituted a kind of *paper foxhole* where someone could hide in order to say, "He should have known." I'm sure everyone assaulting Normandy on D-Day had a similar individual training requirement.

However, I did complete all the components of training expected of me, including things like anti-terrorist training, Leader Development and Education for Sustained Peace, the MNF-I core warrior values training, tribalism in Iraq, law of land warfare, rules of engagement (ROE), operations security (OPSEC), trafficking in persons awareness training, SERE (survival, evasion, resistance and escape) code of conduct training, and several others.

---

23   COIN: Counter Insurgency
24   CPX: Command Post Exercise

Amazingly, there was even a module on general orders, which I had learned and was drilled into everyone during Basic Training. *Really?* You have to verify that people know the three general orders? Paper foxhole indeed! All told, I worked dozens of hours to complete these modules and obtain the required certificates. I dutifully printed out my certificates, expecting to turn them in to someone, somewhere.

———————

It was sometime in early February when Sara called to me with the phone in her ear. "Matt, it's Lea. She's got some good news for us and wants to talk on speakerphone."

"Great. Hi, honey. What's happening with you?" I answered after putting it on speaker, hoping to finally get some good news from our daughter. Lea struggled in her marriage to Tom, an unemployed ne'er-do-well. Last we heard they had resorted to sleeping in their car when Tom failed in the auto garage business he inherited from his dad. *Loser.* They lived on Lea's meager income and tips from waitressing.

"Hi, Mom, Dad," she said, voice trembling a little. "I've decided to take matters into my own hands and join the Army. Tom's sister is a recruiter here in Las Vegas and she got me set up to take the ASVAB[25] test after New Year's. I'll make a decision on my military occupational specialty [MOS] after she gets the results."

Sara and I both looked at each other with incredulity. Lea was thirty-four-years-old, and Army Basic Training would not be easy at that age.

We both answered in unison. "That's awesome, honey."

"How can we help you?" I added.

"Please just pray for us," she said, her voice almost breaking with tears. "I can't go on living like this, and so I'm taking charge of my life again."

———————

25   ASVAB: Armed Services Vocational Aptitude Battery test to determine training suitability

We spent the next hour or so talking about her decision and what she could expect. It was uplifting for all of us. She vowed to make it. She also came to visit and we trained together on the Army APFT events to help *both* of us prepare for the Army—me after thirteen years out of uniform, and her getting ready to put on that uniform for the first time. We prayed she would make it.

"Hi, Mom, Dad," Lea opened on our weekly speakerphone call. "I did really well on the ASVAB and qualified to become a combat medic. I'll be enlisting and heading to Fort Jackson sometime in March so I can finish Basic Training before the next medic course in June at Fort Sam. I have to tell you that you've both been an inspiration to me to become a medic."

Needless to say, there wasn't a dry eye in the Jerome house as Lea honored us with those words. Even more so, our tears of joy were for her as we hoped this would change her life for the better.

I arrived in Columbia, South Carolina, on March 1, 2009, where I grabbed a seat on a military shuttle van. After filling with other soldiers headed to Fort Jackson, the van headed out from the airport. The driver dropped off the others at the fort's reception station, leaving me as the only one left in the van as we drove down Leesburg Road east of Fort Jackson toward Camp McCrady Training Center. There I would sign into Task Force Marshall.

In a little under three weeks, Task Force Marshall would attempt to transform me from grumpy old retired military into an active-duty soldier once again. *Hooah!* The regreening at the training center, local training areas, and ranges at Fort Jackson would encompass medical screening, drug testing, physical fitness, basic skills refresher training and common task training/warrior task training. I would have to complete these items successfully before continuing in the mobilization and deployment process.

Personal pride told me that I would not fail in these things. I had lost those thirty pounds and trained diligently enough to pass the APFT for my age group. With a hip replacement only two years earlier, I went the extra mile and had my orthopedic surgeon re-inspect his work and certify me as fit for duty.

The taxi dropped me off at the door of the headquarters building for Camp McCrady. I went inside, dragging my newly bought duffle bag and laptop case with me. I was met by the staff duty NCO (SDNCO).

"Evening. Looks like you're checkin' in?" he remarked as he looked me over in my civilian jeans and jacket, not knowing if I was an officer or enlisted.

"Yes, Sergeant Epps," I read from his nametag. "I'm Captain Matt Jerome reporting in. I'm a retiree recall. Here, let me dig out a copy of my orders," I offered as I pulled one free from my laptop bag.

SFC Epps looked over my orders approvingly and without hesitation remarked in his Southern drawl, "Yessir. We gotcha on a list. We got an officer hooch for all y'all, but we might gotta put some other people in there, too. More people comin' than there's bunks. Oh, I'm fixin' to go to supper, so if you can officially sign in here." He placed the official sign-in log in front of me. "I'll get you to the hooch quick like, you can drop yer stuff, and then I'll give you the nickel tour to the DFAC,[26] sir . . . iffnyawanna."

"No thanks for the tour, Sergeant Epps, but when does the DFAC close? I'll probably head over a little later if there's plenty of time," I said.

Sgt. Epps seemed relieved at not having to escort an officer to supper as he remarked, "No problem. The DFAC just opened twenty minutes ago and won't close for another hour and a half. It stays open extra time on reporting-in days."

We walked the fifty yards or so to the officer hooch, which was merely an open bay barracks with bunk beds.

"Owwww!" I exclaimed to Sgt. Epps. "Bunk beds? Really? Oh

---

26   DFAC: Dining Facility (pronounced "Dee Fac")

my God. What's the bathroom like?" So much for rank hath its privileges. At least all the officers, company and field grade, would enjoy the same splendor.

Luckily, a community bathroom served us at the back of the barracks rather than outside and down the trail over yonder. *Phew, dodged a potential bullet there.* Unlike my Basic Training barracks just down the road at Fort Jackson, SC, back in March of 1975, there were no community shower rooms or a row of toilets side by side or a long trench-type urinal to use. By the way, it was sitting on those commodes during Fire Guard with another basic trainee that I learned how to play the card game Spades. This upscale barracks sported four individual shower stalls and four toilet stalls with doors. *Thank God for simple pleasures.*

Fortunately, I found a bottom bunk with a corresponding double-door wall locker, which hadn't been spoken for. There appeared to be a locker for each bunk, but many were in disrepair. *And no damn hangers,* I said to myself.

"Hi, I'm Matt Jerome," I said to the younger major unpacking his bags on the bunk next to me. He stopped midstream, grabbed my outstretched hand and shook it. With a smile he said, "I'm Mike Corso, glad to meet you. Are you IRR?" he asked.

"No," I said. "They scraped the bottom of the retiree barrel to find me. How 'bout you?"

"Hey, me too," he said as we both sized each other up, and in the silence that ensued, I think we both started wondering how bad the situation must be that the Army was pulling in retirees.

I broke the silence. "Any other retirees like us here yet?"

"Probably, judging by the gray hairs on their heads. They all wandered over to the DFAC already. Some have been here a couple of days and most of them are IRR and not fully retired yet. With you, there are two retirees for sure; me and you. I think everyone else is either IRR or IMA."

There were four of us with assignments to Iraq. Maj. Corso, Maj.

Kevin Smith, Capt. Carl Buckley and me. We called ourselves the Four Amigos. However, the moniker would not last once we got split up in Iraq.

Mike and I were both retired, but Kevin and Carl were IRR. Kevin told us, "Hey look, I've got a lot of active-duty service. If I can stay on active duty long enough to go over eighteen years of active service, I should be able to claim *sanctuary* for retirement."

"Good luck with that, Kevin," I remarked dryly. "The Army has safeguards against that. Don't you remember some of those forms we had to sign? One of those forms specifically addressed the issue of someone coming back on active duty who could possibly achieve enough years for retirement. Some Remington Ranger at HQ or a computer database query is going to pop out your name as fitting this description. They'll cut you free before you get too close."

"Maybe, but I'm going to try," Kevin said.

"I'm just trying to get me some tax-free money," announced Carl, who was from New England and recently unemployed. He relied on the *Huffington Post* and the *Daily Kos* for his news and political information. To say he was a dyed-in-the-wool liberal was putting it mildly. I tried to steer clear of Carl as I was not liberally minded. Carl also mentioned that he had been passed over for promotion because he hadn't completed an OAC. He hoped to clear some debts with the money he'd make on deployment.

Maj. Corso, Army Ranger, called Louisiana his home. We bonded as friends because we were both retired, and I had spent almost nine years living in the South. I could speak the lingo. Mike was in great physical shape at forty-five years old and showed off some of his mountain climbing pictures. Once a Ranger, always a Ranger. Although it was unspoken between us, we became battle buddies who unconsciously looked out and cared for each other.

I had not heard the term *Battle Buddy* before I got to Fort Jackson. Of course, I recall the term *Ranger Buddy* from my time at Fort Lewis in the '70s. I often taught Specialist Four Rangers when I worked the NCO Academy, and it was common practice to use the term. Ranger Buddies were soul mates!

While undergoing medical screening on Fort Jackson, we came into some limited contact with Basic Training soldiers and their drill sergeants. "Private Robinson," a large and imposing drill sergeant yelled across the waiting room. "Where's your Battle Buddy?" The private, drinking from the water fountain, stopped and turned toward the drill sergeant with eyes wide open. He suddenly ran back over to another private sitting in a waiting room chair about twenty feet away.

"That's me, Drill Sergeant," the sitting soldier said while quickly standing up as Robinson came to stand by his side.

"DROP," was all the drill sergeant said to the two soldiers standing there. The soldiers immediately assumed the front-leaning-rest position,[27] prepared to execute push-ups on command. They waited while the drill sergeant moved closer to the group.

The drill sergeant now stood close to his Basic Training charges, who were all near each other in the large waiting area of the troop medical clinic. He glared at them and spoke with an even tone and focused voice. "Robinson and everyone else here. Do *not* let me wonder where your Battle Buddy is again. You don't have to be joined at the hip, but you better be pretty darn close to each other so I know you haven't been abandoned. I don't care if you are just getting a drink of water at the fountain or heading off to the bathroom. You had *better* take your Battle Buddy with you. Am I clear?"

"Yes, Drill Sergeant," came the indoor-voice response from the group.

"Give me twenty, you two," bellowed the drill sergeant as he spoke to the two privates still waiting in the front-leaning-rest position.

The two Battle Buddies started cranking out push-ups in complete unison while counting, "One Drill Sergeant, two Drill Sergeant. . . " until they had completed twenty push-ups. "Request permission to recover, Drill Sergeant."

---

27   Front-leaning-rest position: Push-up position

"Get up, then sit down!" came the terse reply. "I'm your worst nightmare."

During the medical processing, I saw a doctor who gave me a thorough exam. He read through my medical history and asked about my hip repair.

"So, what is this with your right hip?" he asked. "It says your hip was resurfaced two years ago. Tell me more."

"Yes, sir," I answered. "I had a procedure called Birmingham hip resurfacing. It is not a hip replacement. They clean up the head of the femur and install a new ball on it. After cleaning out the socket, a new metal socket matched to the ball is installed."

I showed him a copy of the X-ray I had in my wallet, along with a letter from my orthopedic surgeon clearing me for duty.

"So, you're not having any problems with the right hip, I presume. Otherwise you wouldn't be here, going back on active duty." The doctor smiled.

I was ready for that question. "The hip is fine, sir. In fact, I logged almost four hundred miles hiking in preparation for this recall."

"OK then. I'll mark you good to go. Your hip was my only concern. Everything else, including your labs, looks pretty good. Your blood sugar is at 105, but your A1C, which is a better measure for diabetes, is fine at 5.2 percent," said the doc.

Another hurdle cleared.

We performed the first week training in civilian clothes. If anyone was going to wash out, that would be the time to do it, before they bought several hundred dollars' worth of Army uniforms. In fact, that *was* the reason our platoon guide gave us for restricting us from the uniform store.

Staff Sgt. Shirley Mills functioned as our platoon guide or babysitter, keeping us on track, on time and in the right place.

"You can't wear Army green, until you've been officially regreened," she said. "That occurs near the end of the second week, when you complete the last civilian-clothes phase of training. You'll need ACUs[28] for training after that as we'll go to the field to fire weapons and do convoy IED[29] training and all sorts of good stuff. Why buy all those expensive uniforms before you really need to?"

I spoke up weakly. "To at least get the boots broke in?"

Weapon familiarization provided another hurdle I needed to clear. I needed to qualify with an individual weapon to be able to deploy. I didn't think I'd have a problem since I had always qualified and usually at the *expert* level. This time around, the marksmanship familiarization training phases were all conducted on an automated, indoor 3-D simulator range. "This is kinda cool, Matt," Mike said between firing lines.

The simulator allowed a lot of people to get trained without a lot of expense in time, money and ammunition. "My problem, Mike," I groused, "is my progressive bifocals are giving me a problem. If I put my nose to the charging handle for a proper and consistent cheek-stock weld like I was taught thirty-four years ago, the sights are blurry. I have to tilt my head back to get the right view, or move my head off the charging handle. Maybe I should try without my glasses." I qualified on the simulator, but I knew I could do better.

We headed back to Fort Jackson to the record fire rifle range, which provided some melancholic moments. I spoke about it to Mike, who was sitting next to me, and who had gone through Basic Training several years after I did.

"The last time I went down this road I was in Basic Training, thirty-four years ago in March and April 1975. My, how time flies when you're having fun. We did all the marksmanship familiarization phases on these ranges. The one we're headed to is for conducting record fire. We usually walked to these ranges, but on occasion if the training schedule was tight, we'd get a lift in the cattle trucks. What a time it was."

"Cattle trucks?" Mike asked.

---

28   ACU: Army Combat Uniform
29   IED: Improvised Explosive Device

"Sorta," I said. "They were basically cattle trailers like the kind you see being pulled by an eighteen-wheeler. They weren't as tall or long. Maybe twenty-five feet long and about eight foot tall and had slats in the walls for airflow. There were some benches to sit and a pipe framework hanging down from the ceiling that you could hold on to. Every time we got in those trailers people would start mooing. I think all the Basic Training schools used them in the seventies."

"That's why I don't remember them," Mike added. "We used Army buses by the time I got there in the eighties."

All told, record fire went well. There were a couple of IRR people who had to refire, but they ultimately qualified. Meanwhile with my glasses on, I still qualified as a sharpshooter. I was pissed that I didn't do better. Old age strikes again.

Task Force Marshall provided a lot of first aid training. The training team didn't provide a full Combat Lifesaver Course of sixteen hours, but it seemed like they covered a lot in the four-hour block of instruction.

Coincidentally, I almost needed first aid when I literally fell out of the back of a Humvee during training. As the resident expert on communications, I was directed to man the radio in the back of a Humvee during a convoy-type exercise. Sitting for a long period of time wedged in between the radio mount, cases of meals ready-to-eat (MRE) and other impedimenta made my hips cramp up. I had to squirm a lot to keep them from hurting. We stopped to do an after-action review (AAR) with the instructor after the convoy, and as I exited the vehicle, I briefly caught my trailing foot on the door ledge as I stepped out. *Whammo*, I landed hard on my left hip while wearing Individual Body Armor (IBA) and helmet. Graceful it was not.

"You all right?" Mike ran back to the Humvee as I was sprawled out on the dirt road next to it.

"Besides my pride?" I asked. "I think I bruised my left hip, but I should be OK."

Truth be told, I learned a few nights later that maybe I wasn't OK. I started waking up in the middle of the night because that hip started aching. I said to myself, *That ache feels just like my right hip ached the year before it needed replacing. I better get checked out at Fort Benning when I get there.*

When we completed our regreening at Camp McCrady on Friday, March 20, I noted it was the thirty-forth anniversary of the day I originally joined the Army in 1975. I also learned my daughter, Lea, was headed to Fort Jackson, the same fort where I endured Basic Training thirty-four years earlier. *Coincidence?* Unfortunately, I would miss her as I'd be heading to Benning as she was headed here.

Task Force Marshall held no big graduation ceremony. They merely provided us with individual packets containing certificates of the various required training modules we completed. I found out later these certificates were next to worthless at CRC, Fort Benning. They offered us bus tickets to Fort Benning.

Rather than take a bus, Kevin offered to put up everyone at his house in South Carolina on Friday after we signed out.

"Guys," he said. "Here's an idea. Rather than go by bus to Benning, I can get everything in my truck. We drive to my house after we sign out of here, have a day of R&R[30] on Saturday at my place, grab a rental truck on Sunday morning, and then head to Fort Benning. I'll put the rental in my name and we drop it off in Columbus when we get a chance."

We kicked it around, but could not find any problem with the rental car concept—on paper.

We had a great Saturday in Augusta just lounging around watching Kevin cut his grass one last time. In reality, the rest of the plan went to crap when Kevin dilly-dallied around on Sunday morning. Before leaving, Kevin said he wanted to have a big breakfast at a local restaurant.

30   R&R: Rest & Recuperation

The four of us plus Kevin's wife spent nearly two hours at a packed Cracker Barrel restaurant. Then we headed out to get his rental. Once we got the car and hit the road for our four-plus-hour trip to Benning, it was almost noon. We arrived at the CRC late Sunday afternoon with only a couple of hours to spare. Meanwhile, just about every other replacement reporting to the CRC for that cycle had already signed in to the company and taken up all the best bunks available.

The training at CRC, Fort Benning started at 1800 Sunday. Remarkably, the training schedule at CRC covered a LOT of the same subjects we had just conducted with Task Force Marshall at Camp McGrady. Unlike Task Force Marshall, the CRC intended to complete this training in one week versus three weeks, with some classes scheduled as late as 2300.

I looked at the CRC training schedule and remarked, "This looks a lot like what we just finished at Fort Jackson. I'm going to show them my training certificates and see if we can skip some of these classes. We did SRP at Fort Jackson and now CRC is going to do it again? It looks to me like the CRC is trying to stuff ten pounds of shit into a six-pound bag."

"I agree," chimed Mike. "We've already done 80 percent of these classes and qualified with both the M-9 pistol and M-16 rifle. We do need to go to RFI,[31] though, and get all of that stuff issued."

We found the CRC training NCO and tried our gambit, presenting our certificates, but he wouldn't accept them.

"The problem, sirs," the training NCO told us, "is that the CRC commander must certify you as *trained and ready* to deploy. To do that certification, our colonel insists that CRC conduct the training and that we not rely on any pieces of paper from other units. You'll have to do it all here."

---

31   RFI: Rapid Fielding Initiative, a program designed to put the newest military gear directly into the hands of those deploying overseas

"Trust the Army to be redundant," Kevin said.

When there was a small lull in the training schedule that first day, I got a ride over to the emergency room at Martin Army Community Hospital. I needed something for the left hip, which pretty much woke me up every night. I saw a real doctor who ordered an X-ray.

"Captain Jerome, I don't see anything broken in your hip. You've got a little osteoarthritis just like all of us over fifty, but that's it. I'll write you a prescription for Mobic;[32] that should help," said the lieutenant colonel doctor on duty.

"OK, ma'am. I will soldier on," I said.

We endured the short week of early mornings and late evenings in training at CRC. To be honest, there were a couple of classes taught we hadn't received at Fort Jackson.

By the time Thursday rolled around, we were very ready to get out of Dodge on the charter flight to the Middle East. We dropped our baggage at the covered formation area and then headed over to the DFAC. The DFAC put on a bigger than normal breakfast for us, which was awesome, and we headed back to the formation area for a 9 a.m. muster and manifest check.

We went by bus to Lawson Army Airfield and arrived around ten. We offloaded and just sat around using Wi-Fi on laptops until a final manifest boarding call.

"Anyone hear when we're going to board the aircraft?" Kevin asked, but we all shook our heads no.

"I did hear that the DFAC is preparing a special going-away lunch for us," Carl piped.

Kevin popped over and added his two cents. "There's a reason for that. DFAC just arrived and they're settin' up for a meal. Take anything they give ya cuz it's going to be a long ride with no meal service on-board . . . only snacks. That's why DFAC is here, to feed

---

32   Meloxicam: a nonsteroidal anti-inflammatory drug

us right before we fly out. The Operations NCO said we fly into Shannon, Ireland, for fuel. No tellin' how long we'll be there. We could be on the ground two or three hours. Then another long-ass flight into Kuwait."

CHAPTER 5
Welcome to Iraq

March 26 – 28, 2009

The Operations NCO back at Benning was spot on with his timetable. After a nearly eleven-hour flight from Lawson Army Airfield, we then sat on the ground in Shannon, Ireland, in the middle of the night for almost three hours. After reboarding our charter, we learned we were in for another eight-plus-hour flight to Ali Al Salem Airbase in Kuwait.

As the Brits would say, "We all got sorted on arrival at Ali Al Salem." Ali Al Salem Airbase functions as the theater gateway and transportation hub to and from the Middle East combat zones. Everyone coming or going gets processed through there and routed to their gaining commands. The Air Force has this part of the operation down to a science.

One of the first orders of business after arrival at Ali Al Salem was to swipe in with our Common Access Cards or CACs[33] to start our boots-on-the-ground time in theater. Next, we checked in with the 1st Corps liaison officer (LNO), a master sergeant who directed us to a line of buses nearby and told us, "Catch one of the buses going to Buehring.[34] Once there, check in with the 1st Corps LNO and

---

33 CAC: Common Access Card (Military ID)
34 Buehring: A U.S. military base in Kuwait known as Camp Buehring

get yourselves a place to crash. Other main body aircraft are due in from Fort Lewis over the next couple of days. The LNO will get you hooked up with them for the flight into Baghdad."

"Kevin!" Mike screamed over the idling line of buses. "Get your bags over here. That bus is going to Camp New York." Mike pointed to a small handwritten sign in the corner of the passenger side window.

Kevin, who was a bit out of it from the flight, looked up, nodded and then grabbed his bags just before someone was about to load them on the New York–bound bus. He was two buses down the line from the buses headed to Buehring.

"Sorry," Kevin apologized. "I guess I was just following Lisa and wasn't thinking. I figured we were all going to the same place."

Capt. Lisa Bowen was a Medical Corps officer whom we all met back at CRC at Benning. She was unpretentious and outgoing, and Kevin and she became friends. We all wondered how friendly they had become since Kevin had a wife at home. Regardless, she and the rest of the medical people from the CRC headed out to Camp New York for more training.

Camp Buehring provided us some needed rest for a couple of days. When the 1st Corps main body started arriving, the LNO hooked us up with the assistant chief of staff for Personnel (C-1), a full colonel. The C-1 office handled augmentees like us pretty much as replacements.

The colonel talked to us in the tent. "Gentlemen, I'm happy to see you all made it here. I'm going to make sure we bring you into the fold, so to speak. The LNO gave me your names and we'll make sure you get on the main body manifest to fly into Iraq with us. If you've got any questions, feel free to catch me here or later in-country and I'll do what I can for you."

The colonel was true to his word; a lieutenant dropped by our bunks a few hours later to give us a warning order for movement. The lieutenant gave us the lowdown. "Gentlemen. We'll need you out on the other side of that tent row with bags and baggage," he said, then pointed outside our tent flap, "at 2300 hours. We'll have transportation waiting. The uniform for the flight into Iraq is full IOTV[35] body armor with SAPI[36] plates and weapons. If you pack your IOTV at the top of your bag so you can pull it out easily, you will not have to wear it on the transportation to the preflight tents. Once we get to the tents, you'll have time to put it all on. There's wait time in the preflight tents for people to get settled and to verify the manifest."

"Thanks, Lieutenant," Mike answered. "We'll see you in a couple of hours."

The manifest for our C-17 Globemaster III aircraft included about 130 or so armed troops from the 1st Corps headquarters and Special Troops Battalion. The chalk commander again verified our names on the manifest as we exited the preflight tent and walked over to the flight line before dawn. It was about effing time. We'd been sitting in that preflight tent for hours, ready to go.

As we got near the flight line, an Air Force NCO wearing earmuff hearing protection appeared and lined us up to march single file behind him. The NCO led the way toward the back of an aircraft, where he stopped short and then pointed us to the loadmaster at the back of the open cargo hatch. We kept walking with our weapons and assault packs into the cavernous body of the aircraft. The Air Force loadmaster dutifully counted us as we entered "his" aircraft, and he pointed us forward toward another loadmaster at the front of the cargo hold.

The straps of my Kevlar advanced combat helmet, or ACH, were anchored at the back and sides, wrapping down around my ears, across my cheeks and underneath my chin. Head and helmet were balanced and moved as one while I lumbered forward wearing twenty-five pounds of IOTV body armor with SAPI ceramic plates and with deltoid and groin protectors in place. In this uniform

---

35   IOTV: Acronym for Improved Outer Tactical Vest which replaced the Individual Body Armor (IBA)

36   SAPI: Acronym for Small Arms Protective Inserts made of a ceramic trauma plate (pronounced "Sap E")

configuration I felt like saying, "Play ball!" Maybe "Strike three, you're out" seemed more appropriate.

The other loadmaster at the front of the cargo hold inside the C-17 motioned us forward and herded us like cattle into the center palletized seats and permanent sidewall seats, loading it from front to rear. We sat side by side in the dim, tactically lighted cargo hold, cradled in the combat gear provided by the RFI at the CRC at Fort Benning, GA. I tried to latch the seat belt. I guess some people had success with that.

If you were unlucky enough to be placed in the five-across seats of the centerline seating pallets, you could not move. Thank God I peed before I got on! By the way, did I write *sit*? I meant to write we squeezed in like sardines in a can. In full combat gear with our pack and other carry-on crap in our laps, we were wedged in right up against the seats to the front. This position did make it easier to snooze, by the way. The fifty-four soldiers in the sidewall seats fared much better as they at least had a little bit of leg room as they faced the center of the aircraft.

Figure 1: Inside the C-17 Globemaster III

The flight from Kuwait was not very long, but it was eventful as the pilot started a tactical descent into BIAP.[37] Pilots performed tactical descents to reduce aircraft exposure to anti-aircraft weapons fire by descending, landing and stopping on the airfield tarmac as quickly as possible. I would find out later that the C-17 Globemaster III could descend like the space shuttle at a rate of 20,000 feet per minute. For the math wizards, that's a loss of over 300 feet per second.

The word *descend* is open to interpretation. I think it's more accurate to say this plane dropped at a rate of nearly 333 feet per second while performing an exaggerated turn or two. The tactical descent can all be a bit unnerving when you're immersed in the whine of jet engines while packed in the dimly lit space with no windows and the faint bouquet of jet fuel and hydraulic oil. Does James Stewart in the movie *Vertigo* come to mind?

During that awful drop with a couple of radical, steeply banked turns thrown in for good measure, the soldier sitting next to me asked, "Sir, do you smell that?" He was truly my brother in arms as we sat shoulder to shoulder with our arms squeezed between us, his arm resting mostly on top of mine.

"No." I stopped mid-sentence as the waft of someone's vomit crept into the nearby airspace. "Oh yeah, now I do. And that's why we took off *before* breakfast," I told my neighbor.

We heard a couple of people choke up over the jet noise; perhaps a little dry retching may have occurred. I don't remember the loadmaster handing out any air-sickness bags when we got on board, either. It's like going fishing aboard an open-boat charter out of San Pedro, CA. Once someone gets seasick on the deck and the smell gets around, it can spread like wildfire.

Fortunately, the smell in the aircraft didn't get any worse. Besides,

37   BIAP: Baghdad International Airport

we had more important things to think about, like getting down to earth in one piece. Now, if someone crapped their ACUs, that might have changed the attitude on board.

Once the wheels touched down, the pilot reversed engines and put the foot on the brakes to quickly bring the aircraft to a taxi speed. No one was clapping, but a collective sigh of relief from the assembled masses seemed appropriate.

As Army luck would have it, by the time we deplaned at Sather Air Base on the west side of BIAP and headed over to its DFAC for breakfast, it was closed. The Operations sergeant major from 1st Corps headquarters tried to get us in, but the DFAC NCOIC[38] said, "No way, GI. Come back for lunch in three hours."

The sergeant major spoke up. "OK. Listen up, people. DFAC is closed so we're going to head over to Hope Chapel for an in-briefing. So, you need to load your bags onto that truck." He pointed at the large mountain of duffle bags, trunks, footlockers and other extraneous baggage still loaded on a couple of Air Force pallets which had been placed there by forklift.

No one moved an inch toward the baggage. This wasn't surprising given that a significant number of fellow passengers were field-grade officers and senior NCOs. You could sense their attitude: "The smadge[39] isn't talking to me since I don't do manual labor."

The sergeant major looked around and said, "We can't go anywhere until those bags get on the truck."

More silence ensued with no movement toward the bags.

Looking around at the expressions, you could almost sense someone about to say, "You talkin' to me?"

A major standing nearby turned to me and said, "Whaddaya say, Captain? Shall we get this ball rolling or what?"

"Absolutely, sir. I'll organize the truck end of it, I guess." I moved toward the truck and said under my breath, "If you want something

---

38 NCOIC: Non-Commissioned Officer in Charge
39 SMADGE: Nickname for Sergeant Major

done, I guess . . ." As my voice trailed off, I jumped into the back of the truck to organize the load plan.

The major started giving orders to form a handler's line from the baggage pile to the back of the truck. "OK, let's get a line going from here to the truck," he said as he pointed at the baggage. "And let's do it *now*, too," as he saw no one moving very fast. He pointed at some officers and junior NCOs standing around picking their noses, and he wagged his finger in a yes-I-meant-you method.

He looked toward the truck and spoke up. "You three people standing near the truck," he said as he pointed at them, "y'all jump in the back with the captain and start stacking the bags."

Finally, people started cooperating. I could not believe the laziness.

Once it got going, it went pretty smoothly. Still, we had way too many bystanders. *Too many chiefs and not enough Indians* came to mind. We filled the truck with little room to spare, and it headed out toward the chapel while three forty-five-passenger buses arrived for the people part.

We made it to Hope Chapel, where we filed in and settled down in uncomfortable metal folding chairs too close to each other for any comfort. Several guest speakers briefed us, all of whom had their own little spiel of "whatcha can do and whatcha can't do while here at Camp Victory." The briefing seemed to go on forever, my stomach growling intermittently. But at least we could take off our body armor and helmets while sitting there.

At the end of the briefing, it was time for everyone to get keys to their containerized housing units, or CHUs.[40] An NCO started calling out names in alphabetical order to come up and sign for their CHU. We all stood there disappointed as we watched while 126 other people got lodging, but not us. We walked up to the counter and said, "What about us?"

The NCO looked at our name tags and then to her lodging list. "I'm sorry, sirs. I don't have your names on my list."

---

40   CHU: Containerized Housing Unit

"Well ain't that a fine how da ya do?" said Kevin. "Will a set of my orders help you to find me some lodging?" Maj. Kevin Smith pulled a copy of his orders from his cargo pocket as we all decided that was a good idea and did likewise.

"Sorry, sir. You're not on my list. There's really nothing I can do for you because I have no more keys to give out," she explained. She called over to the Operations sergeant major for help.

To say we were all a bit pissed would be an understatement.

"What a fuster-cluck," Carl said. "It's not like they didn't know we were coming. I mean, they *did* get a copy of our deployment orders. After all, they had us manifested on the bird, didn't they?"

Mike and I stood there quietly, knowing sooner or later it would all get sorted. No sense in getting any more frustrated. Besides, I was too tired and too hungry to worry about it.

Fortunately for us, the sergeant major took pity. He also had a HUMMER with a trailer, where we loaded up our bags for a trip over to the Freedom Village lodging office, where they broke up the four of us over our impassioned protests. They said they had a policy to follow for vacant CHUs. The office gave the two majors, Smith and Corso, individual CHU rooms which were not close to each other at all. The two captains, Carl and I, got stuck with each other in the same CHU, F-23AB on the north end of Freedom Village. I was hoping that at least the four of us could be in nearby CHUs.

I knew from being around Carl for the last month at Fort Jackson and Fort Benning that because of his political views, being his roommate would not be fun. He did not like being called a liberal, preferring the term *progressive*. "Whatever," I had previously told him.

The HUMMER with trailer could only drive us so far into the village before it ran out of space. "OK, sirs, I'll get you as close as I can to your CHU, but then you'll have to hump it in from there," the sergeant major's driver told us.

We learned that the spec four drove the two majors around Freedom Village and dropped them close to their CHU rows in the field-grade officer area. He came back and picked up Carl and me last. He dropped us as close as he could get, which was nearly 100 meters from our CHU row. We then humped our four duffle bags, assault packs and laptop cases to the sixth row, where we found CHU F-23AB—our new home! We accomplished all that while wearing body armor and helmets.

It was now almost noon and I'd been awake over twenty-four hours. *Food or sleep?* Being served lunch in bed could have worked nicely. Alas, it was to be neither as our presence was requested at the company orderly room.

CHAPTER 6

The Al Faw Palace

March 28, 2009

The schedule for FNGs (fuckin' new guys) involved getting issued personal defense ammunition from the supply room before heading over to the palace under escort for further in-processing. The staff sergeant from Operations would lead us on a little three-quarter-mile-or-so hump over to the Al Faw Palace from the nicely air-conditioned orderly room.

"Can we stop by our CHU on the north end?" I asked. "I need to drop something off and pick something up."

"Me too," Carl chimed.

"Sure, sirs. No problem cuz it's not that far out of the way," the staff sergeant responded. "Besides, we've gotta walk the whole way anyway.

"And sorry about the distance to the palace, sirs, but all the NTVs[41] were taken," the staff sergeant remarked. "We've got a few NTVs like the Toyotas and Mitsubishis you see running around camp, but all the higher headquarters brass are now in-country, if you get my drift. If you ever get an NTV license while you're here, the roads are very narrow. You'll see that most of the driver's side mirrors are broken." He paused.

---

41   NTV: Non-tactical vehicle, usually a Toyota or Mitsubishi SUV

"OK, I'll bite," I asked. "Why are the driver's side mirrors all broken?"

"Seriously, sir," the NCO remarked. "The streets are so narrow and the mirrors stick out so far that we wind up clipping the mirrors against oncoming traffic as we pass by each other. It's a real problem."

"Ah yes," we all said in unison.

We strolled westward towards the palace following a well-worn dirt path on the north side of Freedom Village. About three feet to the other side of the path, the ground dropped off into a drainage ditch about twelve feet wide with weeds and stinky, lazy water. "This path is gonna be a bitch to walk at night with no lights," I suggested. "Don't wanna fall into that shit there." I pointed to the unknown muck.

On the other side of the ditch was a small two-lane access road lined with T-wall-protected,[42] one-story buildings on the opposite side. Behind the buildings, we could make out a perimeter wall running the entire length of the road to protect and shield the Camp Victory helicopter airfield. We stopped walking as we heard the increasing sound of helicopter rotor wash. We turned to watch a Black Hawk rise slowly a mere 100 meters from us. The aircraft hovered motionlessly in ground effect about ten feet off the ground. After about thirty seconds, the pilot slowly rotated the aircraft until he pointed away from the airfield buildings. We heard an increase in turbine power as the aircraft moved slowly forward and then upward and away from the helipad as the pilot began to pull pitch.

"Oh, this is going to be fucking great," Carl opined. "I've got an active helipad a hundred meters from my bunk. Hopefully, they'll only fly during the day."

"Hey! Don't say that. What if you work a night shift and wanna sleep during the day? Karma might visit you with that wish," I cautioned.

"Not near my bunk," Kevin added. "My CHU's on the other side of Freedom Village. And by the way, that might be Zembiec Helipad. General Petraeus renamed a Camp Victory helipad in honor of

---

42   T-wall: Concrete blast wall shaped like an upside-down T

Marine major Douglas Zembiec who was killed in action in Fallujah back in 2007, but I'm not sure which helipad. I did a little research myself on Camp Victory."

I learned later on my trips around the area the helipad was named Mercy Helipad.

As the Black Hawk disappeared, we continued our march to the palace. To get there, we needed to cross the ditch at some point. Another fifty or so yards down the dirt path, we climbed up the side of a small dirt levee, which crossed over the ditch. We walked along the levee to the other side while large drainage culverts below allowed water to flow through. We could either walk down the two-lane road or along the dirt shoulder. We observed someone driving an NTV crazily down the road towards us.

"I think I'll stick to walking the dirt shoulder . . . facing traffic," Mike offered as a solution.

"No shit, Sherlock," Kevin said.

At the end of the dirt path, the ditch ended, but seemed to go underground towards the lake surrounding the palace, since a small electric pump of some sort noisily churned on. We all stopped to look at this marvel of Iraqi engineering.

Mike seemed to be the most thrilled with the pump. "Guys. Y'all know I'm from Louisiana and I've seen some redneck engineering on lots of projects before. Hell, I've even done my share of it, but this pump contraption takes the prize. There's more duct tape and baling wire keeping that thing running than seems possible."

Mike pulled out a small camera and took a picture of it. "For the folks back home. They'll never believe this shit."

The crazy Iraqi ditch-pumping station ended at a five-way road intersection. We waited for traffic to subside, and then ventured into the intersection. Ranger Mike spoke up as we crossed, and he pointed to the road hugging the lake's east side.

"That road there runs north along the side of the lake and will get you to Camp Liberty."

"Ah, it's about time that he goes all Ranger on us again," I said with a bit of admiration. "You can take the soldier out of the Rangers, but you can't take the Ranger out of the soldier."

"Hey, so I did a little map recon earlier," Mike offered. "Besides, it might be a decent place to run, too."

"You're going to run while you're here? Isn't that against regulations for retirees to do?" I asked in jest.

We reached the other road, which ran closely along the bank of the lake and turned left toward the palace. We approached the first checkpoint for entrance to the Al Faw Palace area on the perimeter road about 100 meters inside the eastern corner of the palace's lake, and yet still about 700 or so meters from the front door. As we got closer to the checkpoint guarding this vehicle entrance, we could see the guards were not US forces. The staff sergeant informed us, "If you end up working in the palace, you'll go through this checkpoint every time and show your badge. The Army uses third-country nationals from Africa to man some of these less-critical spots. Most of them do not speak English. Just show your badge and they'll let you through."

Two soldiers from Nigeria or Uganda, or wherever, were standing just outside a small building that looked more like an old drive-up kiosk from the 1980s, the kind of small, two-man hut where you just dropped off your film to get pictures developed. Two small wooden barriers leaned up against the guard building. Ostensibly, the barriers could be pulled up across the road if necessary. The guards spotted us and smiled broadly as we approached.

"Well, that's reassuring," I remarked.

The staff sergeant led the way through this first checkpoint, displaying his badge and basically showing the guards with hand and arm signals that "these guys are with me." There was no complaint from the guards. I'm sure they were quite happy to be making some US dollars to send home. "Don't stir the pot" was certainly their watchword.

We kept walking about another half klick[43] to the next checkpoint, a much larger building that stood with fence gates at the entrance to the palace access road. The two-lane road was a bridge from lakeside to palace side with a center median sidewalk used by pedestrians.

Figure 2: Walking across the bridge to Al Faw Palace

A six-foot-high chain-link fence blocked our entrance at the building. *No entrance without ID,* read a sign on the gate. Two US soldiers manned the building, and one of them came out to see our identification.

"Hey, Specialist," the staff sergeant said while showing him his palace access ID. "I'm escorting these new officers to get their access badges."

"Sure, Sarge," the specialist said as he whipped out a salute, which we all returned.

The specialist pulled the chain-link gate open enough for us to pass through and then closed it.

---

43   Klick: Military slang term for a kilometer

We walked past a large pallet of water bottles staged on the median just inside the gate, stopping just long enough to grab one each. We then moseyed on the median the rest of the way down the length of the bridge, only stopping to see a boiling in the water below us at the palace end.

The staff sergeant pointed out what the ruckus in the water was all about. "Those are the Al Faw Palace lake fish."

Figure 3: The Al Faw Palace fish

"I heard these are specially bred Saddam bass, only they just look like carp to me. Everyone feeds them. They are here at this end constantly and they'll become your friends. A word of advice; if you see someone out here fishing and wearing what looks like cook's whites on Thursdays, do not eat the fish in the DFAC on Fridays."

"Thanks for the heads-up," Carl said. We all laughed heartily at the legitimacy of his warning.

The staff sergeant had more to say as we stood there watching the fish boil below. "By the way, gentlemen, Camp Victory has two great DFACs and a great gym on this end of Freedom Village. It's called the SFC Paul R. Smith Gym, named after a Medal of Honor recipient here in Iraq. The gym stays really busy because there's not much else to do except work out or go eat lots of food in the DFAC. So, here's your dilemma. When you redeploy to CONUS, you'll either bench-press three hundred pounds or you'll weigh three hundred pounds."

That last comment really got us all laughing because it was more than likely dead-on true.

We moved on from the fish and on to the next and last checkpoint, inside the very tall palace front door.

Figure 4: Front Door to the Al Faw Palace

Armed US servicemen were just inside the door, blocking the entrance beyond them while checking badges. A large counter area was behind the guards and to our left as we entered. Looking beyond the guards and through an open passage, we could see what looked like a large rotunda area.

Once we got waved through this last set of guards, the staff sergeant turned us over to another tour guide, a civilian, to take us through in-processing. At the counter we turned over a copy of our orders, and they took our pictures and presented us with nifty ID badges. The rest of processing through personnel and IT sections went smoothly, too. We were their only customers since everyone else presumably processed at Fort Lewis before deployment.

"I don't know about y'all," I mentioned to my three amigos, "but that was actually pretty smooth getting checked in here. We got bullets, badges and access to the palace. Let's get to work."

I cautioned my friends as we waited for another tour guide to join us.

"Hey, guys, one thing you should know while we are here in the palace. Don't refer to 1st Corps as Eye Corps. Way back in the late '70s while stationed at Fort Lewis, Washington, I learned that 1st Corps is referred to as First Corps. Yes, the unit name often appears as I Corps, where a Roman numeral one is used in the name and looks like a capital *I*. Still, the unit name is First Corps. Don't forget it because someone may correct you."

The Four Amigos who came together during regreening in South Carolina were all assigned to 1st Corps as it took on the command and control mission of Multinational Corps-Iraq, or MNC-I for short. MNC-I directed the tactical operations in Iraq while Multi-National Force – Iraq (MNF-I) managed the strategic-level issues in the country. To give major commands operational experience, the Pentagon rotated corps-level headquarters into the MNC-I duty on a regular basis.

The various MNC-I staff organizations for personnel, intelligence, operations, training, civil affairs and other coordinating and special staff sections resided in the Al Faw Palace and other buildings around the lake. Smaller lakeside buildings on the north end provided lodging for some general officers with a convenient helipad and aircraft parking ramp right across the street. 1st Corps merely became the most recent landlord or host unit to take residence and occupy all these buildings.

One of the more prominent buildings on the lake was nicknamed *The Juicer*, because of the hemispherical dome rising from the main building roofline. The dome ended in a point at the top, with eight vertical ribs extending down the sides of the dome. If you've ever manually squeezed an orange or grapefruit with a juicer, you'll know what I'm talking about. The Juicer provided office space mainly for the assistant chief of staff for Personnel, C-1 and his subordinates.

Figure 5: The Juicer (note the dome)

The palace also provided working space for other long-term tenants not affected by the MNC-I rotation. They included allied forces as well as civilian contractors involved in IT, logistics, personnel and other support-type fields. These people remained in the palace for the duration of their civilian contract or until their country pulled forces out of Iraq.

The MNC-I rotation from one corps headquarters to another occurs as a transition. Officially, it is referred to as a relief in place/ transfer of authority. In other words, units may come and units may go, but the mission never ceases. Someone always has to have their hand on the tiller. Consequently, the transition process provides an overlap time so the gaining unit can train-up with the losing unit to take over the battle space. In practice, this transition process is known as right seat, left seat, which basically refers to pilot and copilot positions in an airplane cockpit.

The gaining unit sits in the right seat to observe the losing unit conduct operations from the left seat. After some time of observation, the losing unit moves to the right seat to observe and mentor the gaining unit. When fully ready, the losing unit officially hands over the command-and-control mission in a transfer of authority ceremony.

In practice, I thought it looked more like a game of musical chairs. When the transition music started playing, XVIII Airborne Corps functioned as MNC-I while 1st Corps walked around the chairs with them. Once in a while the music would stop and 1st Corps would start occupying chairs once held by XVIII Airborne. Finally, the only people walking around the chairs were from 1st Corps.

We all had specific job assignments related to a paragraph and line number in the Special Troops Battalion, 1st Corps table of organization and equipment (TO&E) manning document. And now here we were in Al Faw Palace getting taken to those respective assignments.

A staff sergeant from the 1st Corps personnel section finally showed up and led us upstairs to the C-3 Operations office to meet up with our working sections. I'd met my future supervisor, Lt. Col. Hellard, back at Fort Lewis, where we talked about my working as an electronic warfare officer in his section. He had advised me to start up the process for a TS clearance, too. As we entered the C-3 area, Lt. Col. Hellard was walking towards me with a cup of coffee.

"Hello, sir," I said as I extended my hand to shake his. He gave me a rather queer look, stopped and shook my hand, then with merely a "Hello, Captain," he continued walking down the aisle away from me.

I stood there looking a bit confused and probably embarrassed. I turned around in time to see him also turn around and walk back towards me. "I'm sorry, Captain," he said with some puzzlement. "Have we met before?"

"Yes, sir. I'm your retiree recall from Arizona to serve in one of your electronic warfare officer slots." His puzzled look endured. "I came to Fort Lewis a couple of months ago and met with you," I said cautiously. The light bulb in his head turned on, but maybe only about forty watts' worth.

"Oh, yeah," he said with some resignation. "There's been a change of plans. You won't be working for me." And without further ado, he turned on his heels and exited stage left.

OK, I said to myself as I watched him walk away with his coffee.

I linked back up with the other three amigos standing by themselves near a cubicle partition. "What's up, guys?" I asked.

"We're waiting for that staff sergeant to come back," Mike replied. "He seems to be a bit confused about where to take us."

"So, what else is new?" Kevin asked sarcastically. "After the FUBAR[44] lodging assignments at Hope Chapel, I'm surprised anyone is looking for us to show up."

The staff sergeant returned with a smile on his face and said, "OK, sirs. I know where we're going now."

He ushered us off to another area with an office. Inside was another lieutenant colonel. A very fit-looking fellow named McGregor. Since he had his own office, I presumed he probably was filling a full colonel position. As we entered, he picked up his telephone and called someone. He motioned for us to come in as he finished his call.

"Welcome to Iraq. I'm Kerry McGregor." He offered his hand as we introduced ourselves. Lt. Col. McGregor briefed us as we stood there.

"We're going to get you guys into the scheme of things here shortly after Lieutenant Colonel Willis, Tom Willis, gets here from the reconciliation cell. As part of COIN, the CG wants us to really work the KLE process through the reconciliation cell. The corps reconciliation cell supports the efforts of the force strategic engagement cell, or FSEC."

The lieutenant colonel must have gotten some blank stares from us, so he started to explain. "Sorry, are you all retirees?"

"Just the major here and me, sir," I offered while patting Mike's arm.

---

44   FUBAR: Fucked Up Beyond All Recognition

"We're both IRR," Kevin offered for himself and Carl.

Lt. Col. McGregor looked at me and Mike and asked, "How long you been retired?"

I deferred to Mike. "Five years, sir."

"Thirteen years, sir," I added.

"Thirteen years?" Lt. Col. McGregor asked with some incredulity. "How'd they get you?"

"Well, sir, I believe the person that called me from HRC was dyslexic. I told him he should be looking for a twenty-five-year-old captain, not a fifty-two-year-old captain."

Only Lt. Col. McGregor laughed as my three amigos had already heard this story.

"Well, that sounds about par for the course at HRC, and don't tell them I said that, either," the lieutenant colonel said. "But hey, no problem. Glad you're here. We throw these acronyms around and forget sometimes we have newcomers who've been outta the business a while."

He slowed down, took a breath and then said, "COIN stands for 'counter-insurgency' and KLE stands for 'key leader engagement.' KLE is how we engage the populace through their leaders, hoping to turn them towards us. The reconciliation cell runs point on KLE to help 'reconcile' the country."

Lt. Col. McGregor had started to explain the concept of winning over the hearts and minds of the people as the focus of the reconciliation cell when Lt. Col. Tom Willis arrived. "Gentlemen. This is Tom Willis, chief of the reconciliation cell."

"Thanks, Kerry, for bringing these men to my attention," Lt. Col. Willis remarked. "I'll take them down to our conference room, where we can get to know each other a little better."

Willis led the way out of McGregor's office, and down the corridor and to a conference room about the same size as McGregor's office. "Let's all sit down. I'd like to hear about your backgrounds."

We all settled in behind the table into rather comfy chairs, and looked around at briefing easels along the wall and a large LED monitor on the wall at one end. "Yup, it's a conference room all right."

Willis started. "Before you begin, though, let me tell you about the reconciliation cell and our mission. As you're aware from all the pre-deployment training we endured, COIN is the name of the game for winning and it's working . . . so far. We're turning the once-bad guys into our good guys by fostering a reconciliation process with the government of Iraq. At the heart of the reconciliation process is KLE, or key leader engagement. KLE involves targeting, but not in the traditional kinetic warfare sense. In KLE, we identify targets such as influential community leaders and those insurgent leaders who might otherwise be engaged by outreach, negotiations, and other beneficial interactions. We try to show them that there is a better way to stabilize their country and begin reconstruction efforts.

"That's it in a nutshell. I need people to help with this who have an open mind and perhaps a background in community services, outreach or volunteering, which could be brought to bear during these KLEs." He paused. "So, let's go round the table and you tell me a little about yourself and your background, starting with the junior captain." Willis opened a notebook he was carrying and was ready to take notes. "I'm ready," he said.

Carl and I had already had that discussion about who was junior back at Fort Jackson, so he spoke first. "Sir, I'm Carl Buckley. I'm an armor officer currently assigned to the IRR. I have nine years of service. I'm on temporary leave from my job during this deployment."

Technically, that was a lie. Carl had told all of us back at Fort Jackson that he was let go because of a lack of work as a consultant at his company. He'd told us he only pursued the individual augmentee deployment as a quick way to make some decent, tax-free money while he waited (hoped) for his company to have work for him. I suppose he was just sugarcoating it by saying temporary leave. I gave him the benefit of the doubt. After all, I was going to have to share a cramped CHU with him for some time to come.

"What do you do as a civilian?" asked the lieutenant colonel.

"I'm a consultant, sir, for a personnel services company. I'm kind of like an on-call fireman. If and when they see a problem somewhere in the organization or with clients, they ask me to research it and deliver a report on my findings."

"How long have you been with this company as a consultant?"

"Two years, sir."

Lt. Col. Willis nodded then turned toward me. "And you, Captain Jerome?"

"Sir, I'm Matt Jerome and I'm a retiree recall from Arizona. I retired from active duty as a Medical Service Corps officer in 1996. I am also branch-qualified as a Signal Corps officer. After leaving military service, I retired in late 2004 from my second career as a health care administrator and information systems manager at a veterans' nursing home in Georgia. Prior to coming here, I was doing some volunteer work at the VA hospital, my HOA and some other community organizations. I also pursue my hobby of woodworking."

"How would you feel about going out to these Iraqi towns during KLE with an eye towards assessing health care needs in general?"

"That would be fine with me, sir. My post-graduate education is in health care administration, and I would see this as a new challenge. Besides, the fundamentals of providing health care don't change much around the world."

Lt. Col. Willis nodded and then turned toward the two majors. "Who's next?"

Mike spoke up. "That's me, sir. I'm Mike Corso and I'm also a retiree recall, but I'm from Shreveport, Louisiana. I retired as an MP[45] officer five years ago and then became a deputy sheriff in Shreveport. In my off time I like to climb mountains, skydive, scuba dive and go fishing."

Lt. Col. Willis smiled and asked Mike the same question. "How

---

45　MP: Military Police

would you feel about going out to these Iraqi towns during KLE with an eye towards assessing policing needs in general?"

"Wherever I'm needed, sir. That sounds OK to me because I enjoy being outdoors. Working at a desk all day with computers is OK, but only for a brief time."

Lt. Col. Willis nodded and looked at Maj. Kevin Smith.

"I'm Kevin Smith, sir, and I'm from North Augusta, South Carolina. I work in Directorate for Plans, Training, Mobilization and Security (DPTMS) for the Signal School at Fort Gordon. I'm branched Intel and serving in the IRR."

"Which component of DPTMS do you work in?" asked Lt. Col. Willis.

"I'm an assistant chief in the security and intelligence division, sir. My focus is on the Garrison INFOSEC[46] mission."

Willis finished making his notes and then looked up. "Gentlemen, I am impressed. Thank you for joining 1st Corps as augmentees. I'm not sure I can use all of you in my mission, but we'll see."

The lieutenant colonel got up from his chair, went to the door, opened it and motioned for someone else to come in. The personnel sergeant who served as our current tour guide entered the conference room.

"Gentlemen, if you'll go with the sergeant here, he'll take you to your next destination," Willis said as he held his arm up while pointing to the staff sergeant.

As Mike approached the door, Willis pulled him aside. "Can I have one more word, Major Corso?"

"Yes, sir."

"I need to talk with you too, Captain Jerome. Can you join me?" Lt. Col. Willis motioned me to Mike's side. He closed the door behind him and turned towards us.

"Gentlemen, I'd like you on the reconciliation team. I like the fact that both of you are retired and serving in your communities.

---

46   INFOSEC: Information Security

I also like that you both have current experience working with the public. You as a sheriff's deputy," he said as he nodded at Mike and then looked at me, "and you with your experience in working with families in the nursing home environment. I think we can use your unique perspectives in conducting KLE with a variety of folk outside the wire. I need you back here at 0900 tomorrow for our daily huddle. No field gear, just soft caps, weapons and ID. I'll introduce you to the rest of the team and get you integrated. Have any questions for me before I head off to another meeting?"

Mike spoke for both of us. "No, sir. I'm sure Captain Jerome and I can think this through tonight and bring our follow-up questions to tomorrow's huddle."

I nodded my assent.

"Good. Until then."

We followed Lt. Col. Willis out of the conference room to the corridor, where the staff sergeant was waiting with Carl and Kevin. Lt. Col. Willis walked over to the staff sergeant and gave him instructions.

"Staff Sergeant Walker, please take Major Smith and Captain Buckley back to Colonel McGregor's office for further assignment. Major Corso and Captain Jerome are released until tomorrow's reconciliation huddle."

"Yes, sir," Staff Sgt. Walker replied as he headed with Kevin and Carl back down the hallway.

"Maybe we'll catch you two in the DFAC for supper?" Mike said as they walked away.

"Sure, Mike. I'll drop by your CHU later," Kevin replied as he waved adios.

Mike and I headed out of the palace and toward CHUville. We both lived in Freedom Village, just different areas, so most of our walk we talked about the upcoming challenges working in the reconciliation cell and doing KLEs.

"I hope you like wearing all that IOTV, because when we start doing KLE outside the wire, we'll be fully geared up," Mike said.

"It is what it is," I remarked. "I thought I was going to be doing a lot of desk jockey work with maps, routes and frequency management, but I'm a field soldier at heart. My wife won't like it, but we're all in."

We went our separate ways at the west end of Freedom Village right next to the laundry drop-off point to go to our respective CHUs.

Carl woke me from my afternoon cat nap around 1630 hours. "Hey, Matt, we're going to meet Mike and Kevin at five at their CHU, then head over to the DFAC."

Mike and Kevin were standing outside Kevin's CHU when Carl and I arrived. Kevin looked pissed. "Let's go," he said, storming off toward the DFAC.

Mike shrugged.

"Kev, you might as well air it out here," Mike said. "What's wrong?"

Kevin took another deep breath. "1st Corps just screwed me. That's all. I have a paragraph and line number on my orders for a lieutenant colonel slot in the C-2 Intelligence planning cell. I have a TS clearance for the assignment, too. That's what I volunteered to do. One of the reasons I'm in the IRR is I couldn't get promoted in my USAR[47] unit; no slot available. I only need about thirteen months to go over eighteen years of active duty service, too. I was hoping to use this colonel slot to help me get promoted and then possibly to stay on active duty. If I can get to eighteen years of active duty, I can claim sanctuary for an active duty retirement. Instead, the C-3 chief rerouted me to the fusion cell in the JOC—a major's slot. The C-2 said that the C-3 chief has priority on replacement assignments right now. So, I'm going to the JOC. At least I'm not going to be managing SCIF[48] access or some shit like that."

---

47   USAR: United States Army Reserve
48   SCIF: Sensitive Compartmentalized Information Facility (a classified information facility pronounced "Skiff")

"If it's any consolation, Kevin," I chimed, "they changed my assignment, too. The paragraph and line number for my assignment was to function as an electronics warfare officer. I'd be sitting around with maps and plans to manage frequencies to defeat IEDs on convoys and such. Now, I'm going to be going outside the wire on a regular basis on these KLE meetings. Not exactly what I planned for *or* trained for, either. I'm sure the same thing is true of Mike and Carl."

Carl jumped in. "Me? I don't care where they put me. Just show me the money. That's why I'm here—tax-free income. Remember, I was unemployed when I took this on. They can extend me if they want."

"Actually, I'm signed up for a position in the provost marshal's office, but I'm obviously not going there either," Mike added. "We know how you feel, Kevin. It seems like you had a lot more riding on your assignment than we did. You rolled the dice and gambled that the Army would honor the deal. Those kinds of deals have a low percentage of going according to plan, especially as an augmentee on a deployment slot. The sun, the moon and the stars all have to line up. In your case, it was worth a try I suppose. But hey, maybe God will open a new window in the fusion cell for you?"

Kevin's mood lightened as we headed off to the DFAC to soothe our wounds with freshly made Panini sandwiches and a visit to the ice cream bar.

"Good morning, Carl," I said as we both got up the next day. "How'd you sleep?"

"Fine. I was dead to the world."

I wasn't as gleeful as I looked around the cramped, ten-foot by twelve-foot room designed for one person but occupied by two persons, each with a double-door wall locker and a bunk. A small desk occupied the space between the bunks at the head end, with the foot of the beds at the door end. A small two-cubic-foot refrigerator sat hidden just inside the door to the right. It was only large enough to hold a handful of water bottles and a few snacks.

Carl and I occupied Room AB, an end unit of CHU F-23. Twelve-foot-high, concrete T-walls surrounded all the CHUs to provide for blast protection. Although CHU F-23 was about forty feet long, it was only ten feet wide and sectioned into three rooms for AB, CD and EF. A wall-mount air conditioner hummed merrily just to the left of the entrance door, flooding the room generously with its cool wind.

Figure 6: Entering CHU F-23, Room AB (unit porch rugs strewn by wind)

I looked over at Carl tying his boots. "I thought it was fairly comfortable sleeping with the a/c on last night. However, there's a problem with the bathroom in here. *We don't have one!* There's a porta-potty without lights about seventy-five meters away outside CHUville. Or we can get up, put something on our feet and then walk a little bit farther to the middle of the village where we can use the comfort trailers. That's what I did because at least the bathroom trailer had lights. I was up another hour until I could get back to sleep. I gotta find another way."

"Coffee can from the DFAC might work," Carl offered with a shrug. Being thirty-something, Carl wasn't getting up in the middle of the night that often. His suggestion did, however, spark an idea, which I would pursue on my next trip to the DFAC.

"I really need to let my uncle Mike know about the bathroom and toilet facilities around here," I said while putting on my over-the-shoulders pistol holster.

"Why's that so important? Did he raise you or something?"

I shook my head. "Nah. I just remember him coming back from Vietnam forty years ago in 1968 and he told me a story about the latrines he used. He talked about fifty-five-gallon drums which were cut in half and placed underneath the latrine seats. Periodically the drums would be removed and the contents burned with either gasoline or kerosene. He said that was a real *shit duty*, pun intended. And here I am complaining about not having a bathroom *in* the CHU, even though we've got a porta-potty and a bathroom trailer just a short walk from here with real toilet paper. Most people around here probably never had to use C-ration TP[49] either. Regardless, I think he'd get a kick out of knowing how far the Army has come. I'll have to tell him about Saddam's toilet facilities in the palace, too."

"Yeah. I bet he'd get a kick outta that," Carl said. "Well, I'm outta here. See you later."

"Me too," I said as I opened the door for us to leave the CHU.

Carl went to the DFAC while I headed off to my first meeting in the palace—an 0900 huddle with the team in the reconciliation cell. Mike was standing outside the doors of the palace waiting on me as we had pre-arranged. I saluted him as I approached, he returned it with a smile, and then we entered.

We flashed our badges to the front door guards and went through to the rotunda and onto the highly polished marble floor,

---

49   C-ration TP: A small folded-up packet of toilet paper found in the accessory condiments packet.

Figure 7: Al Faw Palace Rotunda (note marble staircase to left, JOC foyer to the right)

past Saddam's Chair on our right,

Figure 8: Saddam's Chair (a gift from Yasser Arafat)

and then we crossed over to our left, where we ascended the winding ornate marble staircase to the second-floor offices.

Figure 9: Marble staircase from rotunda to upper floors

We made our way down the hall to the reconciliation cell office and checked in at the first desk we came to; we were about ten minutes early. The lieutenant sitting there acknowledged us. "Please wait here a second, sir. Lieutenant Colonel Willis needs to talk to you before the huddle." The lieutenant then scurried off.

"Very good. He was looking for us," I said. "It's nice to be recognized for a change."

Lt. Col. Willis exited a cubicle nearby where the lieutenant had disappeared into, and Willis walked over to us. "Good morning, fellas. I've got some bad news. My decision to add you to the reconciliation cell was vetoed. I guess Operations has priority on replacements and they decided they need you somewhere else more than I do. I'm really sorry."

Before we had a chance to say anything, the lieutenant wandered back to his desk and Lt. Col. Willis turned to him and said, "Can you take the major and captain back over to Operations assignments? You know that Marine major who was here earlier? The one who was working the assignments desk?"

"Yes, sir, I know him."

"He's waiting for them to come in this morning."

We each shook the lieutenant colonel's hand, and Mike answered for both of us. "We understand. Fast-paced change of assignment appears to be normal around here."

"Unfortunately, you got that right, Corso. I wish you success in your assignments." Lt. Col. Willis added as he slinked away. "Sorry. Off to team huddle."

The lieutenant had been twirling a yo-yo and placed it into his pocket before leading us away down the hallway to another office. *A yo-yo. How appropriate*, I thought.

We entered and the lieutenant quickly introduced us to the Marine major, and just as quickly exited the room, having accomplished his mission. I thought, *He's probably going back to master his "walking the dog" yo-yo trick.*

The Marine major working the assignments desk was not a pleasant fellow. He motioned for us to follow him, and we did to a small unmanned and quieter cubicle. He spoke to Mike first. "Major Corso, you're being assigned as an LNO. You need to take the Rhino to the Green Zone. The Rhino loads up at 1230 hours and leaves promptly at 1300 hours down at the east checkpoint to the palace. You'll need to put on full body armor, weapon, and it wouldn't hurt to take an overnight bag with clothes for a couple of days. They've got lodging there. Everything else you need to know is in this packet, including a TDY order. Better get lunch here before you get on the Rhino."

The major handed Mike a sealed manila envelope. "Questions?"

"No. I guess not. I'll read my packet and orders and get on the bus," Mike said with some resignation as he turned and headed out the door. "See ya later, Matt."

The Marine major seemed pleased. One down, one to go. "Come with me, Captain."

Without another word, the Marine major led me out of the office and back toward the marble staircase. We glided down the stairs and literally marched in step across the empty rotunda to another foyer on the left, where he checked us in at the guarded access point to the JOC. We showed our badges as we approached the guard, who acknowledged us as we headed to the closed door of the JOC.

Still without a further word, the Marine major opened the door to the JOC and went through with me close behind. After we passed through the first entry door, we entered a long, narrow corridor with small, individual wall lockers on the left side.

A doorway to the right was open, and the major walked in. Just inside and to the right through the door, I saw a young Army specialist four sorting mail at a small desk and posting names to a you-got-mail list. I said to the specialist, "If I'm working here, is this where I pick up my mail?"

"Yes, sir," he replied as he shoved a card in my hand with the standard mailing address as I followed the Marine major.

The card read,

Rank First Name Last Name
HQ, MNC-I (JOC)
1st Corps
APO AE, 09342

The major walked past the mini post office desk into a rather wide room with amphitheater-type seating that ascended quickly from floor to ceiling. The amphitheater reminded me of an IMAX theater, which is both wide and tall, but not very deep. I saw ten to twelve rows, the rows situated at a steep angle from floor to ceiling.

A long workstation cabinet of sorts ran from one side of each row to the other. Atop this cabinet I could see computer monitors placed every four or five feet. The steepness of the rows reminded me of getting nosebleed seats in the upper right field deck of Anaheim Stadium. If you turned around to talk with the person behind you, you were staring at the person's crotch.

The major led the way up some stairs on the right-hand side. The stairs were narrow and without handrails. You almost had to place your boots sideways on the stairs to get any grip because if you put your foot on it straight, the tread would only accommodate about half of your boot. It reminded me of climbing to the top of the Chichén Itzá temple in the Yucatan.

The major stopped climbing about five aisles up. He stayed on the staircase and pointed to an Air Force captain sitting about four or five chairs inside the narrow row, and behind a computer workstation. He was busy typing away, not aware that the Marine major had pointed him out to me. As I reached the major on the stairway, he said to me, "You work for him now." I stood aside, holding on to the workstation cabinet of the row above and behind. The major went back down the stairs without another word.

Within about thirty hours since arrival, I went from having no lodging, to no electronic warfare officer duties, to no KLE duties in the reconciliation cell, to some unknown job description in the Joint Operations Center. I pondered, *What's next on the agenda; the suspension of my desserts in the DFAC?*

CHAPTER 7

The JOC

End of March 2009

I landed in the JOC and found Carl sitting at his workstation. He motioned me into the cell.

"Hiya, Matt. I thought you were going to be in the reconciliation cell. What happened?"

I shrugged, "Oh hell, I don't know."

I brought Carl up to speed quickly. "Willis just told us he got overruled. They made Mike an LNO in the Green Zone[50] and sent me here. Mike's headed over there via the Rhino today. They told him to take some clothes with him, too. He's not sure when or if he'll be back at his CHU. Whatta they got you doin?"

"I'm doing PowerPoint Ranger stuff . . . presentations. Probably the same thing you'll be doing. I heard the OIC[51] talkin' about needing someone else for the night shift. I've done this before, but at a brigade level. Shouldn't be much different, I suppose. Except it looks like only the officers are doing the PowerPoints,"[52] Carl added.

Carl introduce me to his boss, Captain Collins. "This is Captain Matt Jerome. He just happens to be my CHUmate."

---

50   Green Zone: The International Zone of Baghdad
51   OIC: Officer in Charge
52   PowerPoints: Presentations created with Microsoft Office PowerPoint software

Capt. Collins stopped typing just long enough to give me a quick glance and say, "Oh. That'll work out fine. You'll be on night shift, Jerome. Buckley is on day shift; that way you can have the CHU to yourself when you're off shift. Captain Valderama is my assistant and is in charge when I'm not here. Captain Cabrera is working a swing shift and I'm hoping for another lieutenant or captain as fillers."

"Is there an SOP[53] I can bone up on before I start a shift?" I asked.

"Nah. It's all OJT, I'm afraid, but there's little time for that either. You gotta get up to speed quickly. Have you ever worked in a TOC[54] or other operations center as a captain?" he asked, trying to gauge my experience while continuing to type.

I tried to give him a quick twenty-five-cent tour of my resume since he was obviously multitasking with his workstation. "Yes, I have, but not as a captain. I was an infantry sergeant back in the '70s when I worked a TOC. In the late '80s I was an assistant S-3 for a Signal battalion, before I branch-transferred to Medical Service Corps. I retired in 1996, so I don't have any recent experience working an operations center."

Capt. Collins motioned for Capt. Valderama, who was sitting a couple of workstations down from him on the other side.

"Jesus, I need you to bring Captain Jerome up to speed so he can join the night shift tonight," Capt. Collins said bluntly, then went back to his keyboard without so much as another word.

Capt. Valderama spoke up as he squeezed past Collins's workstation. "Sir, I'm going to take Captain Jerome down for a cup of coffee to talk with him."

Capt. Collins nodded his approval. Capt. Valderama and I then went down the stairs, grabbed some coffee, and then headed out the door of the JOC and into the rotunda.

I learned from Capt. Valderama that I was now assigned to the presentations cell. He gave me the nickel tour.

---

53   SOP: Standard Operating Procedure
54   TOC: Tactical Operations Center, usually at brigade and lower levels

"The presentations cell normally has a major OIC, a senior NCO as NCOIC, one to two captains and a couple of junior NCOs for each of the two shifts. A third shift has one captain and a junior NCO which do a split shift to augment the other shifts. Day shift works 0700 to 1900 and night shift works 1900 to 0700. The third shift works noon to midnight. In reality, due to mission or briefing requirements, the shift times often float a bit. It's doable, sometimes aggravating, but doable," Capt. Valderama explained in between gulps of coffee.

He kept going like the Energizer Bunny. "The JOC briefs the MNC-I commanding general, Lieutenant General Jacobson, and his senior staff officers in the morning. These briefings can happen just about any time. Once the briefing gets started, they lock the doors to the JOC. Sometimes we do the briefing using video teleconferencing or VTC with the MNC-I commanding general. Rarely, but on occasion, General Osmand might attend the briefing in person. We also do a CHOPS[55] briefing most evenings. The intent of that briefing is pretty much a dry run to get it right for the CG's brief."

Technically, I outranked Capt. Valderama by date of rank, having been promoted in June 1992 compared with his DOR of June 2007. I probably had more time standing in Army chow lines than Capt. Valderama had in total military service since the young captain mentioned he'd joined sometime after the 9/11 attacks. Nonetheless, he owned the position by virtue of being assigned to Headquarters, 1st Corps, and he had recent operations center experience. I was merely a temporary guest, so to speak.

We headed back into the JOC, where I stopped at the mini post office to talk with the postal clerk.

"Hiya, Specialist. Do you also handle incoming packages?"

"Yes, sir, we do, but it depends on the size," he replied. "I can handle about ninety percent of the packages most people get. If it's a really big package, I have to leave it at the orderly room. If you get packages, I'll post your name here on this list."

---

55   CHOPS: Chief of Operations

"Thank you. I appreciate the info. I suppose I may get the occasional priority mail care package."

"That's the best way to get stuff here, sir."

"Thanks again," I said as I wandered over to the coffee service to refill while Capt. Valderama walked up the narrow stairs to the presentations cell.

I headed up after him with a fresh cup of coffee in hand. Somewhere around the fourth or fifth step, as I stepped forward to plant my foot, my toe caught the front of the stair tread and I went down pretty hard, spilling the coffee.

As I gathered my senses and my pride, I noticed other similar coffee stains in the area where I tripped. I wasn't the first person to trip here.

"Sign the book," someone yelled out from a small group of people snickering to my right.

I looked at them dumbfounded, not knowing what they were talking about. One fellow pointed down behind me. "Down there," he said.

I turned around to find a major motioning me to come to him. I descended the stairs slowly, not wanting to do a repeat performance on the way down.

"Hey, Captain," said the major behind me at row two of the JOC stairs. "You need to sign the JOC Trip Log. Look," he said with finality, "everyone trips on these fuckin' stairs. We're required to have everyone sign this journal when it happens. Even General Petraeus has signed it. It's happened so much this is the third journal we're working on. Right now, I'm the designated custodian of the JOC Trip Log." He gave me a half-assed smile.

I took the trip log and found a place for my name, date and remarks. I wrote, *Caught* in the remarks because that was all I could think of at the moment.

I picked up some paper towels from the coffee service area and returned to clean up my spill. Fortunately, most of the coffee had already soaked into the mostly bare plywood masquerading as stair treads.

I performed my next transit up the stairs to row five presentations cell successfully without a coffee cup. I almost expected a round of applause. I spent the next hour or so watching how they conducted business in the cell. Capt. Valderama gave me a running commentary.

"After the CHOPS briefing, we get settled down into the grind. The captains work on presentations while the NCOs read SIGACTs,[56] track down supporting information, grab things from the printer, post the briefing books, or whatever's needed for getting the job done. We do things a little differently compared to lower level operations centers. Normally, a captain would provide direction and guidance to the NCOs and functions as editor at large for the presentations being prepared by lieutenants and senior NCOs. The captain would provide over-the-shoulder editing, but not here in the presentations cell. Briefing the three- and four-stars is too high-profile."

Capt. Valderama whispered, "We don't do that here because we don't have any lieutenants and the OIC doesn't trust the NCOs to do the PowerPoints. Hence, the captains do all the PowerPoints while the NCOs sit around picking their noses and watching movies."

A young junior NCO made his way up the JOC stairs and entered the presentations row. Capt. Valderama acknowledged him as he sat down in the empty chair beside me and introduced us.

"Sergeant Manley, this is Captain Jerome. He'll be working the night shift."

Sgt. Manley gave a weak, almost forced smile and offered a handshake. "Sir."

I replied in kind—"Sergeant"—as I watched Sgt. Manley take the seat to my left, log in to the workstation and begin some kind of research.

"Manley works the swing shift with Captain Cabrera, who should

---

56   SIGACTS: Significant Activities reports

be coming in soon, too. In fact, that's him down by the coffee pot." Capt. Valderama pointed out another captain dutifully topping off his coffee mug.

After Capt. Cabrera ascended the treacherous staircase and entered the presentations cell, Capt. Valderama introduced the twenty-something captain. "Vince, this is Matt Jerome. He's gonna take the night shift."

"Hiya, Matt. You're Carl's CHUmate, right?" Capt. Cabrera asked with genuine interest. "Heck, you don't look nearly as old as what Carl suggested."

I turned toward Carl to give him a dirty look, but he was too engrossed in typing to see or even hear what was going on beyond his own little world. *I'll get his ass later,* I thought. I looked back toward Capt. Cabrera.

"That's right, and I can still pass a PT test, too, but not sure if Carl can. If anyone dares call me pops or grandpa, there'll be hell to pay. Hey, Vince, Jesus, if I'm coming on shift at seven tonight, I'd like to wrap this up and get some downtime," I suggested.

We spent another hour going through some of the routine procedures I would need to know. I took notes.

It was now 1330 hours, but before I strolled off in the hope of getting at least a nap before my shift, I asked Capt. Valderama, "Jesus, what do you do when you've got to pee in the middle of the night?"

"I use the porta-potty in my room. Don't you?" He smirked.

"You've got a porta-potty *in* your CHU?"

"Sure. Don't you?"

"No. Did lodging provide that?"

"Nope. The guy who had the room before me bought a small camping porta-potty and left it behind when he rotated home," Capt. Valderama said. "It holds about three gallons of water and uses only a pint to flush it. Every few days I go dump it and refill the holding tank. I figured everyone had one."

"That's a decent idea. Does the PX sell them?" I asked.

"Naw. He said he had to order it and it took a couple of weeks to get here."

"I've got to find a quicker answer than two weeks. You may not have to get up that often in the middle of the night, but I'm over fifty and . . . well you get the picture," I said. "And here's the other rub, there're pallets of drinking water all over the place; inside the bridge checkpoint, inside the palace doors, inside the JOC doors and all around Freedom Village. On the palace bathroom walls they've got warnings about the color of your urine and how to tell if you're drinking enough water. OK, OK, I'm drinking lots of water and keeping hydrated. And that's my problem; I'm fully hydrated when I get to bed."

Somewhere during my explanation, the twenty-something captain started smiling . . . or was he laughing?

"Well, I'm sure you'll find a solution. Why don't you go get some rest and come in late at twenty hundred hours?"

"Thank you, I think I will," I replied then moved out. I looked at Capt. Valderama and his dumbass smile to say, "You too will get old someday!"

Carl came into the CHU about 5:30 p.m. and woke me up in the process. "Hey, sorry, buddy. I cut out early for dinner and then home."

"No problem, man," I said as I opened my eyes. I was on my back wearing just my pants and a T-shirt with my woobie, a folded camouflage poncho liner, underneath my head. It made for comfortable napping.

"And hey, I took your advice about a can from the DFAC to go pee," I mentioned triumphantly. "I thought about getting a urinal from the TMC,[57] but didn't want to walk that far in the heat. Plus, it might be a little funny asking. Anyway, I got me a couple of those

---

57   TMC: Troop Medical Clinic (aka medical dispensary)

wide-mouth Gatorade bottles from the DFAC," I said as I showed him a half-filled bottle.

"Oh yeah. Forgot about those. I've used them, too. The nice thing about a Gatorade bottle . . . it has a wide mouth." Carl grinned.

I jumped on his answer, "You're right. Those bottles are really deep, too. I can use it without ever getting out of bed. I figure when I leave for work, I'll just take the bottle and dump it in the real porta-potty on the trail to the palace. Easy-peasy!"

"Speaking of work, not sure if you noticed, but Captain Collins is a twenty-four-carat asshole. Be careful," Carl offered. "Oh, and by the way, he's a jet pilot and he's absolutely pissed that he's not flying on this deployment. He opened his notebook yesterday when he was briefing me and I saw his aviator call sign scrawled on the inside cover. Guess what it is."

"Hell, I don't know. How 'bout *Gold*, as in twenty-four-carat?"

"Oh, that's good. Quick too, but no," Carl shot back. "His call sign is *Rocketman*. Captain Chris 'Rocketman' Collins. And so far as I can tell, it absolutely fits him because we are moving at light speed here."

We both shook our heads. "It figures," I said.

"Hey, let's go to dinner. I'm buyin'," Carl joked. "I'll give you the fifty-cent analysis of our predicament at the DFAC."

On our way over, we fell in behind a foursome of soldiers leisurely strolling toward the DFAC, too. The pathway was too narrow to play through the foursome and get ahead of them, so we had to stay behind. It was a bad decision to follow.

"Whoa. Someone up there shit his pants," Carl said loudly. "Hey y'all, how about a little warning before you go crop dusting[58] on the way to DFAC. OK?"

All four soldiers turned around smiling until they realized we were officers. One of them spoke up, "Oh sorry, sirs. Didn't realize anyone was behind us."

---

58   Crop Dusting: Slang term for the subtle art of passing gas while walking

Carl replied, "Well, OK. Hope you were only crop dusting and not fertilizing."

With that comment the three soldiers busted out laughing and started poking fun at the crop duster. One soldier said, "Gee, Miller, maybe you better check to make sure," punching his buddy in the arm.

During our meatloaf dinner, Carl spoke candidly. "Collins is an asshole. He spends more time trying to kiss the DCHOPS's[59] ass with lots of make work and whitewash crap than anyone I've ever seen. He tells me our job is to make *him* look good, and he points down to the DCHOPS. Rocketman expects the presentations to be letter and word perfect, period. He even goes into the presentations while still in draft mode and magnifies the view to two-hundred percent to look for flaws."

"Whoa. That's a bit of overkill isn't it?" I suggested. "I *do* understand the concept of making the boss look good. Everyone wants to do that and I've certainly done that in my career. However, accomplishing the mission should be the focus. Making the boss look good becomes a real problem when that becomes the *only* focus. Subordinates will know when you are gilding the lily to make the boss look good at their expense.

"Besides, isn't everyone working on these presentations over a period of days as the info trickles in? I might type something one way and then when you come in or someone else works on it you might change what I wrote or display it differently.

"It's kind of like we're all creating an oil painting by committee," I said. "I might paint the background with color and sketch in a vanishing point reference to the horizon. Then you come on shift and sketch in some details and then someone else adds their artistic muse to the equation. If someone changes what is already on the canvas because of personal preference, that's going to be a problem."

"We do have kind of a general template or format, but I've already

59   DCHOPS: Deputy Chief of Operations

seen Rocketman wanting to tweak it unnecessarily for show, to make him look good," Carl said.

"Well. As we say in the woodshop after we've tried our best to line up the miter joints, 'It is what it is.' That's why God created Wunderfil, to fill in the small cracks," I said.

"What's wonderful?" Carl asked.

"Sometimes, in spite of our very best efforts to have perfect cuts and angles, we don't. It shows up as small gaps or space between the wood surfaces. Wunderfil™ is a type of wood filler which you can use to fill holes and voids in your work. Hopefully, you only have small holes and voids. It comes in colors to match the wood and it can be easily sanded. Miter joints are notorious for having gaps. Rather than throw the work out and start over and waste a lot of time and wood, we use Wunderfil™ if the gaps are very minor."

"Oh. OK, sure," said Carl. "Well, I'm here to tell ya that Rocketman expects perfect at light speed—no cracks, no gaps. Cabrera told me Collins once said to him that a presentation needed fixing. Vince said he looked it over and could not find anything wrong so he asked Collins, 'What needs fixing?' and Collins said, 'Right there,' and points at the screen. 'Don't you see it?' Vince says to me, 'I look again and I don't see anything wrong and I tell Collins that. So, Collins zooms the magnification to two hundred percent and then shows me a *period* at the end of a sentence. I look at the period and say to Collins, 'OK, I still don't see it.' Collins is now pissed and says to me, 'Captain Cabrera, that period is not black; it is a bolded scarlet color. You need to change it to black.' Vince says he just looked back up at Collins with as sarcastic a smile as he could muster without being insubordinate and told Collins, 'Roger that, sir.'"

"Why didn't Collins just fix it on the fly instead of wasting everyone's time over something you could only see on two hundred percent zoom?" I asked

Carl looked me in the eye and said, "Like I said, twenty-four-carat asshole. This place is stressful enough without getting hammered over a non-black period at the end of a sentence, which could have been placed by any one of five people who worked on that presentation!"

"I really liked the meatloaf. Did you?" Carl asked as we headed out of the DFAC exit.

"Oh, I don't know. I think I'm losing my appetite and taste for some reason," I suggested as the reason I threw out half my dinner. "I'm going to head over to Green Beans for a nice cup of coffee before I go on shift."

"I'm going to grab a shower, then watch a movie," Carl added with some delight. "I'm thinking about ordering Wi-Fi. They say it's simple."

"It is simple," I pointed out. "In fact, I've already got Wi-Fi up and running in the CHU. No need for you to purchase your own. Let's just share mine. Since we're on different shifts, we can each use it fully when we're in. It's seventy-five a month. We can settle up as we go."

"Oh man, that's awesome," Carl exclaimed.

I gave Carl the Wi-Fi password and he walked off to relax while I walked over to Green Beans for a big jolt of extra caffeine before working with Rocketman. I told myself, *Rocketman's just another in a long line of assholes I've had to deal with and work with during my career. Nothing new here.*

I got settled in for my first full shift at a workstation where I sat next to Sgt. Barry Manley. A young, twenty-something soldier, he wore his light-brown hair short along with wire-rimmed glasses. He was a smallish figure, but appeared lean and fit. He wore the 10th Mountain Division patch and explained to me, "I'm a 35F intelligence analyst. I worked in the 2nd Brigade TOC, but they attached me here to work for MNC-I. Things were slow at the brigade, and they said

MNC-I put out a request for people to work the JOC. I've got a TS/ SCI clearance, so they sent me."

"How long did you work the brigade TOC?" I asked.

"A couple of months," Sgt. Manley said. "It was slow for me out at FOB[60] Hammer. When I was on shift, I found myself just looking through the networks to keep abreast of what's happening. Every now and then we'd have a TIC[61] and I'd get involved, but things are slowing down in that AOR. We spent some of the time listening to music and watching movies, too."

Sgt. Manley worked the in-between shift along with my new friend, Capt. Cabrera. Sgt. Manley did not evoke any warm fuzzies from me about his work. It didn't take long for my spidey sense[62] to start tingling when Sgt. Manley was on shift.

"Sergeant," I said. "What are you so diligently looking for on the SIPRNet?[63] I don't think I've seen you off it since I came on duty three or so hours ago. You're almost ready to go off shift, too."

Barely acknowledging my inquiry with a slight turn of his head, Sgt. Manley responded, "Same ole shit, different shift, sir." He seemed to be studiously reading. "I'm almost done, sir."

When he finished reading, the sergeant turned to me from his workstation and quietly said, "Sir, you wouldn't believe some of the stuff I've seen. It's a bit mind-blowing. Captain Cabrera asked me to do some additional research for our own presentations. I keep coming across other incidents that make some of our SIGACTs pale in comparison. Some of these incidents look pretty dicey."

I wasn't sure what he meant by *pretty dicey* but I suggested, "Don't you think we have enough to trouble our souls with our own SIGACTs?"

"Yes, sir. You're probably right. But some of these things just

---

60   FOB: Forward Operating Base
61   TIC: Troops in Contact report
62   Spidey sense: one of Spider-Man's super powers
63   SIPRNet: Secret Internet Protocol Router Network (a computer network for storing and accessing "Secret" classified information)

come up in the search field when I'm trying to do this research. It's sometimes hard to avoid," Sgt. Manley offered as an excuse.

"Just be careful. Remember that even though you've got a TS/SCI clearance, you must also have a 'Need to Know' that information before you go diving into the details. I wouldn't open and read some of those files unless doing so is necessary for our mission," I cautioned. "If you have any concern about a file and your need to know, ask Cabrera for guidance. If he's not here, you can ask Captain Collins or me."

"Yes. While working at the 2nd Brigade, it was suggested that I try to learn what's going on around us by checking out other incidents within the theater. I would brief the battle captain on anything of extraordinary significance," Sgt. Manley said.

"All right, carry on. Just don't get too wound up in it. Perhaps to clear your head before going off shift, you can switch over to the NIPRNet[64] and do some bird watching on YouTube," I joked.

I left Sgt. Manley alone as I was elbow-deep into a presentation someone had started four days earlier. I wanted it finished, but was still waiting for EOD to send their forensic report on the SIGACT.

I learned to hate EOD's online AARs. EOD conducted CSI[65]-type investigations regarding any explosion, usually caused by some type of IED,[66] which included graphic photo evidence, measurements, analysis and manufacture. The photos included in these reports could be heart-wrenching. The inside pictures of destroyed MRAPs and Humvees clearly showed the effects of when an IED literally burned a hole through several inches of door armor, splattering the inside with molten steel. The occupants would have little chance to survive.

The EOD reports also included an analysis of how an attack occurred. Unfortunately, this analysis provided more substance and detail to the data and pictures in the report.

64　NIPRNet: Non-classified Internet Protocol Router Network (a computer network for storing and accessing non-classified information
65　CSI: Crime Scene Investigation
66　IED: Improvised Explosive Device

I don't want to read the details of this attack. It's bad enough that I have to see pictures of the scene, learn how big the explosion was and how much damage it produced, I'd say to myself, but then read it anyway because it was my duty to know all the details to summarize the event.

The EOD reports generally were the last item we needed to finish a presentation. In that respect, we were happy to get an EOD report because it meant we were close to publishing the final presentation.

CHAPTER 8

The JOC - Drone War

April 2 – 3, 2009

Near the end of the week in the JOC, I settled in next to Vince Cabrera in our side-by-side workstations. We noticed a change to the TV monitors at the front of the JOC. One of the two extremely large LED TV monitors at the right front of the JOC, which were normally tuned to US network broadcasts, changed to a live, night vision camera aboard an overhead MQ-1 Predator drone instead of the usual CNN broadcast on that monitor.

Figure 10: MQ-1 Predator Drone

Meanwhile, the other TV monitor on Fox News was showing *The O'Reilly Factor*. The JOC was predominantly pro-Fox News, but showing CNN seemed like the politically correct thing to do. However, when there was important stuff to show, CNN got the thumbs down ahead of Fox News.

The other twelve linked, large-screen LED monitors, which formed a matrix display at the center front of the amphitheater, continued to display a map of the MNC-I area of responsibility (AOR). The map displayed the boundaries for the MNC-I order of battle: MND-N,[67] MND-S,[68] MND-W[69] and MND-Baghdad.[70] In March 2009, the United Kingdom had turned over command of MND-SE,[71] which was then merged with MNC-C[72] to create MNC-S.

Vince and I each put on a pair of headphones tied to our workstations to listen to the monitors. Channel 1 audio gave you *The O'Reilly Factor* off the left-most monitor, while Channel 2 provided audio on the right-side monitor showing the drone targeting camera. This was only the second time I had watched live drone thermal camera footage since working the night shift.

"Looks like a convoy of MRAPs going somewhere with a drone in ISR[73] support," I hypothesized as I could clearly make out the unique vehicle profile compared to a Humvee.

I saw the MQ-1 Predator provide eyes-in-the-sky overwatch protection for the convoy against potential unseen enemy ambush sites. The drone pilot repeatedly scanned in wide-angle view ahead of and to the sides of the convoy, looking for hotspots. This gave the pilot a very wide and expansive field of view to locate threats. Whenever a hotspot was detected, the pilot would change the camera resolution and contrast to zoom on the hotspot, giving a

---

67   MND-N: Multinational Division-North
68   MND-S: Multinational Division-South
69   MND-W: Multinational Division-West
70   MND-Baghdad: Multinational Division-Baghdad
71   MND-SE: Multinational Division-Southeast
72   MND-C: Multinational Division-Center
73   ISR: Intelligence, Surveillance, Reconnaissance

much clearer image of the threat. Convoy commanders loved drone support since drones were responsive, efficient and deadly; a really nice security blanket.

"Oh, there's a hot spot," I heard Vince exclaim over the workstation-to-workstation intercom inside my headphones. "Watch him zoom it."

In wide-view low-resolution and low-magnification camera footage, hotspots were just that—almost formless white spots that occasionally moved with only a little definition to assess the threat. A hotspot could be a person, an animal, a leftover campfire, a warm engine cowling, etc. Scanning in this fashion was the equivalent of looking a mile wide and an inch deep for any hotspot. When the pilot found a hotspot, he would change to higher resolution and magnification to expose the threat. In high resolution and maximum magnification, the video feed was so precise and focused that a good drone pilot could literally see a terrorist taking a leak and shaking it off. That would be the last time that terrorist would have a full bladder.

Vince and I watched as the drone pilot shifted the crosshairs of the targeting camera over the top of the newly discovered hotspots in wide-angle, zoomed-out view. The pilot then switched the camera resolution to high definition and zoomed in with magnification. To better define the target, the pilot changed the video contrast, and the target's silhouette popped into view.

Vince and I looked at each other as the silhouettes of some animals, probably goats, could clearly be seen on the monitor. The animals were facing the road on which the convoy would pass. The animals in this position almost mimicked the same profile of people lying in the prone position as if waiting in an ambush hide. The high-res video ruled out the threat.

"Well, thank God it was some goats or something," Vince remarked. "At first it looked like somebody waiting in ambush because it didn't move."

I pointed out, "This can be a bit mesmerizing, watching the search go on. I think I'll just listen and get back to work."

I switched my gaze briefly over to *The O'Reilly Factor* as Bill teased the next segment, a talk with Code Pink's Medea Benjamin on why her group had raised the ire from some in the Daily Kos groups. I listened while I returned to my never-ending PowerPoint Ranger duties.

While the convoy continued with drone support on the right monitor, I watched Bill O'Reilly come back on air with his Code Pink spokesperson. I half-heartedly listened to the Code Pink nonsense while pounding away at the keyboard on the presentation du jour.

Ms. Benjamin then made some comment to O'Reilly about the United States using drones to kill people in Iraq and Afghanistan. She didn't think that was appropriate. Bill kinda rolled his eyes, but it then dawned on me. I looked up at the side-by-side TV monitors and was struck by the timely juxtaposition of the Code Pink interview immediately next to the live armed drone footage on the other monitor. Hollywood couldn't have written that scenario any better.

"Hey, Vince. Are you watching or listening to O'Reilly right now?" I asked over the intercom.

"No, man. I'm watching *Drone Hunter*, starring an Air Force captain in Nevada on Channel 2," he shot back, laughing.

"You have to appreciate this situation," I said. "This Code Pink person just complained to O'Reilly that our drones are killing people in Iraq and Afghanistan, while I'm watching live drone video on the monitor right next to *The Factor* broadcast."

Vince shifted his eyes to the O'Reilly monitor and listened for a moment before speaking. "She doesn't know what she's talking about. She's an ejit!" Vince said. "But hey, looks like we've got somethin' cookin' on *Drone Hunter* for sure," he blurted. "Look at all those hot spots up ahead. Come on. Zoom in for Christ's sake," Vince implored the pilot.

As if on Vince's cue, the drone pilot shifted the crosshairs to the potential threat which lay several miles ahead along the convoy route. Plenty of time to assess, seek permission to engage and destroy the target if needed before the convoy even came close to the area.

The pilot adeptly centered the targeting crosshairs on the fuzzy white-hot shapes on the black background of much cooler ground cover. Then, whammo, the pilot switched from wide field of view to a much more focused and magnified camera view of the hotspots.

I could clearly make out the details in the high-res, high-magnification video stream as I mentioned with some trepidation, "Hey, man. Those are bad guys. Looks like a small technical vehicle with a PKM[74] machine gun on the back and several more dudes just walking around with AKs. They're sitting there at the bend of the road to the east behind some shrubs facing west toward the convoy!"

---

74   PKM: A Soviet Union made 7.62mm general purpose machine gun

Suddenly the camera crosshairs shifted to another location not far away, but farther up the road from the bend on the south side of the road the convoy would be traveling. There we made out an equal number of hotspots which were clearly lying in wait along the convoy's route of travel. The pilot zoomed magnification again and manipulated the video contrast to get better detail. It paid off.

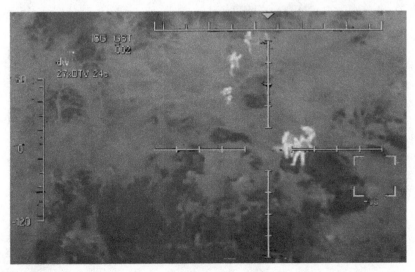

Vince foresaw what was unfolding.

"Holy shit, Matt. There're seven more guys with AKs and backpacks. Could be satchel charges or bandoleers or something. If they stay right there, they'll have a perfect L-shaped ambush with the technical vehicle shooting down the length of the convoy."

Vince and I had read more than enough ambush SIGACTs to understand what could happen. As the convoy approached from the west along the road, the technical vehicle would open up against the lead vehicle to try and disable it near the other part of the ambush team. If the convoy got stopped during this opening engagement, it would likely be stopped right in front of the attackers on the south side of the road. These attackers would then open a crossfire into the side of the convoy while the technical vehicle would strafe it with fire from the front.

At some point when the convoy's return fire was suppressed, the technical vehicle would hold fire while some of the broadside attackers wearing suicide vests and possibly carrying explosive satchel charges would assault the now-stalled vehicle convoy. The convoy members would not have much time to react to these attackers running into the convoy from as little as twenty meters away.

"Yeah, I see it, too," I added. At that point everyone in the JOC started seeing it and the place became eerily quiet. In fact, even Rocketman Collins stopped working, which was rare for him since he was doing everything in his power to make his boss look good.

Breathlessly, all of us in the JOC watched the drone pilot scan the ambush area for additional threats or perhaps reinforcements arriving. Not finding any more targets, the pilot focused back on the technical vehicle, the more immediate threat. The south side ambush team would not attack if the convoy didn't stop, and the convoy would only stop if the technical vehicle opened fire and caused it to stop. Eliminating the vehicle threat was the beginning.

This threat needed to be neutralized and now. The Channel 2 audio picked up the warning to the convoy commander.

"They probably won't stop, but they will slow down to give the drone some time. Convoy route manager will be calculating an alternate route around the ambush, if needed," Vince said.

We then watched the dismounted insurgents loitering around the technical vehicle depart the area, leaving the driver and gunner with the vehicle. These seven terrorists headed over to the other ambush team on the south side of the road, running to cover the 100-or-so-meter distance quickly. They must have received intelligence from someone up the road that a convoy was approaching.

They lied down next to the others already in place, bringing the south side ambush force up to fourteen insurgents. Fortunately, the fourteen insurgents were packed tightly and only spread out about twenty-five or so meters. If they all got up and ran in different directions when the technical vehicle got hit, they would be a more difficult target for the drone to engage with a missile. The pilot would have to be quick on the trigger. This was a big to-do, and everyone in the JOC knew it. Work in the JOC essentially halted in place while we watched the scene unfold. We basically knew we were going to seriously rain on the insurgents' parade real soon.

It seemed like hours had elapsed since the start of this engagement as we watched impatiently. In fact, it had been no more than about fifteen minutes since the hotspots were found to be insurgents. The drone pilot got both ambush teams in the camera view, switching magnifications to ensure no other teams or vehicles were entering the engagement area unnoticed. Finally, the pilot centered the crosshairs on the technical vehicle and stayed there. The technical gunner and driver were in the vehicle in a stand-to attitude, obviously waiting on the arrival of the convoy.

"Come on, man. You need to launch. Don't let those bastards get away," Sgt. First Class O'Rourke whispered in our cell intercom. Heads were nodding in agreement.

"There it is!" Sgt. O'Rourke said with anticipation as we all watched the drone camera momentarily blur and shake as a Hellfire missile was launched. Someone on the intercom quietly announced, "Shot, over." Someone else responded with, "Shot, out." These being standard artillery fire direction center to artillery forward observer calls to announce the shot, and the other to acknowledge it. The first Hellfire was on its way to the vehicle team.

"OK, baby. Go get the other team," Vince commanded to an unhearing drone pilot. Once again as if on command, we watched as the drone pilot quickly moved the crosshairs from the technical and then line up on the center of mass of the deployed insurgents along the south side of the road.

After a moment, we saw the familiar blur and shaking of the drone targeting camera, which silently announced the launch of missile number two speeding on its way towards the second ambush team. The same someone once again spoke, "Shot, over," but before anyone could reply with "Shot, out," someone else excitedly said, "Splash, over," indicating the hit of the first missile. The JOC erupted with a shout as the first Hellfire found the target vehicle to the right of the second ambush team.

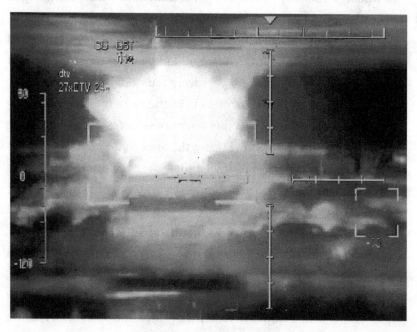

"And that is why we say splash!" Sgt. O'Rourke informed as the vehicle and its passengers exploded in a violent eruption of white-hot mess erupting from where the vehicle was parked.

"Did you see the pieces of vehicle and people flying through the air?" I asked. "And look at ambush team two; they're starting to get up and *di di mau*[75] from the site," I added, using an old Vietnam term I picked up in the '70s from other veterans. Seeing a strange look from some of the younger generation near me, I spoke into the cell intercom, "It's Vietnamese for *let's get the eff outta here.*"

However, it was too late for the lazy ones wondering what the hell was going on at the ambush site. "Splash, over," Sgt. O'Rourke announced again. The drone pilot was right in the middle of the group with the missile, instantly killing all but three, who were on the outsides of the formation and trying to *di di* out of the immediate impact area.

As we watched the three obviously dazed and confused insurgents scamper away, we saw white spots exploding around them, killing them too, all in a matter of moments. Unbeknown to us in the JOC, an Apache helicopter had arrived on station and performed target area cleanup with its 30-millimeter chain gun.

After the second Hellfire splash, the drone pilot once again resumed a wide field of view of the target area. We could see the convoy up the road several kilometers away. It was safe. Meanwhile, the drone pilot resumed searching the immediate target area. He would do a battle damage assessment, or BDA, and ensure all threats were neutralized with no reinforcements coming. Sometimes after the dust settled from an airstrike, you might find other insurgents crawling out of the woodwork to escape.

"You know, that drone jockey did a pretty decent job of bringing steel on target quickly," Vince observed. "Fortunately, the ambush site was pretty far outside that last village . . . little chance for collateral

---

75   Di di mau: Vietnamese for "Go Quickly." Military slang to "unass the AO" (leave now).

damage. Otherwise, he would've spent a lot more time checking and assessing ROE. You know, civilians in the way, markets, local mosques, etc. The ROE would have tied his hands up pretty well. He might not have been able to launch. But there, out in the countryside, it's almost a weapons-free engagement area. All he needed was to identify hostiles and get the airborne FAC[76] to green-light it."

Sgt. Manley weighed in. "That drone pilot was good. It's amazing—the power of unmanned drones being flown by pilots thousands of miles away attacking and neutralizing a hostile threat like that so quickly and efficiently. I guess you could say that the mouse is mightier than the M-16."

"Oh, that's a good one, Sarge," Vince said. "You know, the same could be said about our PowerPoint presentations; the mouse is mightier than the M-16. In theory at least, our presentations are supposed to give other planners some insight into how the enemy fights. Sometimes we develop countermeasures and other plans based on these presentations."

"My thoughts exactly," declared Sgt. Manley. "The things I can do with a mouse, keyboard and network access, you just wouldn't believe."

Yessirree Bob. All was right with the world at that moment, but Sgt. Manley appeared to be a bit pained.

"You OK, Manley?" I asked.

Sgt. Manley's expression appeared to change from grim to just a little bit disturbed.

"Yes, sir. I guess it's just that engagement happened so quickly. I was concerned there might be civilians nearby. I'll admit I didn't see any while I was watching. There've been some instances where the chopper jockeys were a little too quick on the trigger and caused some collateral damage."

"Really?" I asked. "Where and when did this occur? I haven't seen

---

76   FAC: Forward Air Controller who manages airspace and aircraft operating in a given area

any SIGACTs about that. Certainly, it would have been reported."

"Yes, sir. It's happened," Sgt. Manley stated. "I've seen some incidents from Afghanistan as well as here in Iraq when I was working at FOB[77] Hammer. Some of these look like the kind of incident where someone might blow it off as the fog of war or something to try and shift blame away from their responsibility to adhere to the ROE."

"Whoa, son. Stop right there," I cautioned. "Are you talking about something which could be classified as a war atrocity against the Geneva Conventions, law of armed conflict and the law of land warfare? Where're you getting these ideas from?"

"I've seen some videos and other footage that was uploaded along with the after-action reports. I don't know if you could classify it as war atrocities or against the Conventions because the written reports seem reasonable enough. Some of these things just don't look right."

Being a bit worried that our cell may have missed something, I asked Sgt. Manley, "Have we worked on any of these incidents? Did we miss something here?"

"No, sir. Most of these things I saw while at FOB Hammer."

I asked with just a hint of suspicion in my voice, "How is it that you know about incidents in Afghanistan if you were working at FOB Hammer here in Iraq?"

"The battle captain at Hammer instructed me to see if there were other similar incidents to what was happening in our area, to see if we could learn from it," the sergeant said. "It was research."

I was still a little suspicious, but Sgt. Manley seemed truthful in his reply.

I said, "Well, OK. But look, if you ever question something that's happened, you ask one of the officers for guidance on it. We need to keep our heads together while working on these SIGACTs. If you start letting your imagination run wild, you could find yourself at the Combat Stress Clinic. We can't afford to become stress casualties."

---

77   FOB: Forward Operating Base

"Roger that. I'll keep it in check," Manley replied.

I looked over at Vince, who had gone back to watching *The O'Reilly Factor*.

"You know, Vince, if Medea Benjamin only knew that her interview with O'Reilly on April 2, 2009, was playing opposite a drone strike on Iraqi insurgents, I think she'd lose it."

The CHOPS came over the intercom. "Thank God that drone strike went well. I really don't want to do any more hero salutes."

CHAPTER 9

The JOC - Hand-Off

Saturday April 4, 2009

It was a big day for 1st Corps. I'm glad I was off duty and out of the palace before 1000 hours, when the official transfer of authority ceremony took place in the Al Faw Palace Rotunda. The place was packed to the gills.

Figure 11: Cover of the MNC-I Transfer of Authority program

After the TOA ceremony, Lt. Gen. Jacobson informed the command we could officially wear either the MNC-I or the 1st Corps patch as our combat patch on our right shoulder sleeves. 1st Corps was now MNC-I and in the left-seat position all by itself.

After the TOA and a full weekend of twelve-hour shifts learning and doing, I found the routine in the JOC exhausting and stressful. Not much changed from day to day. Another day, another SIGACT, more research, another dreadful EOD report and another presentation. I skipped too many meals because I just wasn't hungry and was losing weight.

Everyone else in the JOC, and especially my section, seemed to operate on coffee or Red Bull energy drinks in between spitting smokeless tobacco juice into whatever container they had at hand— peanut cans, Coke cans, Gatorade bottles. You couldn't smoke in the JOC, but you sure as hell could chew tobacco and spit. Disgusting!

It made for some good theater when I was enjoying a cold diet soda retrieved from the drink bucket at the front of the JOC. I would often just get a Diet Coke and drink it back at the workstation.

One night I downed my soda in two long pulls. I tossed the empty twelve-ounce can in the garbage under the workstation. The bubbles inside reacted accordingly and I let out a well-earned soda belch.

"Captain Jerome. Do you think you could quit doing that when you're on shift? It's kind of rude," Capt. Collins huffed from his workstation.

"Yes, by all means I can do that. Can I ask a favor?" I inquired of the OIC.

"Sure. What is it?"

"While I'm refraining from my open soda belching, would you mind not spitting your tobacco juice into any empty cup on the counter, and can you also stop saying *goddamn* or *fuck* in just about every conversation I hear? We all have to work together here and that can be a little bit rude, too."

"Well, I don't know about that, Captain. Been here a couple of months and this is how I operate. Hard and fast with little time for niceties," Capt. Collins shot back, obviously pissed that I exposed his hypocrisy. He went back to his keyboard. Engagement over. Tactical win to the old guy!

I saw Vince looking at me sideways with wide eyes, sitting on the other side of Capt. Collins. He had one of those looks as if to say, *"What the hell are you doing, dude?"*

Vince got up, squeezed past Capt. Collins, and then headed down to the coffee service. I followed.

"Boy, you got some balls to call him out on that," Vince chided. "Collins can make life hell for us."

"He can't get much worse than he is now," I said. "Besides, him calling me out on belching, seriously? When he and others go around cursing nonstop while spitting into cups and sometimes dribbling it onto their own chins? He's got no room to bitch about an occasional belch. Besides, he may have the position of OIC, but I'm pretty sure I've got him on date of rank—1992!"

I grabbed another soda while Vince topped off his coffee mug, and we headed up the stairs and back to the cell.

Days after my encounter with Capt. Collins, I sensed an underlying anxiety overtake the room after I started my shift.

"Vince, do you know what's up? Both the CHOPS and assistant CHOPS have noticeably turned down their aggressiveness and anger. In a way, they have kind of mellowed. They seem to be preoccupied with something."

"Yeah. It started early this afternoon when I came on. I asked Collins and he said we may have a visitor coming, but he didn't say who or when."

"For a secure JOC, they're sure being tight-lipped about it in here," I suggested. "Gotta be someone pretty important, like from the Joint Chiefs, maybe even the SecDef himself."

"What we do know is they're closing the parking lot outside the palace checkpoint tomorrow beginning at 0700. All NTVs have to be removed by then. No time on reopening it," Vince reported while showing me the email blast we all received.

"That changes the equation. No vehicles near the only entrance to the palace means it's probably a high-ranking civilian. Could be the new president," I surmised.

"Hmmmm. You've got a point there on it being a civilian," said Vince. "I guess we'll hear about it when we need to know."

For the next couple of hours, the anxiety in the JOC remained elevated, even though the work atmosphere actually turned a bit more collegial and team-oriented, something unknown and unseen since I'd started working there.

There was a sense that the JOC would be part of something almost historical, and therefore demanded a better working atmosphere. Around midnight, just before Vince left shift, the assistant CHOPS teased it over the intercom. "All right, everyone, we need to make sure we've got our best foot forward tomorrow for our special visitor. Can't tell you right now who it is, but you'll need to make sure you put on a clean uniform."

"Still so secretive, isn't he?" I asked Vince as he was about to head off.

Vince got serious. "I think you're right. I'll bet Obama is coming to the palace. I've not seen this much secrecy since working here."

The CHOPS walked over to the assistant CHOPS and talked to him for a moment before returning to his workstation. The assistant CHOPS got back on the intercom to speak. "OK, I've just realized we've got people going off shift, so we'll have to let you know now before you come back on duty tomorrow. President Obama will be visiting the palace tomorrow in the late afternoon. There will be increased security at both checkpoints starting in the morning. Do NOT bring any weapons to work—and that includes any kind of knife, too. If you are off shift between 1600 and 1900 hours, we need you to come in to help fill the rotunda for his talk. OK. That's all."

Vince turned and smiled. "See you tomorrow."

Capt. Collins rolled his half-broken chair over closer to mine behind my workstation.

"Hey, Jerome, you got any experience doing graphics or pictures?"

Is he warming up to me? I thought.

"I suppose I do in general, but not necessarily with the graphics package you're using."

"Let me show you what I'm talking about," Capt. Collins said, pointing to the large map displayed across six interlinked monitors at the front of the JOC. "My job is to post items to that map, some of which correspond to the presentations y'all are doing. So, I'm posting that mortar attack from this morning. I'd like to show the path of the mortar rounds through the air from the POO[78] to the POI.[79] Do you think that's possible?"

"Considering how much the Army probably paid for the software, I'd be surprised if it didn't have that capability along with sound effects," I joked. "But I'd need to get into the menu of the graphics software. Is this something new that's needed? I don't see any other types of trajectories posted."

"That's the word I couldn't think of—*trajectory!*" Capt. Collins said. "It's not really needed, but I thought it'd be a nice touch to have on the map. It'll make the DCHOPS look good when he points it out in a briefing."

Here comes the eyewash and the extra work, I thought.

"I don't see why that can't be done," I said. "Most graphic programs allow you to draw lines; straight, curved, point to point to point, etcetera. Here's how I would do it. I'd choose to draw a spline curve or Bezier curve from point A, your POO, to point B, your POI.

78   POO: Point of Origin (pronounced 'Pooh')
79   POI: Point of Impact (pronounced 'Pee Oh Eye')

Then grab the line somewhere in the middle with the mouse and drag it to create an arc from both points."

"OK. That sounds logical. Can you show me?" Capt. Collins asked.

We changed chairs so I could use Capt. Collins's workstation, which was already logged into the software program driving the map graphics. I found the main menu and opened the graphics tool menu. A box opened on the side of the screen with a host of tool icons to perform all sorts of graphic touches. It looked just like my favorite graphics program at home, Paint.net.

"Look here," I said to Capt. Collins. "This is the Line/Curve tool icon. When you click this icon, your mouse can then draw a line. What's the grid for the POO?"

He gave me the grid and I placed the mouse on that point. "So, you start here, click and hold the mouse button. That creates the line start point. Keep mouse button depressed while you draw the line to the POI. What's your POI grid?" I asked.

He gave me the grid for the POI and I moved the mouse to it, creating a straight line when I let go of the mouse button.

"Now watch this," I said. "Do you see those little circles on the line? Those are grab points. See what happens to the cursor when I move it over a grab point? The mouse cursor changes to a hand. When you get the hand, you can then click, hold and pull with the mouse to adjust the line into an arc or trajectory. Like this," I said as I demonstrated, creating the necessary arc from the POO to the POI.

"Lastly, you can add an arrowhead to the end of the line to show direction by clicking on the Shapes tool icon, then choose arrowhead and place it on the POI point."

"Goddamn, all right! That's exactly what I need," Capt. Collins said. "Oh, sorry 'bout that."

"No problem. I understand your excitement. Now it's your turn to do it," I said as I deleted the line and arrowhead so he'd have to do it himself.

"Hey. It's gone," he said.

"Yes, it is," I said. "It's your turn to make the line."

He looked at me like I did something wrong

"You can give a man a ride in your airplane and he'll get to where he's going one time, or you can teach the man to fly the airplane and then he'll never take off his Nomex[80] flight suit!"

Capt. Collins smiled and then drew his own trajectories from that point forward.

When I got off shift the next morning and exited the palace, the weather outside was warm, but comfortable. I started my little overland trek to the DFAC knowing that by noon when I would be trying to sleep in the CHU, the temperature would creep up into the high eighties, but still dry. The air-conditioning in my CHU would keep it comfortable, I hoped.

When I walked across the palace bridge, I found the parking lot empty except for a run-down street sweeper vehicle slowly driving around in a huge cloud of dust. It looked like the Pig-Pen character from the *Peanuts* comic strip driving around the parking lot.

I did a double take; the machine was sweeping the larger rear portion of the overflow parking area, which was not paved but merely a dirt hard-stand with a few potholes and low spots. I thought, *Seriously? They are sweeping a dirt parking lot? I guess we gotta look good for the commander-in-chief.* I just shook my head as I wandered off to the DFAC.

I returned as ordered around 1700 to help fill the palace. I got to the bridge checkpoint and found a line to get in. MPs were using metal detectors to check everyone. I forgot about the little two-inch pocketknife in the bottom of my cargo pocket, and was relieved of it by an MP. "Sorry," I told the MP sheepishly. "Forgot it was there." The MP took it and threw it in a box along with other confiscated items.

---

80   NOMEX: A flame-retardant material popularly used to make clothing for pilots and air crews

There were more MPs at the palace door checkpoint. They were the only ones with weapons, and they looked a bit anxious.

I strode into the rotunda where President Obama was on stage surrounded by a chorus line of soldiers dutifully standing behind him. *Photo Op 101,* I thought.

There were three things I heard him say which meant something to me. He said, "It is time for us to transition to the Iraqis. They need to take responsibility for their country and for their sovereignty . . . and we can start bringing our folks home."

Earlier, the decision had been announced by Gen. Osmand that all US forces would completely leave Iraqi cities by June 30, 2009, if the situation supported it. Now, Obama was talking about bringing our folks home. There was some small talk around camp turned towards downsizing the force. It made me wonder why it was so important back in 2008 to recall retirees for the *surge* in Iraq. *I've been here only about a month and already they're talking about downsizing? You can downsize me right outta here.*

It's almost like the Army was saying, "OK, turns out we really didn't need y'all to come back in. Sorry, our bad!"

The furor over Obama's visit two days earlier was abating, and inside the JOC it was back to business as usual. Back to the normal *Groundhog Day* mode; Capt. Collins still cussed, drank Red Bull and spat his tobacco juice everywhere.

I walked carefully up the staircase towards the presentations cell and the workstation that awaited me. I was determined to not add my name another time to the infamous *trip log;* two times was enough.

I settled back in behind the keyboard to resume work on the presentation du jour—the assassination of a local leader by another neighborhood tribe that felt they had been wronged. *What else is new?*

CHAPTER 10

The JOC - Bloody Easter Week

April 8, 2009

The telephone rang at the JOC workstation.

"This is Captain Collins, sir. How can I help you?"

The conversation lasted just a couple of minutes, and then Capt. Collins passed me the phone saying, "A Chaplain Christopher wants to speak with you."

"Hi, Gordon. This is a pleasant surprise. What can I do for you?" I replied to Capt. Gordon Christopher, the Special Troops Battalion (STB) chaplain whom I had met early on the second day while visiting Hope Chapel.

"Hiya, Matt. I'm kind of in a bind and need your other skills tomorrow—your woodworking skills," the chaplain implored. "I committed to creating a retreat diorama of sorts for Good Friday and Easter weekend and I need a large cross made. Can you help me out tomorrow morning?"

I replied enthusiastically. "Sure. I get off at 0700 or so and can come over to Hope Chapel then. I presume you have materials and tools I can use."

"Tools I've got or can get, but I'll need you to go to the hardware store to get the lumber. You can use my NTV."

"Hardware store?" I asked with amazement. "Victory Base has a commercial hardware store?"

"Oh yeah. I haven't been there yet, but True Value is the AAFES concessionaire on Victory Base. The store is over on the west side of the base along Rivaridge Road, just inside the wire," Chaplain Gordon explained with glee, as if he were exposing a great secret.

I listened as he explained, but was thinking, *Of course there would be a commercial hardware store here. We've only been in Baghdad for about six years now, and where else will all the civilian contractors order and receive repair items? Everything else on base has been turned over to a civilian contractor, why not Class IV[81] military supplies and equipment, too?*

The chaplain explained. "I need a cross about six feet tall, so whatever lumber you need, glue, screws, fasteners, etcetera, you can buy there. I've got an account you can charge it to."

The chaplain continued. "I've got access to a maintenance section that will lend us power tools like a circular saw, hammer, sawhorses, cordless drills and clamps. Anything you might need, I'm sure. Can you come by Hope around 0900? I spoke with your OIC and he reluctantly agreed to let you off around 4 a.m. so you could get some sleep before helping me."

I thought about it and decided there was no way I could say no. "Sure. I'll skip breakfast and go get some sleep, and then come over to the chapel at 9 a.m. Will that work for you?"

"On second thought, I've got a better idea," the chaplain said. "How 'bout I drop by your CHU with the NTV at 0900? We have to go get the tools from maintenance anyway, and I'll bring you a breakfast burrito and a cup of coffee."

"I can't beat that with a stick. Almost as good as breakfast in bed. OK, see you in the morning."

---

81   Class IV: Military class of supplies which includes construction materials, including installed equipment and all fortification and barrier materials.

I found the True Value hardware store the next morning to be well stocked with just about anything you could need, and of course you could order stuff, too. They had located the store inside a small warehouse structure about 5,000 square feet on the perimeter road inside the wire.

I purchased lumber and headed back to the chapel. After making the chaplain's cross outside, I went back inside to touch base with him. Inside the empty chapel I watched a lone soldier wearing just a T-shirt, trousers and boots who seemed to be pacing about the sanctuary. His ACU blouse was draped over the back of a chair with his M-4 rifle leaning against it.

I went to the office and found the chaplain's assistant. "I'm sorry, sir. Chaplain Christopher is out doing ministry work and won't be back until this afternoon," replied the chaplain's assistant.

"No problem. I'll get with him later," I said.

As I left the office and emerged back into the sanctuary, I observed the lone soldier continuing to walk around the sanctuary. He appeared to be talking to himself silently as he walked up and down the side aisles, back and forth. You could tell by his slow movements with his head cast down or looking skyward at times that he was in some emotional distress. I could see that he had shed tears.

I approached him. "Do you need some help, soldier? You wanna talk or something?"

He stopped and looked at me, holding up his hand, palm forward, and then spoke. "I'm OK, sir. I'll get through this."

"I can pray with you if you like."

He smiled weakly. "No thank you, sir, but I appreciate your concern. I'll be all right."

I smiled back. "OK, if you say so. But if you change your mind, the chaplain's assistant is in the office if you need something. OK?"

"Yes, sir, and thank you," the soldier replied and continued his pacing around the chapel.

I debated what to do at that point, but figured he was in God's house. *Have faith. Let go and let God seems the appropriate thing to do,* I told myself.

I actually had an appetite at that point and decided to try and satisfy it at the DFAC, so I left the chapel thinking seriously about the panini bar.

"Attention in the JOC. Attention in the JOC," bellowed the voice over the center's communication system. "MND-North spot report: 2nd Brigade Combat Team, 4th ID reports an SVBIED[82] attacked the Iraqi National police compound in Mosul just outside the FOB Marez gate. Several Iraqi Security Forces vehicles inside the COP[83] Eagle motor pool are on fire. An MRAP from 1-67 Armor was also destroyed in the attack with five US KIA and two Iraqi police KIA. Unknown number of WIA[84] at this time."

The JOC fell silent for a moment, and then behind me where the division LNO cells were located, I heard the muffled sound of someone saying, "Shit." It was April 10, Good Friday. We all knew a suicide vehicle-borne IED or SVBIED could be difficult to stop or avoid.

"That's just hunky-dory; another suicide attack on a Friday. And not just any Friday."

"Vince, I'm going to keep on with this assassination brief until we get the MND-North SIGACT. It should be coming in within the next couple of hours or so," I said.

"No problem, Matt. I'm still working on that marketplace SVIED[85] attack from two days ago. The EOD forensic report is in, so I can add that to it."

"Vince, it just dawned on me. Today's Good Friday," I said. "This kinda shit can't happen today or this weekend."

---

82   SVBIED: Suicide Vehicle-Borne Improvised Explosive Device (pronounced 'Ess Vee Bid')
83   COP: Combat Outpost
84   WIA: Wounded in Action
85   SVIED: Suicide Vest Improvised Explosive Device (pronounced 'ESS VID')

Suddenly we were disturbed by a pounding sound immediately below us. "What's DCHOPS doing?" I whispered to Vince as we both watched him pounding away on his desktop with something in his hand. "What is that, a towel or something he's pounding with?" I asked.

"I have no idea," Vince said as we stared at the DCHOPS flicking this towel thing wickedly against his wooden desktop as if he were trying to rip it apart. It looked like a piece of camouflage towel.

The DCHOPS suddenly turned toward us and stopped his pounding as we stared at him in wonderment. "It's my dammit doll," said the DCHOPS as he held up this voodoo doll–looking thing. He then turned back to pounding the doll against his desktop while now blurting, "Dammit, dammit, dammit," each time he hit the desk. He finally stopped after four or five more hits on the doll, calmly stuffed it back into his cargo pocket, and then resumed his work.

OK, I thought. *No one here is stressed out, are they?*

We continued to slave away at medium cruising speed on the open presentations, knowing we would have to start the Mosul SVBIED PowerPoint once we got the SIGACT.

My luck ran out when the SIGACT showed up on the SIPRNet about twenty minutes before Vince got off shift. "I'll start this one since you're leaving shift," I told him.

"Thanks, man. I'm pretty knackered anyway," Vince replied with a term he'd picked up from working with a couple of Brits.

The SIGACT pretty much mirrored what the MND-North LNO reported during his "Attention in the JOC" announcement. I started the PowerPoint for it, so I now had four active SIGACTs in various stages in progress. I flitted between the open presentations as I obtained more information, pictures and other details that could be added to them. Sometimes I would get new information that corrected earlier details, which is why I didn't publish these too quickly. *Gotta wait for the SIGACT to be finalized and closed. Can't report bad data!*

The Mosul SVBIED SIGACT gave some more details, which I added as notes for others. "The 1st Battalion, 67th Armor soldiers appeared to be in the wrong place at the wrong time. The convoy they were driving in was leaving the base compound as the explosive-laden truck was headed down the road toward the entrance to the Mosul headquarters of the three-thousand-member paramilitary Iraqi national police. The suicide truck came under fire from US soldiers in the convoy as well as Iraqi police at the last checkpoint. The bomber ran into a wall adjacent to the convoy, where he detonated the explosives before he got to the base entrance."

Once I finished the SVBIED notes, I busied myself with the other presentations for the rest of my shift, since these did not have any US KIA. It helped, a little. Just knowing that more gruesome details of the Mosul SVBIED attack would be coming in was troublesome.

The next day I prompted Vince when I came on shift. "Hiya, Vince. I suppose you got some new info for the Mosul SVBIED last night?"

"Yeah, we did. Some info came in from the Iraqi interior minister's office. Iraqi security forces sealed off the area, so we don't have the best access to the point of attack. I'm guessin' EOD will be in there soon enough to document it. The spokesman said it was a dump truck with two thousand pounds of explosive. How the hell would they know it was two thousand pounds this quickly after the attack? Inside information?

"Anyway. We added a little detail to the open presentation. I'm sure more will roll in with pictures once EOD gets there," Vince offered. "For the time being, that presentation can sit on the back burner."

"OK. Sounds good to me. Anything else going on?"

"Nope. Same ole shit. Just another day," Vince said.

"I made an interesting observation just before coming on shift."

"Oh yeah? What would that be?" Vince asked.

"So, I'm out on the balcony getting ready to light up a cigar. I guess it's about sundown because the call to prayers starts up from the mosque. And I'm thinking pretty deeply about this fourth call to prayers."

"The fourth set of prayers is named the *Maghrib*, just so you know," Vince added.

"How do you know that?"

"It was part of all that pre-deployment training at Lewis. That one stuck in my brain for some reason," Vince said. "It's intended to remind them of God when the day is ending."

"OK. Whatever," I responded. "Anyway, I started reflecting on these calls to prayer. Five times a day they pray to remember God and ask for forgiveness and guidance. Right? Considering how many times the Shia and Sunni groups try to kill each other, every day, sometimes within an hour or so *after* the evening prayer, it seems to me these five calls to prayer should really be calls to cease fire. Tell me how many times we've had a SIGACT occur DURING any prayer. Rarely. Ten minutes after they pick up their prayer rugs, they are back at it trying to slit each other's throats. And they call it a religion of peace and love?"

"Yeah. You've got a point," Vince said. "What else can you say? I try not to think about that shit when I'm off duty. TMI.[86] 'Nuf about that; let's get back to work."

It was surprisingly quiet for some time after the Mosul SVBIED attack. Maybe because it was Easter weekend? We made some progress on open SIGACTs and completed a couple of open presentations. Once completed, we printed out copies and posted to the CG and CHOPS briefing binders. We also went through the process of uploading the files to a secure US DoD website portal, as well as a secure NATO portal, for dissemination to those allies.

To keep my sanity, I focused on the facts of the event and not the personal lives that were lost. I took a clinical approach in the

---

86   TMI: Too much information

research by understanding the details and documenting them in the PowerPoint. Reporting five US KIA was a little easier to deal with than saying, knowing, and thinking that five soldiers died. Regardless, it was a fact that had to be reported.

Specifically, for the presentation, I concentrated on who did this, what happened, when it happened and where it happened. If someone offered a cogent reason with evidence of why it happened, I would add that too. *Keep it clinical; keep it impersonal.*

Vince caught me at the coffee service after evening Mass on Saturday.

"Matt, I thought I'd give you a heads-up before you head back up to the cell. Collins wanted to know where you've been for the last couple hours. I told him you were serving at the Easter Vigil Mass at Hope Chapel. He didn't seem too pleased and mumbled something about religious stuff getting in the way of the mission. So be careful."

"Did you know that Archbishop Widhammer of the Archdiocese for Military Services presided as celebrant?" I asked. "He was really nice. I was part of the procession holding a large candle. It's quite an honor that of all the places he could visit at Easter, he chose Victory Base."

I replied about Capt. Collins, "I hope Rocketman doesn't give me any crap about it in person. I don't know what to make of him. He runs hot and cold. One minute he's an ass and the next minute he's asking me to help him with graphics. So besides being a twenty-four-carat asshole, he may be a nonbeliever. I pity his soul."

Three days later, we received a finalized EOD report on the Mosul SVBIED attack. The report came via email to the battle captain account, which we all shared. Currently it was a Navy EOD unit which provided MNC-I with forensic services of post-attack analysis and evaluation. They were good at it, too.

The EOD team performed like the best crime scene investigators of a major US city. They documented in excruciating detail the dimensions of the bomb crater, the amount and type of explosives used, the probable manufacturer of the device, the origin of the explosive, and even the rationale behind the bombing. EOD also provided extensive pictures of the attack site, vehicle damages and any collateral damage.

"I'm surprised anyone survived this," I remarked with astonishment. "EOD assessed the dump truck was packed with approximately ten thousand pounds of unknown explosive, with a bomb crater over fifty feet in diameter and over ten feet deep. Pieces of the heavy dump truck were found over a quarter of a mile away. A US MRAP was completely destroyed in the convoy, with extensive blast damage to COP Eagle, which was adjacent to the wall."

Vince and I tag-teamed the Mosul SVBIED PowerPoint between the two of us over the course of the Easter weekend and into the next week until the SIGACT was closed. We added new information and corrected information whenever it turned up. I knew more about that damned Mosul SVBIED attack than I wanted to at that point.

CHAPTER 11

The JOC - The Heartbreak

April 16, 2009

A couple of days after Vince and I finished the Mosul SVBIED presentation, made the copies, posted the briefing books, and uploaded to the DoD and NATO archives, the JOC chaplain, a Navy commander, presented us with a problem.

While we were busy researching and documenting the outcome of the SVBIED attack, the JOC chaplain was hard at work putting together his own PowerPoint presentation. Where we focused on the impersonal facts of the attack, the chaplain detailed the highly personal aspects of the five soldiers who had lost their lives. It's what chaplains do. He had contacted the next of kin for details on each soldier for his presentation. Unbeknownst to us, it was during that evening's CHOPS briefing that the chaplain planned to give his presentation of the five lives lost.

When his briefing slot came, the chaplain announced the fallen hero salute, and the JOC came to attention. He began the honors, "Sergeant Edward W. Forrest Jr. graduated from high school in 2003. Known as Eddie, he excelled as a long-distance runner and served on the wrestling team. His former coach Rolland Garrison said, 'He was a very enthusiastic member of the track and field program. He was a good kid with a great smile.' Eddie's sister Melissa said, 'I told him I didn't want him to be a hero. I just wanted him to be my brother. But he said he owed it to his brothers—that's what he called the soldiers in his unit—to go back and help them finish up the job.'"

The chaplain continued. "Forrest and his wife, Stephanie, were living in Colorado Springs with their three-year-old son, Bradan, and a newborn son, Jameson. His father-in-law, Ron Foster, said Edward was home last month to witness the birth of their youngest, and then he returned to Iraq for his third tour."

Tears flowed as Edward's words reverberated in my head. *"I owe it to my brothers to go back and help them finish the job."*

Halfway through Edward's eulogy Vince turned to me choked up and whispered, "This is going to be tough to handle."

I returned his gaze and with tears rolling. "I know, but we owe it to them to try. What else can we do?"

We both stood there at attention, tears flowing steadily while we endured four more promising-hero-lives-cut-short eulogies. And for the next five or ten minutes, even though it seemed to me like hours, the chaplain highlighted, in perfect PowerPoint color with pictures, each one of those soldiers' lives: where each was from, their families and friends, their education, their dreams and their honored service.

I was now confronted with the very personal, human side of the SVBIED attack and the soldiers who were killed. Now we knew those guys as well as what happened to them. It was something Vince and I had purposely tried to avoid from the very start.

Of all the people in JOC, we were the only two who *really* knew all the gruesome details of how those men died. For us, this SVBIED attack lasted a *week* as we read the daily reports, viewed the photographs and documented the details.

Now, standing at strict attention, the chaplain immersed us in the personal life details and the personal costs those men paid. It sucked to be us.

After the CHOPS briefing ended, we collapsed at our workstations and tried to recover. "Shitfire," Vince pronounced. "Chaplain should have given us a heads-up on that. You know, damn it all to hell! It's one thing to be intimately knowledgeable about that event like we are. But when you tie that gory knowledge with the personal knowledge of those who died, it's almost unbearable. We now know those guys."

"Don't I know it," I exclaimed. "I started that PowerPoint presentation and I knew I needed to distance myself at the beginning. Then the chaplain brings it all to us anyway."

"Now, just think about the soldiers who survived that SVBIED in the vehicles ahead and behind the destroyed one. Those soldiers know the details and the personal lives of their brothers in arms. That memory will be with them forever, and I think with me, too!"

After the chaplain's fallen hero salute presentation, I had to leave the cell. "Captain Collins, after that presentation, I need to go to the balcony for a while."

He seemed to sense I needed some time away. "Sure, Jerome. Take some time. You too, Cabrera, if you feel the need."

I left the JOC, wandered across the marbled rotunda and up the marbled stairs. When I got outside on the balcony, I was immersed in mist-like fog. I would've thought I was in London.

"What the hell is this? Fog?" I said to someone sitting near the number ten vegetable can he was using as an ashtray.

"Dust," was his matter-of-fact answer.

Figure 14: Typical Daytime Dust Event at Al Faw Palace

The guy was right. Everywhere the eye could see was shrouded in an extremely fine cloud of dust. It was eerie to see the few streetlights glow like magical orbs within the cloud. There was no storm or wind, and it did not necessarily cover the ground. It just hung in the air like a cloud of smoke.

Fortunately, I had an olive drab cravat back in my CHU. I would have to start carrying it so I could wear it over my face like I often did at Fort Irwin or Grafenwoehr Training Center in Germany. Note to self: *Ask Sara to send me some dust masks from my woodworking kit.*

Figure 15: OD Cravat Saves the Lungs

Ultimately, I went back to the JOC after only a few moments in the moondust cloud which had engulfed the palace and surrounding area. I soldiered on through the rest of the shift, not saying much to anyone, but trying to stay focused on work.

I'd kept my mind off the previous shift as I returned straight to my CHU in the morning. I skipped breakfast to try and get some extra rest. It was not to be.

I got in the rack covered only by my woobie[87] and tried to doze off. My mind kept flittering back to the chaplain's presentation, no matter how much I tried to relax and not think of anything. I needed help.

On the wall above my bunk, I had placed the small wooden crucifix my friend Tom Kerrigan made for me in the woodshop. Looking at the crucifix helped me find the focus and assistance I needed in the rosary inside my locker. I retrieved it, got back in bed and started out, "I believe in God, the Father Almighty, maker of heaven and earth. . . "

Somewhere around the end of the third decade of the rosary, I started to garble my Hail Marys and not remember the words. I pressed on, but dozed off only to wake up a little while later clutching the rosary in the middle of the fifth decade. I finished the prayers, then placed the rosary around my neck. I had found my answer. "Hail Holy Queen, Mother of Mercy, our life, our sweetness and our hope. . ."

After doing a few more JOC shifts, I found my muscle memory of how to get things done was pretty solid. Once Capt. Collins approved a presentation for final, we'd "Git 'er done," as Larry the Cable Guy would say. The routine was getting a bit old, tiresome and stressful.

Technically the JOC was a SCIF-light in that we didn't have to sign in, only show our badge for access, and it lacked access to any top-secret information via JWICS.[88] Information was compartmentalized via separate network systems as we would upload to SIPRNet on one computer, change to another network to upload the NATO Forces system, and to a special DoD network location. These networks did not connect to each other, and each had its own procedure for login, passwords and file uploads. We would sometimes forget which network we were using and then use the wrong login procedure or file upload sequence. We also printed two copies of the presentation in living color and posted these to the CG's and CHOPS briefing books.

---

87   Woobie: Camouflaged poncho liner
88   JWICS: Joint Worldwide Intelligence Communications System (Pronounced 'JAY Wicks')

Once you finished one presentation, there was always another one being worked on or freshly created. This routine and achieving the goal of perfect every time took its toll on everyone.

"Hey, Vince, when is this going to slow down?" I asked one night.

"I don't know, Matt. Been like this since I started, which was about three weeks before you showed up," Vince sighed.

"At least we get an hour for going to the DFAC during our shift," I said with finality as I headed off to see if I could eat something. My appetite had continued to wane.

I was obviously preoccupied with things in general around the JOC and at my workstation in the presentations cell as I strode across the lake bridge, through the parking lot and between the buildings on my walk to the DFAC. The outside temperature had increased to the mid-eighties and was not yet oppressive. I've had warmer days in Arizona, but rarely in April. I hadn't felt much wind either, which helped to cool you off.

I perused the typical lunch menu in my mind, trying to create an interest in one specific item or another. They'd probably posted the menu somewhere on the NIPRNet, but I hadn't had time to look.

The walk to DFAC was ten minutes, and I waited in line another ten minutes before I reached the CAC[89] swipe, which would allow me to enter and eat. That's when I realized I'd left my CAC back at my workstation. To be able to use a workstation, you had to insert your CAC in the special reader slot on the top of the keyboard to allow you to log in and use the computer.

I'd been warned about this little mistake when I first started working in the JOC, just like I'd been warned about the damn JOC stairs and the trip log. During the walk back to the JOC to retrieve my card, I wondered why the DFAC didn't have some kind of log to keep track of the walk-of-shame offenders like the JOC stairs trip log. I got embarrassingly smug smiles from everyone as I retrieved my CAC and headed back to the DFAC.

---

89   CAC: Common Access Card (Military ID)

When I returned from eating a little something at the DFAC, I asked my battle captain partner, "Hey, Vince. Except for my walk of shame, doesn't this feel like another damn *Groundhog Day* shift? I guess I'm just gettin' tired of reading the same SIGACTs day after day, shift after shift and then having to draft what seems like the same presentation shift after shift after shift. I mean really, when has there *not* been a protest by Muqtada Al Sadr supporters immediately after Friday night prayers that *didn't* end with a SIGACT? Am I right? Maybe we should create some PowerPoint templates for each type of frequently recurring SIGACT as a starting point. Then, when we get that type of SIGACT that meets the CCIR[90] threshold for reporting, we open that template and just fill in the data points. It sure would save us a lot of time. We can start by creating a *Friday night protest by Al Sadr supporters ends in violence* template. Or here's another one, *Suicide bomber attacks open air market after Friday prayer service: X number killed.*"

Vince looked up from his workstation and smiled knowingly at my frustrations. He turned toward me with his back to Rocketman Collins and lifted the flap of his ACU shirt pocket. On the underside was a Velcro patch which read *EMBRACE THE SUCK*. After I smirked at his patch, he closed his pocket and responded with, "Nice try, bucko. But as soon as we do something as time saving and efficient as that might be, they will somehow change, or should I say improve the presentation format or structure again, which will only make the templates obsolete, turning our effort into wasted hours. Remember how they changed the dashboard on the management portal and sprung that on us without notice? We had to basically relearn where all the shit was located. Great idea of yours, but this is the wrong place to implement it." His voice trailed off with anguished resignation.

"Well, I guess you're right; wrong place, wrong time," I said. "But I'm getting tired of being a slave to these presentations. It's all we do for the entire shift while we sit at these workstations. It used to be

---

90   CCIR: Commander's Critical Information Requirements

that *death by PowerPoint* meant you had to sit through an endless number of presentations for school or something. Now I can honestly say it also means having to *create* an endless number of presentations.

"On another subject, do you know Captain Harry Henderson up there in that other support cell?" I asked.

Vince smiled wryly. "Yeah. His call sign is Houdini, by the way. Thank God he's getting ready to redeploy. Sometimes he joins our little dinner group in the drive over to the other DFAC. He'll start talking about how he spends an hour or two preparing his portion for the briefing, only to use the other ten hours watching fucking movies on his workstation. Meanwhile, the rest of us keep rowing like slaves in the bowels of the JOC galley ship. I'm kinda waiting for CHOPS to bring in a drummer and then give the command, 'Ramming speed.'"

I looked at him with a quizzical smile and asked, "Aren't we already rowing at ramming speed?" We both chuckled.

I told Vince about an admission by Capt. Henderson. "You weren't there, but I heard Henderson mention at the group dinner table the other day that his OIC is going to put him in for a Bronze Star for serving in the JOC. He said he told his OIC no, but I can't accept that. Whaddaya think about that?"

Vince was wide-eyed in his reply. "So, he's getting a Bronze Star? Let me guess. He's also getting a 'V-Device'[91] with the award, as in *V* for video?"

We laughed and Vince continued. "I'm not sure I would have shared that story if I were in his shoes. In fact, I'm not sure I know why he shared it. Is he trying to get out in front of bad press when it happens? He knows he's had a kick-back assignment and been shamming most of the time when he's on shift."

We both shook our heads at the inflation of some awards.

"This would cheapen all the Bronze Stars the grunts are getting. It also kind of reminds me of that adage about the six phases of a military project."

---

91   V-Device: On military awards it denotes "For Valor"

"Six phases? Tell me," Vince said. "I haven't heard this."

"Really? Well it goes like this. The six phases of a military project are: Phase One, total acceptance and enthusiasm. Phase Two, disillusionment. Phase Three, utter panic. Phase Four, search for the guilty. Phase Five, punishment of the innocent. Phase Six, promotion and rewards for the non-participants. I think it's safe to say we belong in Phase Five, while Harry Houdini up there is coasting along in Phase Six."

"I'd laugh if this didn't sound so true," Vince declared.

CHAPTER 12

The JOC - Lieutenant "Sugarbritches"

"Hey, I've gotta hit the head. Be right back," I said to Vince as I pushed away from my galley rowing station.

About ten minutes later, I got back to my workstation and Vince gently grabbed my arm. "Matt, did ya see that Marine lieutenant down by the coffee service?"

"Are you kidding? How could I miss her?" I asked. "I had to walk right past. I decided I would just wait to get my coffee after I logged in. Not your typical Marine, eh?"

The Marine lieutenant was a fit and very attractive twenty-something at about five foot six inches or so. The USMC camouflage blouse she wore did little to conceal her shape.

"Well, guess what, she's working with us," the unmarried Capt. Vince Cabrera beamed.

"Seriously? What's her name?"

"Second Lieutenant Strobridges, USMC. Right now, she's kinda working the swing shift with me, but that'll probably change, according to Collins. She's got a martial arts class at 2030 each night. Collins gave her two hours off during her shift to attend the class until he can work her into a regular schedule . . . or so he says."

Lt. Strobridges was heading back up the stairs with her coffee when, you guessed it, she fell victim to the stairs, dropping her coffee but catching her fall with her hands and upper thighs as her foot slid out underneath her. She lay almost prone up the staircase.

"Sign the book," someone yelled out while a major from the fusion cell on the other side of the staircase got up to help her. The DCHOPS, a Marine lieutenant colonel, also responded.

Luckily, she wasn't hurt. They both looked her over carefully after she stood up, because it was their duty, you see. The staircase trip log custodian down near the bottom of the staircase did the unthinkable and brought the trip log *to* the lieutenant to sign. Never saw that before. The DCHOPS motioned her into the chair next to his and sat her down so she could sign the trip log.

Meanwhile, the rest of the JOC on our side went back to business. The one exception was the CHOPS, who dutifully, one might say, sauntered over to the DCHOPS area from his chair on the right side to make sure all was well. You know, no broken bones, no serious incident report, etc. *Yeah, right.*

"Are you OK, Lieutenant, uh, Strobridges?" CHOPS said while eyeing the nametag on her uniform just a little bit too long for comfort's sake.

"Yes, I think I'm all right," she replied.

Vince and I looked at each other knowingly as we sat at our workstations on the row immediately above the DCHOPS cell. In the JOC amphitheater, our row of workstations sat about two feet higher and behind the DCHOPS row in front of us. This pretty much provided us a front-row seat.

After the perfunctory scene of making sure she was all right, the major went and got her a new cup of coffee after asking her, "How do you take your coffee?"

"Doing better now, Lieutenant, uh, what's your first name?" the CHOPS politely asked.

"It's Kandi, sir. Kilo Alpha November Delta India, Kandi, sir," she replied, spelling her name phonetically with a smile, probably to show off that she actually knew the military phonetic alphabet.

The two field-grade officers chuckled with the DCHOPS adding, "Answered like a good Marine officer should."

Once she was settled with her cup of java, CHOPS asked, "So tell me, Kandi, when did you start working here in the JOC?"

"Actually, sir, this is my first shift."

The two bantered about with Lt. Kandi, who answered their questions about her college, her military specialty, what she liked to do, etc. The conversations appeared to be innocent enough, light and engaging with smiling and joking.

After about fifteen minutes, CHOPS the rooster pursuing this hen, he may have realized things had gone too far with this very junior officer. "Perhaps you should head back to your workstation now, Lieutenant?" CHOPS said coolly.

Ya think? I said to myself. No one else ever got that kind of welcoming treatment upon arrival in the JOC—*ever*.

The lieutenant left the fawning group of field-grade officers and made her way up to our row. We pulled our chairs closer into the workstation so that she could squeeze behind. Along the way, Vince introduced us. "Lieutenant Strobridges, this is Captain Jerome from the night shift."

I got up from my chair and pushed it in under the workstation table as far as I could. "Glad to meet you, Lieutenant." I offered a handshake.

She stopped, looked me in the eye, shook my hand with a good grip and said with a genuine smile, "Good to meet you too, sir."

I moved out of her way so she could pass as she continued to her workstation. I tried saying her name silently to myself *Strobridges, Strobridges.* In my own mind, I referred to her as *Lt. Sugarbritches.* It kind of fit her, just like her uniform.

Lt. Sugarbritches excelled at being a second lieutenant. She had trouble with just about everything. She wasn't very good at PowerPoint, basically because she had some trouble with taking the detailed SIGACTs and summarizing the key points. Vince had to give her one-on-one training on reading the SIGACTs to extract the important points.

She initially experienced some trouble with the CCIR list to determine if a SIGACT met the standard for reporting. After a couple of days reading SIGACTs, she became well versed in determining which ones required a PowerPoint presentation. Vince took the next obvious step, enlightening her on how to prepare the presentation for a SIGACT. *Lucky Vince? Glad it's him and not me.*

The grind continued day in, day out, shift in, shift out for another week or so. Lt. Strobridges improved at the normal lieutenant rate—slowly. One night she learned a valuable lesson at the expense of someone else in the JOC.

We were cruising along on the keyboard looking at SIGACTs for facts and emails for details when the alarm sounded.

"Attention in the JOC. Attention in the JOC," someone behind me announced.

"Spot report. 1st Brigade Combat Team reports an insurgent running away from an attempted VBIED attack in Taji," declared the MND-Baghdad LNO.

Waiting breathlessly, Vince glanced over at me and we both shared a quizzical smile. I think we were both waiting for a little more detail in the spot report. I thought, *Is that it?*

About ten seconds of silence passed before the CHOPS finally spoke up, clearly annoyed. "Well? We're all waiting, MND-Baghdad. You got anything else to add to that stellar report of yours?"

"No, not at this time," the division LNO responded weakly.

"You've got to be kidding?" a clearly upset CHOPS declared. "You interrupted everyone's work for that half-ass attempt at a spot report? Have you not heard of the SALUTE format? You know, *size, activity, location, uniform, time* and *equipment* relating to the event?"

"Yes, sir. We thought it important to get the initial word out as quickly as possible and fill in with details when they became available," offered the LNO.

"That's not how it's done here, son," the CHOPS huffed. "Next time you announce 'Attention in the JOC,' everyone will be waiting with rapt attention for your detailed report. OK?"

"Yes, sir," came back the quick reply.

I looked over my shoulder at the LNO who'd just gotten his tail feathers singed. I had not seen him before, so I suspected he was a late arrival to the JOC rodeo. From my experience, I knew there was little to no training given to arriving JOCsters. When I first arrived, I asked the OIC for an SOP to read so I would know how things were done. He said, "Ain't got one. Ya just gotta watch and learn."

The division LNO was only a sergeant first class, so I suspect that was another reason CHOPS figured he could tee off on him. I really don't think he would have taken on a master sergeant with that kind of response. I hoped the sergeant would do better next time.

We didn't have long to wait as about an hour later, the same MND-Baghdad LNO announced, "Attention in the JOC. Attention in the JOC. Spot report update from 1st Brigade Combat Team." The JOC silenced itself in anticipation that the division LNO would redeem himself.

"Update follows: A suspected insurgent male, approximately twenty to twenty-five years old, with slim build, weighing approximately one hundred forty pounds, was seen running quickly down the street away from the intersection near Taji, at grid three eight sierra lima foxtrot three zero eight two two one zero five. The suspected insurgent had a full beard, was last seen wearing a short-sleeve shirt, khaki-colored cargo pants and carrying what appeared to be a small pack resembling a suicide satchel. This encounter was reported at 2313 hours Zulu, twenty-three April 2009. A small light-brown four-door Toyota sedan with a driver's side front flat tire was parked near the intersection. It is believed the sedan may contain an IED. A 1st Brigade Combat Team interpreter learned from witnesses that the car broke down with a flat. The suspected insurgent then exited the vehicle, looked at the flat, removed the satchel and then ran away as 1st Brigade Combat Team elements appeared, driving up the road to the location. Then, seeing this man run away, some elements of the 1st Brigade Combat Team started to implement a cordon while others gave chase on foot. The chase went down several alleyways and ended with a house-to-house search. The suspected insurgent was not found. EOD team has been called to evaluate for the possibility of an IED. End of report."

The LNO finally stopped talking and took a breath.

We were just a bit overwhelmed by the LNO's overly detailed spot report. A spot report is normally a short bullet list, but his report was over the top. The sergeant walked right up to the line of insolent insubordination without crossing that line. It was true NCO poetry.

I said in a whisper to Vince, "I think the sergeant LNO just responded to the CHOPS with, OK, you want a detailed report, you got a detailed report." Vince nodded his approval and smiled. I think everyone in the JOC got something close to that same message from the division LNO.

The CHOPS just sat there and kind of grinned while turning around to face the LNO, and said rather facetiously, "I really think you left off some information from your report, Sergeant."

This was a bit stunning for the CHOPS to say. *Really?*

CHOPS continued in his still-facetious, but now-condescending tone to let the LNO know he almost crossed the line: "For example, what color was his shirt? Was it a solid color, plaid, or stripes? And what about his shoes? Was he wearing Nikes or just plain sneakers? What color were those shoes? You had no mention of headgear. Was he wearing a hat or scarf? Anyway, thank you for your report. Come see me later."

Having been a sergeant first class before I became an officer, I was belly laughing inside because it was clear the sergeant got the best of the CHOPS. Never underestimate the willingness of senior NCOs to come back at you.

The JOC returned to *Groundhog Day* mode for about another week after the infamous spot report by the MND-Baghdad LNO. People, mostly NCOs, told the story of the LNO's report at the DFAC and the Green Beans Coffee house, according to Sgt. Manley. I was surprised there wasn't an email announcing it.

Also, during the last week, Lt. Strobridges still got time off each night for her martial arts class with no other change to her schedule. She could almost come and go at her discretion. Oh well. At least one of us was getting taken care of by management. Unbeknownst to me, another single officer was interested in Lt. Strobridges, as I would find out later.

"Captain Cabrera, I'm leaving for class now," Lt. Strobridges announced.

Capt. Collins was gone, so Vince had the lead at the moment. "OK, Lieutenant," Vince replied. "See you around ten or so."

The lieutenant squeezed her way behind the row of chairs and headed out of the JOC.

Vince looked at me and thought it needed further explanation. "She gets a half hour to get in her gym clothes and walk to the gym. The class is an hour and then she gets a half hour to recover."

"No sweat, GI," I said, not really caring. "But can I take time to smoke a cigar on the balcony. When is Collins coming back?"

"Well, here's some good news. He's not coming back tonight. He tweaked his back in the gym and they gave him forty-eight hours quarters. Lucky us!" Vince exclaimed.

At 1100 I asked, "Hey, Vince. I'd really like to go smoke a cigar. Unfortunately, I left them in my CHU locker. Can I go get one, come back and then head up to the balcony?"

"Sure," Vince replied. "It appears we're pretty much caught up on presentations anyway until we get more info. Go ahead."

"You don't need to tell me twice," I said as I picked up my stuff, making sure to log off and take my CAC with me. "Be back soon as. . . "

I didn't get to smoke a cigar on shift very much. We were usually too busy. I walked out of the JOC, the palace, across the access bridge, and headed east back to Freedom Village and my CHU to get the cigars. The temperatures during the day were usually mostly hot. In the evening after the sun went down it was still in the mid to upper eighties.

Once I got into the Freedom Village area, I tried to stay quiet. Everyone there had worked a shift. They could be sleeping, watching a movie, or making a video call back home. It stayed quiet around here most of the day, other than the helipad operations and the hum of wall-mounted air conditioners. The latter being a sound which helped to lull some to sleep.

I approached my CHU door using Scout silence techniques. Carl usually watched a movie after he got off work or would be fast asleep. Either way, I didn't want to disturb him. I just thought I'd slip in ever so softly, turn to my locker on the left, extract a couple of cigars and be gone. No fuss, no muss.

We kept the door unlocked when either of us was there, so we could run out and hit the bunker if needed. When I slowly tried the doorknob, I found it unlocked. I pulled slowly on the door to open it as little as possible, and was met with just enough light to see where I was walking and not trip over stuff. I entered sideways through the half-opened CHU door, closed it gingerly and slid to my left.

As I entered, I could now see Carl. Unfortunately, I could also see Lt. Strobridges. They were engaged in oral sex on his bunk with her straddling his face and looking towards the door. Her eyes were closed as she proceeded slowly and rhythmically.

OH SHIT, my mind screamed out. *Can I get my cigars without them knowing I was here? Fat chance*, I thought as I inched leftward toward my locker, keeping my eye on the two of them. Well, actually I could really only see her. *Shit!* My locker wasn't open.

As I got to the front of my locker and gently tried turning the handle to open it, the lieutenant opened her eyes and turned her gaze towards me. She stopped and slowly rose to a seated position, still straddling Carl's face. I don't know why, but she modestly held her breasts with her crossed arms while gently rocking on his face.

With my other hand, I held a finger up to my face and mouthed, *"Shhhhh."* I then pointed to myself and then my locker to indicate I needed something from it. She nodded her understanding.

In his current position with his ears surrounded by thighs, Capt. Carl Buckley wasn't about to hear anything. *Oh well, if he dies, he dies happy.* It seemed the only person who knew I was there was OK with it.

Surprisingly, the locker door opened without creaking or banging as I opened it just enough to extract the small humidor box holding the cigars my friend Marc had sent me. At that point, caught with my hand in the so-called cookie jar, I decided to take the whole box and just leave the locker open and depart as quickly as I came in.

I turned back toward Lt. Strobridges, but her eyes were closed again as she gently rubbed her chest and rocked back and forth. I gingerly opened the CHU door and slipped out as silently and cautiously as I had entered, slowly closing the door behind me.

Phew. I breathed a large sigh of relief out in the CHU village corridor of T-walls.

I walked briskly back to the palace because I'd spent more time than allotted getting my cigars. I thought about my recent encounter with this millennial female Marine. She wasn't perturbed or flustered in the least, and only briefly modest about her body or what she was doing with it when she discovered me. I think she quickly analyzed the position we were both in and just knew to *continue mission* like a good Marine. What else was she going to do inside the small ten-foot by twelve-foot CHU space? Get up and run to the bathroom? All I could say was, "Oorah, Lieutenant!"

I walked back into the JOC and returned to my workstation. I pulled the small humidor from my cargo pocket and pulled out a cigar. "Heading to the balcony, Vince," I said as I held up a cigar.

"Are you treating the whole cell to a cigar?" he asked. "I thought you were going to get just one."

"No, I'm not, but *you* can have one," I said.

I made my way up top to the balcony on the east side of the palace. There were some beat-up chairs and makeshift butt cans all around. It was the go-to place for smoking. Thank God, PowerPoint could wait for a change.

I walked out from underneath the covered area of the balcony into the open area on the east side to take in the starlit sky above. It was a beautiful sight and you could see forever. I lit my cigar, plugged in my iPod tunes and began to relax.

It didn't take long for Iraq to ruin my short sojourn away from the JOC. I was barely ten minutes into my cigar when a steady stream of tracer fire arced skyward from inside Camp Victory.

Figure 16: C-RAM in action

A second or so after the tracers flew, the light show was followed by the unique report of the weapon. . . a steady *brrrrrrrrrrrrrrrr* rang out. After a one-second pause, the Centurion C-RAM[92] weapon system spat out another one-second burst of tracers to the heavens, followed by the distinctive weapon signature. A few moments later, as the tracers burned out, the fired rounds exploded in mid-air.

I knew that weapon signature from my infantry days back in Germany as the self-propelled, M163 Vulcan Air Defense System which fired the M61A1 Vulcan 20mm cannon. The Navy also used the Vulcan cannon in its Phalanx CIWS[93] for defense against anti-ship missiles and helicopters. To protect FOBs and high-value sites in and around Baghdad, the military adapted the Navy's Phalanx CIWS to a land-based weapon for C-RAM duties.

Figure 17: Navy's Close-In Weapons System (CWIS)

---

92   C-RAM: Counter-Rocket, Artillery Mortar defense system
93   CWIS: Close-In Weapon System (pronounced 'Sea Whiz")

The 1st Corps in-briefing at Hope Chapel informed me about the C-RAM protecting the base from rocket, artillery and mortar fire while those incoming projectiles were still in the air. I had not heard any warning over the base speaker system of a test firing. *Are we under attack?*

After three one-second bursts, the firing stopped. I guess it must have been a test firing. *Note to self: Carry a set of emergency underwear in your cargo pocket.*

When I finally got off shift early the next morning, I went back to the CHU to crash without going to breakfast. Getting up after noon, I decided to go and try to eat a late lunch.

The heat was a bit stifling with some added humidity for my stroll over to the DFAC. *What's this heat going to be like in June or July?* I thought. I had already transitioned from wearing my patrol cap to wearing my boonie hat[94] a couple of weeks earlier. The wide-brimmed boonie hat provided extra sun protection for your ears and neck, and had cooling vents in the top.

I got to the DFAC about twenty minutes before they closed the serving line. Even though my appetite was nowhere to be found, I made a salad with some goodies in it. I wandered over to the north side of the DFAC with my tray where there were some smaller, quieter rooms, some with no television broadcasts. To my surprise, I found Lt. Strobridges sitting alone just starting to eat her meal.

She looked up from her meal about the same time I was deciding where to sit. In my search for a seat, she smiled awkwardly and held her hand out as if suggesting I join her.

I gave a quick nod to her invitation, walked over and sat opposite her.

She was first to greet, with "Good afternoon, sir."

"Good afternoon, Lieutenant," I responded. "I decided to get just

---

94   Boonie hat: Formally designated the 'Hat, Sun, Hot Weather'

a salad. I haven't been eating very well. Nothing seems appetizing," I suggested, pointing to the overly stuffed salad bowl and hoping to break the ice with small talk.

"It looks good, sir."

The elephant was clearly now standing in the room next to our table.

Being senior, I spoke first. "Listen, Lt. Sug—" I stopped mid-word, realizing I almost called her Sugarbritches. "Lt. Strobridges. Sorry, I have a difficult time pronouncing your last name."

"No problem, sir. Everyone else does too," she offered.

"About last night," I started out slowly and diplomatically, keeping my voice lowered even though there were only four other people in the room, and they were pretty far away. "I apologize for interrupting. I didn't know and didn't see you two until I got all the way inside the CHU and closed the door. I felt a little trapped myself, actually. But as far as I'm concerned, what happens between two consenting, single adults on their off time is none of my business. Since Captain Buckley is not your first-line supervisor, there should be no compromise of supervisory authority. However, potentially there could be an adverse impact on morale and discipline within the presentations cell if others learned of this. I'm sure you were briefed on the fraternization policy, a very long document with a lot of examples. Don't quote me, but you two are probably OK right now, but if it impacts the mission, it will become a violation for sure." I let that sink in.

"Here's where it could adversely impact our team," I suggested. "Although Captain Buckley was off shift, you were not. You were supposed to be at your martial arts class," I said as I lifted my eyebrows and smiled wryly.

The realization of being on-duty during her tryst suddenly hit her as a major boo-boo. She put down her yogurt and became quite serious. "Yes, sir. In hindsight, I guess I took advantage of the situation even though I didn't see it at the time. I guess I wasn't thinking clearly. Please let me explain and perhaps you might excuse the indiscretion."

"Look, Lieutenant," I said reassuringly. "If it will help, then go ahead, but I'm not taking any action beyond just talking with you. Being senior, I think I have a responsibility to offer advice and counsel to you even if I'm not your supervisor; just trying to show you where the landmines are located. I got called out of retirement after thirteen years to work in this rodeo, so I've been down a few more trails than you."

She let out a sigh. "Yes, sir. Well, that was not planned. I went to my CHU last night, got into my gym clothes and headed over to the gym. Captain Buckley was there too, inquiring about joining the class. We talked about the class while we waited for the instructor to show up. Around 2035 hours or so, someone from the gym office came out and told us the instructor had to cancel the class that night. Captain Buckley suggested that we should just go ahead and use the gym machines instead. He said we could spot each other on the free weights. I went along with it. Well, you know how it is when working out. You can get a little high on the adrenaline and the hormones, the bodies, I guess. Needless to say, one thing led to another. We found each other attractive, and after the workout we went to his CHU, which was really close by. I think we both were tempted by the moment, the opportunity, the sweat-induced euphoria, and me by his charm."

"I see. Thanks for being so open about this. I really do understand how the situation and moment can overtake you," I said. "This is a good example to talk about really. I assume this is your first combat deployment?" She nodded. "OK. You need to know that even though the military tries to make a combat deployment as close to homelike as possible, it is not just like home. As a single female, whether you're military or a civilian contractor, there is a much higher risk of you being sexually harassed or assaulted while on deployment." I let that sink in.

"Yes. I've heard that in training, too," she said.

I continued. "During a combat deployment, everything is magnified beyond normal. There is higher stress, higher workload, adrenaline and cortisol can skyrocket, while emotions and other feelings also become amplified. It takes a lot of personal discipline to understand and keep these in check.

"Also, there are people who exhibit a much different attitude about things in general while downrange. For them, they might think of this deployment as Las Vegas. You know, *what happens in Vegas, stays in Vegas* could just as well be stated as *what happens downrange, stays downrange.*"

I really had her attention, so I continued. "Do you remember your first shift in the JOC? You were walking up the stairs, tripped, fell down and spilled your coffee?" She nodded.

"Those of us in the JOC then witnessed three field-grade officers compete with each other for almost twenty minutes, fawning over you like some kind of high school crush. You probably thought they were just being nice and welcoming since you are new and you tripped. It looked innocent enough, but just be on guard.

"You should know their behavior could be viewed as crossing the line as far as fraternization. It can be a tough call, but in my book, it did cross the line. Why did it? Perhaps it was an attitude of what happens on deployment stays on deployment. Two of those officers are above you in your chain of command and can exhibit influence over your duties. It's not lost on anyone that your martial arts class could be viewed as preferential treatment, so that could adversely impact morale. I might add that even if the behavior only causes an *appearance* of partiality, it can be against policy. No one else gets that kind of time off, but you were registered in the class before you got assigned to the JOC, so they made an exception. We in the presentations cell are OK with it; we don't care. We'd all like to see you get that black belt.

"I guess I'm just trying to point out that there are some situations for all females that are a little more dangerous and can easily happen on deployment. I'd really hate to see you become another statistic. Now, imagine the ramifications of an indiscreet affair or worse.

"Just one last thing before you go," I added. "One of the reasons we work in a Joint Service Operations Center is for the different services to learn to work together. Each service has its own culture, traditions and set of values that guide them. By working with each other, we learn those differences and how to include them in our day-to-day dealings."

"Thank you, sir, for taking the time. I really do appreciate it. I do have to get back to the shift, but I want you to know that I will do better." She pushed her chair away from the table to leave.

"Very good, Lieutenant. I'm sure you will," I added as I contemplated picking up my tray to leave. I decided to get an ice cream. "I suppose I'll see you tonight when I go back on shift."

"Yes, sir," she replied as she was off while I headed to the ice cream bar.

I slurped my ice cream while heading back to the JOC and thought, *Thank God she's a Marine. Collins and the Assistant CHOPS have primary responsibility to keep an eye on her. I did my part and told her like it is.*

CHAPTER 13

The JOC - Bloody May

The last ten days or so of April dragged on slowly as we worked on a seemingly endless list of PowerPoints. "Have you noticed the PowerPoints after Easter have been steady?" I said to Vince.

"Yeah. Then there was that non-hostile-incident death of that Marine corporal on the twenty-second and the non-combat-injuries death of that sergeant major back on the twenty-fourth. Thank God we don't do PowerPoints for those deaths. Did you see the SIGACT?"

"Yes, I did. Although it wasn't explicit in the SIGACT, it sure sounded like possible suicides to me. When the SIGACT reads *non-combat injuries* or *non-hostile incident* with no other details like a vehicle accident, it makes you wonder."

I changed the subject. "After Obama's speech about downsizing and sending people home, I haven't heard much since. Have you?"

"Well, kind of, but it was so speculative that I haven't spread the rumor," Vince said. "So, I heard some chatter that they're building an Iraqi JOC across the street to take over what we do here. That would be nice. They may ask for volunteers from here to help get it online. That'll set the stage for transitioning stuff out of here. With us having to be out of Iraqi cities by the end of June, I suspect something's going to shake out soon."

April 30, 2009, was another bad day in the JOC for the PowerPoint Rangers of the presentations cell.

I tried not to swear, but, "That fucking Fallujah did it again," I said to Sgt. Manley and Vince. "Did ya see the SIGACT from 1st Marines? We lost two Marines and a sailor there."

"No. I'm still working that Kirkuk patrol from 1st Cavalry," Vince answered. "You takin' the lead on that one?"

"Yeah, sure," I sighed as I brought up another window to launch the presentation template. "That makes nineteen people we've lost in April. Shitfire!"

Yes, I was pissed. I was hoping to get out of April without any more US KIAs.

We hadn't even completed the April 30 Fallujah presentation when we lost two 1st Cavalry soldiers in Mosul on May 2. We then experienced almost a week with no KIAs. I said to Vince, "Maybe May's casualty rate will be different than April's."

"I hope you're right, bro. It's getting harder and harder to stand through these fallen hero salutes without completely losing it," Vince confessed.

I spoke too soon. We had a string of daily KIAs on May 8, 9 and 10. Even Capt. Collins was starting to change after almost daily fallen hero salutes during briefings.

He drew his chair over towards me and asked, almost with some compassion, "Captain Jerome. Are you OK? I saw you and Cabrera break down last month at the hero salute for those five KIAs in Mosul as well as several other salutes. And we've had almost a steady string since the end of April, too. Cabrera tells me you've lost fifteen pounds since you've been here. Is that true?"

I was taken aback by his demeanor. "Yes, sir. To be honest, sir, it's not easy documenting these CCIRs with KIAs and knowing all the intimate details of how they died, only to be followed by fallen hero salutes to those KIAs. As much as we try to compartmentalize the work, it's too personal at that point. I think I can handle the weight loss, but my hip's been bothering me, too. It's these stairs. I've already had my right hip replaced, and after falling out of a Humvee back at Fort Jackson in March, now my left hip is angry at me. The pills only do so much."

"You've got a fake hip?" Collins asked.

"Yes, sir. Actually, it's a hip resurfacing with a new ball and socket. So, I'm metal on metal on the right. The left hip is starting to grind a little bit, though," I admitted.

"How did you clear medical processing?" he asked, surprised.

"My ortho surgeon back in Arizona checked me out and gave me a clean bill of health before I processed. And I wasn't having a problem when I had my entrance physical, but I think I did something the third week of March when I fell out of a Humvee during training."

Capt. Collins seemed genuinely concerned for a change. He was silent for a long moment, then said, "Look. I want you to go to the Combat Stress Clinic."

I was stunned, but asked, "Yes, sir, but why CSC? For my hip? I've already been to the TMC for it and they just keep renewing my anti-inflammatory med."

"No. Not for your hip," Collins stated. "You may not have noticed it, but I see the classic signs of stress starting with you and Cabrera, too. You're trying to gut it out like the rest of us, but you haven't done this for a while. So, go to CSC and tell them about the weight loss and the kind of work you do with CCIR presentations."

"Yes, sir. I'll head over there right after I get off shift in the morning," I responded.

"No, Captain. I mean you need to go *now*. I'm not gonna lose anyone on my team because of stress. Better to go now before it might become a bigger problem."

"Roger that, sir." I got my stuff and left the JOC.

I hobbled on out of the palace and made my way toward the Combat Stress Clinic on the other side of Freedom Village. Fortunately, it was a twenty-four-hour operation that accepted walk-ins at any time. I had a lovely little chat with a staff sergeant medic who performed the equivalent of a clinical triage of my condition.

"No, I am not having suicidal ideations," I told her. "Besides, suicide is against my religion, unlike the predominant religion around here."

She looked at me quizzically. "It's a joke, sorry," I offered. "Look. I've lost some weight, which is OK, and I get a little teary-eyed during fallen hero salutes. What do you expect?"

"Well, sir, from the description of your job, your work environment, and your wife's sickness last month, your OIC was right to send you over. You didn't tell him about your wife getting that H1N1 swine flu, either," she replied. "Besides your wife being sick at home alone, you're not the first person we've seen coming from the JOC. We know it's a pressure cooker. Frankly speaking, our team leader thinks twelve-hour shifts in the JOC are inappropriate and has sent word to the CG about it. I'm concerned that you are buried in the research and reporting of these sometimes-gruesome attacks. Your mind is not immune to the scenes of horror on paper, and lots of it can be subliminal."

"OK. I'll be careful and try to take better care of myself," I said.

She seemed to agree that I was at risk for a stress injury. She made a late-afternoon appointment for me, but gave me her card and told me to drop in or call around 1400 in case of no-show appointments. As a dutiful Medical Service Corps officer, I acknowledged her guidance and headed back to work.

"So, what did CSC do for you?" Capt. Collins asked when I got back to work a couple hours later.

"I've got an appointment at 1700 hours tomorrow, but was told to drop in or call around 1400 in case there are some no-shows."

"CSC called me after you left. She said she couldn't divulge anything about your appointment, but did suggest I ask you about how things are going at home."

"Oh, yes. I didn't think of this when we were talking earlier, but my wife contracted that H1N1 flu that's been going around lately. She's home alone and sick. I asked her if I needed to come home, but she said no, that she could deal with it. She's a retired military nurse and I respect that she'd be honest about this."

"All right. If you say so," Capt. Collins said. "You let me know if things change."

"Yes, sir," I replied, then got settled in behind the workstation again.

The rest of the shift fortunately slithered by rather smoothly. I skipped breakfast when I got off shift at 0630, and decided to try and get some sleep.

Unfortunately, the helipad was busy when I got in the rack. *Damn choppers!* Carl was right; we were way too close. I catnapped, then headed to DFAC.

While standing in line to get in, I saw Mike Corso ahead of me. We waved at each other, smiling bleakly. We got together at a table with our trays once inside.

"Hiya, Mike. It's good to see you. How're they hangin' these days?" I asked jokingly.

"I'll tell ya, Matt, this is the absolute worst assignment I've ever had in my life." It was strange for my Ranger Battle Buddy to openly grouse. "I'm not really doing anything as an LNO—nothing. I'm bored stiff. They've got me kind of chained to a workstation to read some emails and stuff now and then. I go to a meeting every once in a while with no real responsibility. I want to tell them, 'If you don't have anything for me to do, send me home.' I didn't sign up for this, Matt. I signed up for an MP position. This is not that. I am totally disgusted. I usually have to stay there during the week. I come back to Victory Base occasionally to make sure they haven't moved my CHU and to exchange some clothes, etc. This sucks."

"Ya wanna trade positions?" I quipped. "Carl and I are working almost nonstop shifts in the JOC doing PowerPoint presentations for CCIR events."

"My excitement each week is riding the Rhino to and from the Green Zone," Mike said. "No thanks on trading. I hate doing prolonged computer shit. I'd rather be in an MRAP turret once in a while, to tell you the truth."

My Ranger Battle Buddy was being brutally honest with his last comment. We spent the next hour or more catching up. I told him about some of the presentations and my CSC appointment, too. He told me about some of the weird shit happening in the Green Zone and not for public consumption.

"Well, I'd love to sit around and jaw-jack some more, but I need to go make a phone call after 1400 from my workstation about that CSC appointment at 1700 today."

"Yeah. Me too. I've gotta catch the Rhino back to the 'zoo' at 1430, so I'm off too."

We got up from the table, hugged and then headed off to the empty tray return.

I thought about Mike all the way back to the JOC, and felt very sorry for him. His situation reminded me of O'Rourke, the Special Forces sergeant recently assigned to the presentations cell. Sgt. O'Rourke had told me very candidly, "I'm a special operator, a shooter. Why am I here behind this workstation? I volunteered for a PSD[95] assignment and was accepted. I show up and they throw me in here. This is a total waste of my time and skills."

I greeted Capt. Valderama as I wandered back into the JOC cell at 1415. "Hi, Jesus. Just need to make a call."

"No problem, Jerome."

I pulled the CSC card from my cargo pocket and dialed the number. After a single ring, I received an automated message that said the call couldn't go through. I tried again and got the same message. I tried a secondary number on the card and got the same message.

What the hell is going on? I thought.

---

95   PSD: Personal Security Detachment

Reaching back to my roots as a Signal Corps Operations officer, I figured the office phone number extensions were probably consecutively numbered. I'd give it a shot. So, I tried the next consecutive number from the last one on the business card. Bingo! It kept ringing.

After about three rings, it was answered by someone who said, with some audible surprise, "Hello, who's this?"

"Good afternoon. I'm Captain Matt Jerome and I've got an appointment at 1700 today. I was told to drop in or call back after 1400 in case there were no-shows."

"This is Colonel Ziegler. How did you get this number, Captain? These are supposed to be blocked right now."

"Well, sir, I couldn't get through with the numbers on the card, so I just tried the next logical extension."

"OK. Well, this is my back-office line, and I really don't have time to talk. We're in the middle of an incident. Where and when is your appointment today? Camp Victory or Camp Liberty?"

"Camp Victory, sir, at 1700."

"I'll be honest, Captain. The CSC is closed and on lockdown here and at Liberty," the colonel replied with a tinge of remorse in his voice. "I can't say anything more, but you won't be seen today. Call tomorrow for a new appointment. I'm very sorry. If you are in urgent need, you can go to the TMC."

"No problem, sir. I'll make do."

"Very good, Captain. I need to go now, but please, Captain, take care of yourself today."

I hung up the phone, wondering what was going on at the CSC.

"Jesus, have you heard anything about an incident at the CSC today? I tried to call them and got an out-of-order message."

"Yes, we did get something just a few minutes ago, but we don't have any details," Capt. Valderama replied. "They've been on lockdown for a few minutes and the phones have been shut down, too. All communications with them are closed. Not a good sign."

"When the phones get shut down to a unit like that, it usually means there's been casualties, sometimes non-hostile-fire type of casualties," Capt. Valderama said.

"Holy crap. Is it at Victory or Liberty?" I asked.

"We don't know yet."

"Shit, man. I was supposed to have my first appointment there today at 1700, but I called and inadvertently got through to some colonel. The colonel told me there had been an incident and that all appointments were canceled today. He told me to call again tomorrow."

Capt. Valderama shook his head. "Then maybe you should call them back tomorrow. Thanks for the heads-up. Captain Collins also suggested that maybe I should go visit the CSC in the coming week. Said he didn't want to lose anybody to stress. I'll let him know when I see him later."

"Well, OK then. I'm heading to the CHU," I said as I decided to cash in my chips for the day and go get some sleep before coming back to work.

I tried to sleep through whatever appointment I may have had at the Victory Combat Stress Clinic. Eventually I got up with enough time to grab a shower and try to get some dinner before my shift.

I greeted my buddy Vince as I came on shift at 1845, "Hey, Vince, what's up with the Combat Stress Clinic? I was supposed to see them this afternoon, but when I called, they were all on lockdown."

Vince's face was as grim as the night we learned of the Mosul SVBIED attack that killed five US soldiers. Vince spoke slowly.

"Matt. A sergeant by the name of Russell from an engineer battalion at Camp Stryker shot up the Combat Stress Clinic around 1330 or so today. That's why all their phones were down when you tried calling. It appears Russell killed five people at the clinic. He killed a doctor and some others just sitting in the waiting room."

"You've got to be shittin' me," I said. "Here at Camp Victory? I was supposed to *be* at that clinic *today*." I felt flush, wondering if I had literally dodged some bullets.

Vince corrected me. "No. No, Matt. At Camp Liberty. This all happened at Camp Liberty CSC, not Camp Victory."

I wandered back over to the CSC on Camp Victory the next day after getting a new appointment time. As a new security precaution, Victory Base posted armed guards at the entrance to the medical complex. Once I got past these guards, more guards confronted me on the short path leading to the CSC. Once I walked through the clinic doors of the CSC, I surrendered my M-9 pistol to the clerk. All of this was in response to the attack at Camp Liberty.

I told Vince about it when I arrived on shift that evening.

"You won't believe what I encountered over at the CSC today. They posted new armed guards outside the facility leading into the CSC. I've got no problem with the posting of more guards, only the type of guards. Victory Base posted third world–country contractor guards there! What the hell does that imply? I'm sure it was a matter of availability, but could it not be perceived as a mistrust of your own soldiers to guard each other? It was embarrassing if you ask me."

Vince shook his head and went back to work.

In the days that followed, we learned that Sgt. John Russell of the 54th Engineer Battalion at Camp Stryker got into a heated argument with the clinic personnel at the Camp Liberty CSC during his May 11, 2009, appointment. While being escorted back to Camp Stryker, Russell took an unsecured M-16A2 rifle and vehicle away from his escort and drove back to the clinic. He assaulted the clinic, where he killed a couple of health care workers and three other soldiers in the waiting area.

By Sunday, May 17, 2009, MNC-I had incurred nine more KIA in addition to the non-combat deaths of the five people at the Camp Liberty CSC. The month was barely half over and we had almost reached the same number of deaths incurred in all of April. This fact depressed most everyone in the presentations cell who worked on PowerPoints.

In addition to the May death count, we were down one person, Lt. Strobridges, who had injured herself during her martial arts class three days earlier. I had to speak out to Capt. Collins, and I did so with some authority as a Medical Service Corps officer.

"Seriously, sir. The TMC put her on two weeks' quarters for a sprained knee?" I said incredulously. "When I worked a TMC before, I would see the doc take an X-ray and give a sprained knee twenty-four-hours' quarters along with a crutch, a knee brace and a return-to-clinic appointment in forty-eight hours."

"At ease, Captain. You weren't there and you don't know the extent of it," Capt. Collins defended.

"I think she could hobble on back to work, sir. I'm sure we could find several people who would volunteer to carry her to work if that was needed. But if a doctor signed the order, it's a done deal. It's just we're down one more typist."

"Actually, I was going to talk with you about that, Jerome. I've been told to expect a purposeful slowdown of action in the cell beginning June 1 as we start leaving the Iraqi cities. We won't need as many people working our cell or the JOC, I've been informed. The Iraqi JOC should start doing a right seat, left seat in order to take over at some point. By then, Lieutenant Strobridges should be back at work full time, hopefully. This will give you a week to bring her back up to speed before you and Sergeant Manley report over to the interpreters cell in the rotunda area."

The interpreters cell. What is that? I thought.

"Are you saying I'm being reassigned on June 1, sir?" I asked, hiding my excitement.

"That's correct, Captain," he announced almost proudly. "You and Sergeant Manley are going to help the lone commander and his petty officer assistant unscrew the interpreter database mess. Your last day of work here in the JOC will be Friday, May 29. When you get off shift here on Saturday morning, May 30, you're released to the interpreters cell. They want you to report there on Monday, June 1 at 0800. You get Sunday off, essentially. Do ya think you can handle that?" Capt. Collins smiled proudly.

"Yes, sir, I will do the best I can," I replied with glee.

"Sergeant Manley will work there too. It's up to the commander over there to figure out how you two can help. And *no*, Captain Buckley is staying right here. Y'all will have to figure out your own sleeping times in the CHU if you're on the same shift. I hope this upcoming change of assignment helps with reducing the stress. Actually, we're all looking forward to this supposed slowdown as we leave Iraqi cities."

What slowdown? I kept saying to myself during the last two weeks of May. We endured eleven more US KIA during that time. We experienced almost one KIA per day, which meant at least one or two more PowerPoints each day.

I said to Vince, "I think the OPTEMPO[96] is just as high as April, if not higher judging by the number of casualties." I was beginning to think my reassignment to the interpreters cell would be called off, but it wasn't. Thank God!

---

96 OPTEMPO: Operations Tempo

CHAPTER 14

The Interpreters Cell - New Life

I met with Cmdr. Gerhard Schroeder, USN, of the interpreters cell during my last two weeks working in the JOC. Cmdr. Schroeder normally served as an instructor at the US Naval Academy. He also spoke a little bit of German. *Sehr gut!* Having spent three years in Germany myself, I looked forward to rekindling my own limited German language skills.

Cmdr. Schroeder explained his cell operation. "What we do here, Matt, is manage all the interpreters used in the entire Iraq AOR. We have several hundred on payroll at any given time. The J-2[97] funds all of these assets. Our job is to figure out the types and numbers of interpreters needed in the field each month. It's a little bit complicated. We do have a reporting system to help us, but we have to project how many we'll need two months ahead of time. That's the hard part."

"How can Sergeant Manley and I be a part of your team, sir?"

"Right now, it's just me and PO Third Class Sanchez. I suspect I'll have Sergeant Manley shadow Petty Officer Sanchez. You and I can work together with the civilian contractor to tweak the database. I've got two open workstations, as you can see," Cmdr. Schroeder said as he pointed to a pair of side-by-side computers, which looked exactly like the ones I used in the JOC presentations cell. "And each has NIPRNet and SIPRNet access. We also have a couple of landlines, too."

---

97   J-2: Directorate for Intelligence, J-2 (Joint Chiefs of Staff Intelligence Section)

"I think we can help," I told Cmdr. Schroeder. "I'm a former Signal Corps officer and information systems manager. I'm pretty competent with just about any database."

"Well, thanks for stopping in, Captain. I look forward to you helping me slay this dragon. See you on the first," said Cmdr. Schroeder. I returned to my JOC job with almost a renewed sense of purpose and hope for better days.

What a difference it made for my outlook on life to be working somewhere with a window to the outside. Working a shift of 0800 to 2000 hours with an extended lunch and dinner hour was also a blessing. Throw in the fact I could head to the balcony with another cigar smoker from the cell a couple of times per shift, it was heaven on earth compared to the JOC.

The interpreters cell consisted of two sections. Cmdr. Schroeder managed one section with Sgt. Manley, PO Sanchez and me. An Air Force major managed a separate section manned entirely by other Air Force personnel. That section was busy all the time.

The other interpreters cell section reviewed dozens of interpreter applications, appropriately vetting the applicant for suitability through an extensive records research. Applications to be an interpreter for US Forces in Iraq arrived from all over the world, especially from in-country Iraqi nationals. Interpreters made big money—if they could stay alive.

The various MNC-I forces required different interpreter translators based on the unit's AOR, their given current mission, and their projected missions. The cell tried to manage the hundreds of interpreters who spoke Arabic, Pashto, Urdu, Sorani (Kurdish), Turkish, or Farsi along with English.

"Good morning, Captain Jerome, Sergeant Manley," Cmdr. Schroeder greeted on our first day in the cell. "Before we do anything, I need to really explain the process; otherwise you'll be totally lost just like I was when I didn't have the benefit of a very good briefing. The outgoing section chief basically said to me, 'Hello, Gerhard. Welcome to Iraq. There's your desk. Here's the phone number for the J-2 interpreter contractor who can bring you up to speed on this quicker than I can. Sorry, gotta catch my Freedom Bird outta here.' Yup, that's all I got."

The commander continued. "So, here it goes. The other section there receives all interpreter applications for service in this theater. They are bombarded with applications from around the world, especially from the US—where a lot of Iraqi ex-pats live—and from a civilian company on contract to the J-2. The J-2 contractor beats the bushes locally to find and recruit qualified interpreters. They say they can find them, but it's recruiting locals that is difficult. No one wants to be seen as helping us.

"That section's mission is to review and thoroughly vet the applications for education, qualification, criminal background and you name it. They have access to Iraqi government resources and other records to do this. They flag those found unsuitable or unverifiable, and forward acceptable applications to our section. The accepted applications go into our pool for future contract.

"We experience a lot of interpreter turnover, plus the language authorizations fluctuate from month to month and from unit to unit. We are in an almost constant state of cross-leveling numbers and languages in and between units to stay within the funding authorizations provided by J-2. It is *not* easy to do. We have a full-time civilian contractor as the manager of our database management system. He tweaks the database every day for us.

"When a unit needs a terp,[98] we look to the approved pool candidates for someone to fill the slot. We then forward that approved candidate's name to the J-2 contractor to put them on the payroll. That's the process."

I responded favorably to the commander. "Thank you, sir. We

---

98   Terp: Slang term for interpreter

are both familiar with using the NIPRNet and SIPRNet systems. Sergeant Manley can shadow the petty officer for a while, but I think you'll be able to count on us."

"I guess I should tell you one more thing about the future of this cell," Cmdr. Schroeder added. "With the removal of US Forces from the cities and the beginnings of downsizing all forces, the need for embedded interpreters will drop significantly, sooner rather than later. J-2 has already warned me of funding reductions. This will affect the number of people who work here, too."

"You already know my situation, as a retiree recall, so I'm readily expendable and not averse to being downsized right back home. I'll do what I can while you have me," I responded.

Cmdr. Schroeder nodded. "Sure, Matt. I'm mentally preparing for the bottom to drop out of interpreter support. If you wouldn't mind checking in with our civilian database contractor to get a feel for the lay of the land, I think that's where you can help right away."

"Absolutely," I replied with gusto. Sgt. Manley had already logged in to his workstation to begin some OJT[99] with the petty officer while I headed over to the database contractor's office.

I walked into the database manager's office and introduced myself. "Hi. I'm Captain Matt Jerome and I just started helping Commander Schroeder with interpreter management down in his cell."

"Hey, Captain. He told me to expect you. I'm Bryan," the civilian contractor said as he extended his hand.

Being a retired manager of information systems, I could relate to Bryan's workload. Being a couple of *BitBrains*, we spent the requisite amount of time relating our respective histories of knowledge, education and work experience in the binary and digital workspace. I learned he was making some serious money doing database management in Iraq under government contract.

"So, what program are you using to manage the interpreters?" I asked.

---

99   OJT: On-the-Job Training

"What else but Microsoft Access 2007. It gives me the most flexibility for this size database, and I can easily import, export, or convert to other formats for non-database users." Bryan beamed. "Come see." He motioned over to his workstation with dual monitor setup.

"Bryan," I replied with equal pride, "I used to teach Microsoft Access at a local vo-tech college in Georgia. I've developed several databases over the years going back to using dBase II and III in the late eighties and then Access in the nineties. I've dabbled in SQL,[100] but I like Access. I used my Commodore 64 way back in the early eighties to create programs in BASIC. I wrote my first database using the Commodore 64, a cassette deck and a program called Cassette Based Information Management System.

Bryan looked at me quizzically. "Sorry. What's a Commodore 64?"

"Oh my God. I am old," I answered. "Never mind. You're better off Googling it or maybe there's a Wikipedia entry to review. Perhaps I can take a look at the back end of your database?" I suggested to get off the old-guy topics.

He gave me a five-dollar tour of the database structure and objects—tables, queries, forms, reports, menus and macros—over the course of the next couple of hours. I praised his work.

"Bryan. This is very good. You've done a great job with it. It's clean!"

"I can't take full credit for this," Bryan replied. "Someone else created it years ago. I merely converted it to Access 2007, and I tweak things as needed for the terp cell when they ask. I have done *a lot* of tweaks over the last year. In some ways it's almost a new database just from the tweaks.

"As you know, the power in a database is being able to search and filter through the data tables to produce requested output as information," Bryan said as we reviewed his long list of custom

---

100   SQL: Structured Query Language, a standard database language

queries designed to search, filter and display. "I've placed the most-used queries on the database front-end menus so the commander can launch them quickly.

"The problem we've got, Matt, is data entry and data editing of records. There's a ton of it," Bryan said, exasperated. "Fortunately for me, that all occurs in your section and not with me. I just try to make that process as user friendly as possible."

"User friendly is good. Simple is good, too," I said. "Can you summarize the data-entry process? The menus and forms look easy enough, so why is it a chokepoint?"

Bryan explained the difficulty. "It's because there's so much fluidity in the terps' assignments and duty status. We have a few interpreters who are rock solid with their unit. Their units of assignment try to protect them from any RIFs[101] or efforts to cross-level them *out* of their unit. But that is the exception. Generally, there is significant turnover in the interpreter workforce across Iraq. It's not like they give a two-week notice before they exit stage right. When a terp figures he's made enough money, he may leave.

"I think the biggest impact results from the forecasting and funding of the interpreters from the Pentagon," Bryan admitted. "It's the old line about the bean counters justifying the cost versus having the flexibility in the field. There's gotta be a verifiable audit trail for the money."

I gave that some thought before answering. "I can see where the potential for fraud, waste and abuse exists and could be easy to hide, too."

"Exactly," Bryan emphasized. "That's where this database comes in. I do archival data dumps routinely to keep the historical paper trail up to date. I pay special attention to this before we start making significant changes when the commander gets his authorizations document."

"How does that work with the authorizations? I presume it's from J-2?" I wondered aloud.

---

101   RIF: Reduction in Force

Bryan swiveled in his chair to face me and used a notepad to scribble. "It goes like this," he said as he started to diagram a timeline chart on the pad. "Gerhard sends the field units a document requesting their interpreter needs two months in advance. He'll be sending that out very soon this week for August interpreter requirements. The units have the month of June to decide what interpreter support they *think* they'll require starting in August. The units have got to figure out their anticipated interpreter mission requirements that far in advance."

"Boy, you talk about having to SWAG[102] your needs." I grimaced.

"You got that right. It's a total SWAG, but it's an educated one," Bryan added. "Perhaps that would be a SWEG?"[103]

We both laughed at his newly created acronym.

Bryan continued drawing his timeline. "Anyway, about this same time of the month, Gerhard receives from the J-2 the final interpreter funding authorizations for the month of July. That gives him the month of June to adjust the interpreter assignments across the entire Iraq AOR. Some units may have to gain terps, some units may lose terps, some units have the wrong language terps. Gerhard then works with the field units to move terp authorizations around to try and give everybody what they say they require within the scope of what J-2 has authorized for the upcoming months. Patience and flexibility are the coin of the realm as Gerhard untangles the mess, and he's gotten pretty good at doing the cross-level shuffle with units. It often comes down to some simple horse-trading. 'I can give you two Urdu interpreter authorizations if you can give up your two Pashto authorizations.' I have to hand it to Gerhard; he's very accommodating in trying to serve the unit needs. You'll see."

Bryan wasn't done. "All the while this is happening, unit missions evolve or change, terps may leave or become no-shows at any time, and some languages are harder to fill than others as the month drags on. Gerhard is constantly working with the interpreter contractor via

---

102   SWAG: Scientific (or Silly) Wild-Ass Guess
103   Silly Wild Educated Guess

the paper-trail forms to hire, fire, cross-level and keep track of their locations as needed. All of the cross-leveling, gains and losses has to be documented in the database. That's where it all gets tracked and managed."

"Like you said earlier, data entry and editing," I said. "As long as the data forms help prevent erroneous entries and offer intuitive pull-downs for some of the fields, that will minimize the workload."

"They do," Bryan said with pride. "And it's my job to make that happen. I've also devised two macros to automate some of the tasks based on the monthly authorizations document. Those two macros save two days of data entry! After I run the macros, I let Gerhard know so he can start working with the units to cross-level as needed."

Bryan's briefing on the database covered everything I'd needed to know, so I headed back to the interpreters cell.

It was lunchtime as I walked to the back of the office past the Air Force section to where our workstations were located behind a short row of five-foot-high, soundproof cubicle partitions. I walked through the opening in the partitions to find everyone gone to lunch, except Sgt. Manley, who was busy at his workstation.

"Have you got phone watch while everyone's at lunch or something?" I asked.

Sgt. Manley appeared startled as I spoke, and I saw his workstation desktop change images as he turned toward me to answer, "Oh, it's you, sir. Yes. Phone watch. Are you heading off to DFAC, too?"

"Maybe in a little while. Why don't you go and I'll head over when someone else comes back," I suggested. "By the way, whadda they got you workin' on already? It looked like you were knee-deep into something. You on the SIPRNet?"

Sgt. Manley responded a bit sheepishly. "Oh, nothing of any real importance, sir. Just trying to familiarize myself with the interpreters cell folders. Sure, sir, I'll head over to DFAC."

He logged off his workstation and pulled his CAC from the keyboard before he headed out of the cell, leaving me alone at my workstation.

I couldn't help but wonder what the sergeant had been doing. He seemed engrossed and a little too startled when I came back. He was reading something, and quickly exited and changed to the desktop when I saw him. I wandered over to his workstation to check it out.

I inserted my own CAC and logged in, which presented me with my own roaming profile of folder access, permissions and restrictions. I needed to get to Manley's profile to look at his history.

My spidey sense was tingling like it had back in the JOC with him. I didn't like that he had done some random walking through the classified SIPRNet in a previous assignment. His reasoning seemed a little dodgy. Maybe it was all aboveboard, but here in the interpreters cell, he would have no real need for that kind of research.

How can I get to Manley's workstation profile? If I really wanted to find out, I'd have to go to the IT desk or the counter-intelligence section with something more concrete than Spider-man sense.

There was just no way I could see his profile unless he was using a shared profile with the petty officer, like the captains did back in the presentations cell. *That's worth looking into when Sanchez returns from lunch,* I told myself.

I was about to log off and go to my own workstation when I saw a small USB flash drive was inserted in the front of Sgt. Manley's workstation. The CPU[104] mid-tower case of the workstation resided on the desktop, but was pushed up against the back and inside of the bookcase atop the desk. A folder was leaning against the front of the mid-tower case, which obstructed its view, but you could still see the flash drive inserted in a USB port at the top of the tower. The flash drive was small and black, just like the workstation case. The sergeant had either forgotten to pull it when he logged off, or had been concerned that I would see him do it.

---

104   CPU: Central Processing Unit

One of the first big warnings I received from the IT desk when I started in the JOC was that USB flash drives, floppy disks and CDs were strictly prohibited on these machines. They informed me that a virus had infected the entire palace system a while back via one of these, and had crashed the system. Hence, no more use of these. The policy also prevented the loss of classified material via downloading.

I opened the File Explorer to review the workstation's resources. The USB flash drive displayed in File Explorer as Lexar (F:). I clicked on the Properties tab for the flash drive. Manley had inserted a 2GB[105] Lexar flash drive into his workstation and formatted it based on the date I found in the root folder of the drive. There were no files on the drive.

Did I interrupt the young sergeant when I arrived back to the office earlier? Note to self; ask Manley about the USB drive.

The second day on the job in the interpreters cell offered even more surprises for me and Sgt. Manley.

"Good morning," I greeted the commander as I walked into the cubicle office on Tuesday morning. "What's hot for today?"

"Never a dull moment, Captain. Never a dull moment," the commander replied with some exasperation as he gathered up his briefing bag. "We got the July authorizations overnight from J-2. I've got a meeting with the contractor to review them, but when I return, the four of us will need to sit down and talk about what's coming down the pike. Sanchez can fill you in on that. Be back in a while," he said as he left the office.

"Good morning, Petty Officer and Sergeant. Did the commander leave anything for us to do while he's at his meeting?"

"No, sir," replied PO Sanchez, "but I can give you a heads-up that there've been some pretty significant cuts. That's all the commander said when I got here about forty-five minutes ago. He didn't appear

105   GB: Gigabyte

to be very happy. There's something else I can tell you about which came in an email from the planning cell."

"Really, what does plans have to say?" I asked.

"The commander wants us to research and draft a response to their email regarding a proposed change to the interpreter uniform," the petty officer said. "As it stands right now, while embedded, interpreters may wear ACUs[106] that have been stripped of all US insignia. They can wear rank and their nametag, that's it. The proposed change is to not allow them to wear any uniform. The Iraqi government wants to disassociate the interpreters from US Forces by doing this."

"You mean put an even bigger target on their backs, doncha?" I replied.

"Yes, sir, that's what it amounts to in my opinion," PO Sanchez offered.

"OK. So, we should start pulling some stats to support the commander. He'll want to know how many interpreters actually get embedded with units going outside the wire. Any terp inside the wire doing translation won't need to be in uniform. Us leaving Iraqi cities by the end of June will also reduce the number of units actively going outside the wire. So, let's see if we can break down the number of terps at static headquarters versus those assigned directly to field units; that would be a start. Let's work on that until the commander gets back, and we can refine it based on his desire."

"Cool, sir. I can do that," PO Sanchez said.

"I'll give him a hand, sir," Sgt. Manley offered.

A couple of hours into our statistics chase, Cmdr. Schroeder returned from his contractor meeting. He sounded a bit glum when he sat at his desk.

"We need to talk. Sanchez, can you go see if the small conference room is available for us to use right now?"

"Yes, sir," the petty officer responded and got up from his desk.

---

106   ACU: Army Combat Uniform

"Why don't you come with me, Sgt. Manley, so I can show you how to schedule the room in the future?"

"Sure. Let's go," Sgt. Manley replied, following PO Sanchez.

Cmdr. Schroeder turned his chair away from his desk to face mine to talk.

"Captain Jerome. Just when you think you've got things figured out, you get changes. I got the J-2 authorizations document this morning. They cut our authorizations in half. I'll give everyone the full details when we get to the conference room."

PO Sanchez and Sgt. Manley appeared at the door to the office and gave us a big thumbs-up on the room. The commander and I picked up our notebooks and headed there. We got comfortable around the conference room table as the commander sat and opened his notebook.

Looking down at his notes, he said, "Guys, the J-2 cut all of our authorizations in half, effective July 1, 2009. I kind of expected a reduction, but not that much." He shook his head in wonderment, raised his head to look us in the eye and then continued. "The other thing is this also affects our cell authorization for manpower. I have to reduce the cell back to me and Sanchez. I have no choice but to release you and Manley back to the C-1, Captain Jerome. Here's the DSN number[107] for Major Weston, the assistant C-1. He wants you to call and come see him this afternoon to talk about your future assignment."

"On July 1, correct, sir?" I asked with no emotion.

"That is correct," said the commander.

"At least we've got a month to reconcile the authorizations," I said. "You know, sir, I'm not surprised. I'm kind of getting used to changing jobs on a moment's notice. Remind me to tell you sometime of my first forty-eight hours in Iraq."

"Sergeant Manley, I've already had a conversation with the assistant C-1 about your future," the commander continued. "You'll

---

107   DSN: Defense Switched Network telephone or data communications number

be relieved of your temporary attachment to 1st Corps headquarters and returned to your normal unit of assignment at FOB Hammer next month.

"The two big things we need to work on *erste und schnell*[108] are the reconciliation of interpreter authorizations for July and a response to the interpreter uniform proposal."

"Sir, we've been working on the uniform issue while you were meeting with the contractor this morning. We've been gathering some interpreter statistics to support the response," I replied.

The commander appeared pleased. "Thank you, I was going to suggest that before I left this morning, but forgot. There's nothing this headquarters likes better than facts and evidence to support a course of action. I guess we should head back. Here's my plan of action for this week: the NCOs will work on gathering the statistics, I will work on the reconciliation with units directly, and I'd like you, Captain Jerome, to start drafting a response to that idiotic idea about uniforms. I guess you might know how I feel about it. You can float the statistics and other data into the response as the data is developed, OK?"

"Yes, sir. That sounds like a good plan to me," I replied as I watched the NCOs nod in agreement.

"Sanchez, if you and Manley have any trouble with statistics, Bryan might be able to pull some of those from the database. You might also need to contact units to ask them. I'll give you a more detailed list of what I think we'll need later," the commander said.

"Sure, sir," Sgt. Sanchez replied.

"OK. Let's get to it, then. We're burnin' daylight," said the commander as we picked up and headed back to the cell. We had a lot of work ahead of us.

While we walked back to the office, I talked about emails with the commander. "Sir, I've noticed I'm getting a ton of email. When I worked in the presentations cell, I was one of five people with access to

---

108   erste und schnell: German for "first and fast"

the battle captain email account. We received quite a few emails there, too, but not as many as I seem to get here. Is this normal?" I asked.

"Ah, they must have found you," Cmdr. Schroeder quipped. "Before you got assigned to it, the position as C-3 liaison officer went unfilled long before XVIII Airborne Corps turned over the MNCI rein to 1st Corps. That was almost nine months ago according to my predecessor. XVIII Airborne gave your duty position a much lower priority to fill than other positions in the palace. That's why you also have to pop in now and then on the in-house interpreters to make sure they're doing their job. By the way, a lieutenant colonel used to perform the job of babysitting the palace interpreters as her only duty. I heard it was boring as hell."

The commander continued. "On my daily manning report, I show that you and Manley have joined our little workshop here, and so you are now officially in the email loop. Some emails will merely inform you, but others may require your input or feedback for estimates and plans. You'll learn how to sort through all the ash-and-trash and find the important ones to read. It'll take a little time, but you'll get the hang of it."

"God, I hope so. This is a bit of a deluge. Definitely information overload," I remarked while shaking my head. "Besides the emails from our supported field units, I'm getting CC[109] emails from almost every staff section in the palace—plans, logistics, fusion cell, security, intelligence, aviation, reconciliation cell, you name it. I've read these emails and sometimes fail to see why we were included on their distro[110] list. This is in addition to the frequent emails from Victory Base Complex, the MWR Center, and Freedom Village mayor's office. I could spend all day doing nothing but reading email."

A knowing and sympathetic smile formed on Cmdr. Schroeder before he said soothingly, "Matt, here's the deal. We serve at a three-

---

109   CC: Carbon Copy (an email feature to provide a copy to an additional recipient)
110   Distro: Slang term for distribution list

star flagpole. Careers can be made or derailed here very quickly. Some of these emails create the twenty-first-century *digital foxhole* that staff officers jump into to protect themselves. Back in the '80s and '90s before the widespread use of email, my Army friends told me how they built themselves paper foxholes with typewriter correspondence. They would provide a copy-furnished list at the bottom of the memo or letter, and then send a copy to everyone on that list. That way they could say, *Hey, you got a copy, you were aware!* Now, with the ability to create group email lists, we can literally send memos to hundreds of CC addressees from the DoD Global Address List with the touch of a button or two."

The light bulb in my head turned on and I smiled. "We did the same thing in the '70s and '80s with a CF[111] list at the bottom of our memos. We used to say *copy to One over the World,* which basically meant send to everyone we could think of. Back then we used typewriters and *copysette* manifold[112] paper for copies before the widespread use of copy machines. Copysette paper was easier to use than regular carbon paper and less messy. Ah, those were the good old days."

When we got back to the office, I called Maj. Weston's office and made an appointment to visit him that afternoon. I kept wondering, *Where am I going next month?*

I walked over to the C-1 office at the Juicer on the northwest side of the lake around 1500. It was nearly a good twenty-minute stretch of the legs from the interpreters cell. I entered the Juicer looking for the assistant C-1, Maj. Weston, and found a duty NCO sitting at a reception desk in the building foyer.

"Good afternoon, Sergeant. I'm here to see Major Weston. He's expecting me," I said.

---

111   CF: Copy Furnished
112   Copysette manifold: A two-part, lightweight paper that resembled onion-skin with an attached piece of carbon paper. After typing, the attached carbon part of the copysette pages could be pulled out all at once.

"Yes, sir. The major gave me a heads-up to look out for you. If you'll follow me, please," the sergeant said pleasantly as he got out from behind the desk and led me through another set of doors.

The ten-foot-high doors opened into a large area with countless partitions creating individual workspaces for about two dozen people. Walking past the cubicles revealed many to be occupied by a diverse group of company-grade and field-grade officers at workstations. Some cubicles were unmanned, save for the accoutrements of pictures and keepsakes from home on the desktop or pinned to the walls of the partitions. The sergeant led me through the maze of cubicles to the back part of the room and a triple-size cubicle.

He introduced me. "Sir, this is Captain Jerome," and he turned and headed back to his own desk.

Maj. Weston got up from his chair, extending his hand. "Hi, Captain Jerome. It's good to finally meet you. Please, take a seat. I'm Jake Weston. Would you like some coffee or tea?"

"No thank you, sir. I'm fine. Got filled up at the DFAC at lunch."

"I've wanted to talk with you since you got here, but it's been busy. I'm pretty much responsible for you being assigned to 1st Corps as an augmentee, since I submitted all the WIAS augmentee requests back in 2008."

I answered with some trepidation. "Yes, sir. My slot was supposed to be in the G-3 as an electronic warfare officer."

"Well, that's one reason I wanted to talk with you. We developed that list of augmentee requests in early 2008. Back then the G-3 believed he would need that EWO position filled to augment the other people in that section. He maintained that belief until we got here in early March and started the right-seat, left-seat transition and received the decision for US Forces to leave Iraqi cities by the end of June. By then you were already training and in the replacement pipeline with an order for up to 365 days of active duty. The G-3 figured he would just cross-level you somewhere needed when you got here."

"Oh. That's where the KLE assignment came in."

"Yes," Maj. Weston replied. "Lieutenant Colonel Willis wanted you and Major Corso for his operation. We thought that would work, but then the CHOPS in the JOC said he needed bodies to fill seats. The C-1 argued against it, but the chief of staff decided the JOC had priority; hence that's why three of you went there. We needed another LNO for the MNC-I cell in the Green Zone, and that's why Corso got that." He paused for a response.

"Well, I appreciate your explanation, sir. But now I'm in the interpreters cell and Commander Schroeder tells me his staff authorization will be cut in half on July 1. In less than three months I will have had five assignments—EWO, KLE, JOC, interpreters cell and whatever is next."

Maj. Weston nodded. "Yes. Commander Schroeder told me about his authorization cuts. And that's the other reason I wanted to talk with you—to see what we can do at this point, if anything, to keep you here . . . if you want to stay."

The last part of his statement piqued my interest.

"Look, Matt. I know you've been kind of dicked around by us, but the mission focus changes and we all have to be flexible. It's just not a good practice to do that to augmentees. In my opinion we should expect our own folks to be flexible, not retirees or other augmentees we've asked to help us and who have been recalled for a particular assignment. I'm really sorry for that."

"Well, sir, in your defense, this is now a Joint Services Command. You *do* have embedded officers from other military branches involved who might make decisions impacting your plan, but serve their own service's agenda."

The major raised his eyebrows. "You've touched on a lingering suspicion I've had."

"Along that same line of thinking, sir, when we arrived in Iraq and attended the briefing at Hope Chapel, everyone got a CHU assignment, except the four augmentees on the flight. They didn't have us on their lodging list. We told them we were on the flight manifest, and just couldn't understand how we could be left off."

"Yeah, I heard about that, Matt. If it's any consolation, I personally chewed out the battalion S-1 over at STB.[113] What happened is they got the aircraft manifest when that chalk took off from McChord.[114] They used that manifest to request CHUs for everyone. The four of you were added to the chalk manifest when it arrived at Camp Buehring before the flight into BIAP. The STB S-1 didn't get the updated manifest. Our LNO at Buehring didn't inform STB here at Victory of your arrival. He just put you in touch with the incoming chalk flight so you could be added."

"Well, I can't tell you how much I appreciate you telling me all of this, sir. It does explain a lot and helps to restore my faith a little bit. I was also beginning to feel like a utility player on a baseball team who could be sent in to fill any position on the field."

"You're right, Matt. To be clear, we had to project our personnel needs over a year in advance of getting here. Then, late in December '08 President Bush signed the SOFA[115] with Iraq, which established that US Forces would withdraw from Iraqi cities by June 30, 2009. Our mission planning and projected personnel needs could not predict the outcome of the SOFA negotiations or the impact of a June 30 deadline. Then President Obama was elected, and he visited here in April specifically to make the point that we were leaving and downsizing. We are responding to that inevitability. That's it in a nutshell. We gotta be Semper Gumby."

"When you explain it like that, sir, it really all does fall into place on what's transpired," I acknowledged. "Earlier you said, *if you want to stay.* Is that an option for me to be downsized back home?"

"If you want to, yes," he acknowledged. "We understand that augmentees plan for being on active duty for up to a year. I've got

---

113   STB: Special Troops Battalion
114   McChord: McChord Air Force Base
115   SOFA: Status of Forces Agreement

some other augmentees who purchased expensive items because they were relying on their tax-free deployment income."

"That's not the case with me. I was fully retired when the Army called me over a year ago and asked me if I could help you. I'd been out of the military for thirteen years too, but HRC said you needed me, so I said OK. I'd been stationed at Fort Lewis back in the '70s and I thought I might get a PCS[116] there to deploy.

"I really expected to work the EWO assignment. In fact, I almost took a three-week EWO class at Huachuca at my own expense to get some fresh knowledge. Huachuca is only about ninety minutes from my house in Arizona. Right now, I'm glad I didn't take that class. Anyway, there's no money issue for me to stay deployed a year."

"I read your CV so I know you're dual-branch qualified," the major said. "I could double-check with the Corps surgeon's office to see if we could squeeze you in over there. Then there's the Signal Battalion, which is running all the commo around this place. The G-3 is thinking we'll need an LNO crew to work the Iraqi JOC once they get that up and running. The Iraqi JOC will *not* be the same as our JOC. You'll probably sit around all shift drinking tea, to tell you the truth. The C-1's intention is to try and retain people if possible."

"As much as I like tea, I think I've had my fill of JOC duty. I'd love to work Signal again, but I think I'd be more in the way. I'm sure I'm not up to speed with their current technology or TTPs.[117] I may have a mind like a steel trap, but the hinges are very rusty. It would be OJT for six months. The same is probably true for the surgeon's office as far as TTPs. No, sir, I think I'd like to head home if you can make that happen."

The major was conciliatory. "I understand. It's the C-1's decision on whether to release you, but if anything, augmentees, especially retiree recalls, should be given that option as the mission in Iraq starts winding down. We may be able to justify redeployment in July

116   PCS: Permanent Change of Station (relocation)
117   TTPs: Tactics, Techniques and Procedures

to coincide with the commander's authorization cut. I'll get back to you."

The major stood and extended his hand.

"Thank you, sir, for the opportunity to serve here in Iraq with 1st Corps. I'll be waiting on your call."

I walked back to the interpreters cell with my spirit lifted. *Shit. I might be going home next month. I better wait until it's confirmed before I tell Sara. No need to have her hopes dashed by a change.*

CHAPTER 15

The Interpreters Cell - Exiting

June 3 – 7, 2009

Over the course of the next three days, the cell team worked hard toward developing a cogent response to the interpreter uniform issue. The NCOs developed lots of statistics, while I drafted the memo. We had until COB[118] June 7 to submit our response. Meanwhile, Cmdr. Schroeder wore out his keyboard and telephone while reconciling the July authorizations directly with the units. He kept us informed along the way.

"Here it is Friday, June 5· and I've got about eighty percent of the authorizations reconciled between this month and next month—a new record. Bryan's tweaks on the database helped a lot, but then again, I've got half as many slots to fill, too. It's just too easy to call a unit and tell them they no longer get five interpreters, only two or three. It'll be up to them to manage at that point."

The commander had given me a secondary mission of writing an SOP[119] for future interpreters cell teammates when he said, "Captain Jerome, you know what we need in this cell? A *how-to* book on what we do."

"Do you mean an SOP?"

---

118   COB: Close of Business
119   SOP: Standard Operating Procedure

"Call it what you will—SOP, how-to manual . . . whatever. I think we need to document the interpreter management process with an emphasis on how to use the database to its full capability. Could be a step-by-step process or manual, I suppose. It's not a first priority, but if you can work on it this month, I think it will benefit whoever replaces us. It's the best thing we can do to help them."

"Roger that, sir," I replied.

During the drafting of the interpreter uniform response, I found time to create an outline for the SOP mission. Whenever I started to get burned out on the uniform response, I'd work on the SOP. It kept me going.

On Friday afternoon, June 5, I received an email from Maj. Weston. *Redeployment to CONUS approved effective 7/1/09. Attached you'll find your installation clearing documents, release authorization memo and redeployment instructions. It's up to you to get scheduled for transport to Ali Al Salem via BIAP. Instructions for scheduling on the rotator aircraft (Freedom Bird) can be downloaded from their website (refer to redeployment instructions). Commander Schroeder can release you at his discretion to work on your clearance papers. Typically, you need two or three days.*

During my daily Skype video call to home that night, Sara asked me, "What's going on with you? You look a little happier today than normal."

"That's because I have some very good news," I announced. "I've been granted authority to come home in July. Downsizing here begins with me."

Sara could not contain her excitement and started crying. "Oh, that's wonderful, darling. Do you have a firm date?"

"July 1," I said. "But that date is to leave here. I go from here to Kuwait to Fort Benning. I don't know how long I'll be in Kuwait waiting for the CONUS rotator aircraft, and I don't know how long it takes to out-process at Fort Benning. There's a weekly Freedom Bird from Kuwait on the weekends, so I could be flying to Atlanta on

Saturday, the fourth of July if I can get out of Baghdad and scheduled on the rotator manifest. If out-processing at Benning takes a week, I could be released to fly home on July 10 or 11."

"OK," she said with excitement. "This could be interesting timing. Christine and I just made reservations to fly to South Carolina on July 9 to see Lea graduate from Basic Training on Saturday the eleventh. There's also an event on Friday the tenth at 5 p.m., where they get to see their families, too. Maybe you can join us there."

"It's a possibility. That would be outstanding if the timing comes together," I said. "I will work towards the goal of meeting you and Christine in South Carolina on Friday, July 10. I might be able to schedule my flight home for Sunday the twelfth from Columbia instead of Atlanta. I can probably get a rental car to drive from Benning and drop it at the Columbia airport."

With writing an SOP and drafting the response to whether interpreters should be allowed to wear uniforms, I found it difficult to question Sgt. Manley about his formatted USB flash drive. I resolved to find time that first weekend. That opportunity presented itself when the commander took the petty officer to lunch and left us to hold down the shop and answer the phones.

I had let it slip by too long. "Sergeant Manley," I said as we sat at our workstations. "I've been meaning to ask you about something from this past Monday."

"Sure, sir. Whaddaya got for me?" he replied.

"When I returned from my meeting with Bryan that morning, you were here alone to answer phones while everyone else was at lunch. You said you were getting familiar with things around here before you headed off to lunch. What concerned me was this." I held up the USB flash drive I'd removed from his workstation.

"Oh. You found it, sir. Thank you. I've been looking all over for it. I thought I'd lost it. Where did you find it?" Manley asked innocently.

"I found it plugged into your workstation."

"Duh. That's right. I had just finished formatting it. Thank you, sir," Manley said.

"You do know that we are not supposed to use USB flash drives or CDs in these workstations, correct?"

"I was just formatting it, sir," the sergeant replied with a hint of irritation.

I said with the same irritation, "It doesn't matter. We *do not* plug anything into these machines. *Period.* There are plenty of personal laptops available to format flash drives without using a workstation that is connected to the SIPRNet. You signed the same warning notice I did about using these machines. Why didn't you just use your own laptop to format it?"

Sgt. Manley seemed to be searching for words as he didn't reply right away. He finally answered. "I found it in my pocket, sir. I knew that it needed reformatting because my laptop wouldn't read it anymore. I got errors. I guess I wasn't thinking when I pulled it out and figured I'd just try and reformat it here."

"Here's the caution; workstation, USB flash drive, SIPRNet. As Kermit the Frog might sing on Sesame Street, *one of these things just doesn't belong,*" I said.

"You're right, sir. I'll do better."

Was it an innocent mistake or covering up by Sgt. Manley? It was hard to tell.

The last three weeks of June seemed to drag on forever. I did accomplish my objectives: 1) I worked with Bryan on the database queries and import macros for the new interpreter authorizations; 2) I wrote the interpreters cell how-to manual for the commander; 3) I drafted the commander's response for the interpreter uniform question; and 4) I got standby manifested for the Freedom Flight out of Kuwait on or about July 3. I could leave Iraq with a clear conscience.

I completed one other important, albeit non-military, mission in June. I put some weight back on. I had deployed from CRC weighing 195 pounds, and that was before the big meal send-off by the CRC DFAC. While working the JOC presentations cell, my weight got down to 180. I had lost fifteen pounds in those two months. Once I started working the interpreters cell, I started eating better and gained three pounds back. I was at 183 pounds, which was my weight when I retired from the Army in 1996. I hoped I could keep it there.

Sgt. Manley seemed to become fast friends with PO Sanchez. They were almost inseparable after meeting. They went to lunch together, got coffee at the Green Beans Coffee hut, and were working on a plan to meet up for a future R&R trip to Qatar.

The commander for his part was tireless in protecting the interpreters, as well as their units. He reconciled the new authorizations document by June 15 with all the units and the contractor. He reviewed the cell how-to manual I'd drafted and liked it so much he decided to include it as part of an interpreter conference he was co-hosting in July along with the contractor. He attended all the CG briefs in person or via teleconference link. Sometimes he seemed to get a little too far in the weeds on some issues, but you couldn't say he wasn't thorough.

June 26, 2009, would be my last shift in the interpreters cell, and I would be allowed to start clearing from Camp Victory. The Air Force penciled me in for a C-17 flight manifest from BIAP to Ali Al Salem scheduled for Wednesday, July 1, at 2100 hours. I would need to show them my letter of release from CENTCOM AOR memo to get on this Freedom Bird to Kuwait.

Clearing a military post requires you to visit various places around the post and get their signature or stamp on your clearing papers. Part of the reason for this is to make sure you're not scootin' out of town without taking care of business, with lingering debts, or failing to turn in supplies or equipment belonging to the post. These check-off locations usually include the Post Exchange, the library, morale/welfare/recreation facilities, lodging, supply rooms, security office, commercial activities and any other location or briefing the post wants to make sure you complete.

In the case of clearing Camp Victory, I needed to attend a class by the medics and a briefing by the chaplain's office. It's not like you can just walk in, give someone your clearing papers and get the class. You must schedule yourself to attend. You get the signature and the stamp after it's over. I found out in my research that the chaplain's briefing and the medic classes were given frequently. I made a note of when to sign up and attend.

I would also need to complete a post-deployment health assessment (PDHA) through the medics to get their stamp and signature. The PDHA identifies any immediate physical and behavioral concerns from your deployment. It also incorporates traumatic brain injury (TBI) questions to improve sensitivity, as well as animal bite questions to address the risk of rabies exposure, and features women's health symptoms questions.

Most of the other clearance locations only needed me to show up with my papers. Someone there would check their list to make sure I didn't owe them anything. In the case of supplies, I found I could turn in my protective mask inserts and chemical protective clothing on Camp Victory without having to lug them all the way back to the CIF[120] at Fort Benning. Uniforms and equipment not scheduled for turn-in back at CIF I mailed home to momma. I still had two duffle bags to carry, but these were not the same weight as when I had brought them here.

I decided during the month that my only recourse with Sgt. Barry Manley was to say something to the C-2 counter-intelligence folks in the palace during my camp-clearing process. I was going to be there anyway to get their stamp on my clearing papers.

---

120   CIF: Consolidated Issue Facility for uniforms, equipment, etc.

I visited the security office since I would need to turn in my palace ID. Before I did, I asked the civilian contractor if I could speak to the counter-intelligence people.

The civilian holding my clearance papers looked up from the form at me like he'd never heard the question before. "I'll have to think about that for a second," he said. After a few moments, he picked up the phone and dialed a number.

"Hey. This is Sparkman down at the front desk. I've got a captain here who wants to talk with someone in counter-intel. What would you like me to do?" he said.

After a few moments of listening, he said, "There's a warrant officer coming down to talk with you. We can finish clearing you when you're done with him."

"Thanks," I said and moved away from the desk.

It didn't take long before a chief warrant officer appeared. "Hello, sir, I'm Gary Smallwood. How can I help you?"

"Is there somewhere a little more private we can talk?"

"Sure, sir. Sorry. Come with me," the chief said, and we headed off down the hall to a secluded cubicle with a table, a couple of chairs and a telephone. "Let's have a seat and talk. What's on your mind, sir?"

"I worked the JOC presentations cell for a couple of months and then worked over at the interpreters cell this month. There's a sergeant there in the interpreters cell who also worked the presentations cell. We both got reassigned to the interpreters cell the same day. It's the sergeant I'm a little concerned about. I had a few dealings with him in the JOC. His name is Barry Manley and he's got a TS/SCI clearance."

CWO Smallwood nodded. I told him about Manley's claims of atrocities being committed, finding the flash-drive in his computer, and giving a verbal counseling.

"Sir, when you worked in the JOC, did you mention any of this to his supervisor there?" the chief asked.

"I regret to say that I did not. We got pretty wrapped around the axle on doing presentations and it fell off my radar screen to say anything," I replied. "Chief, I was recalled out of retirement to be here. The last time I was on active duty, the digital wonders of SIPRNet did not exist. We had people sign in to our war room. We signed in and kept a log when we opened our classified document safe. We checked people's security clearance and their need to know before they gained access to secret documents. We kept a log of those documents and the people who signed them out. The materials rarely left the war room. In other words, access to our classified materials was strictly controlled to a small group. The SIPRNet on the other hand seems to grant access to anyone with a clearance, a workstation and a logon."

The chief smiled. "When you put it like that, I suppose you're right. What we have with the digital system is a way to quickly grant access while also keeping track of who, what, when, where and how a document was accessed. The system also tracks viewing, downloads and printing. So, it's really impossible to make a covert copy without a trail. The system has to rely on security managers at all levels to perform due diligence for access to workstations, like checking for appropriate clearance and the need to know."

"Look, Chief, this is your bailiwick. I'm clearing camp and headed back to CONUS. This might all be innocent enough, but I don't know. I have a sense about this young sergeant that doesn't fit my impression of how someone with a security clearance should talk or act, particularly someone with a TS/SCI."

"All right, sir, I understand. I appreciate you bringing this to our attention. We have daily huddles, so I'll run it up the flagpole," the chief said as he rose from his chair to indicate we were done talking.

The chief took me back to the front desk, where I completed my out-processing at this office by obtaining a stamp and initials on my form. "Thank you," I said and headed off to the next checkbox on my list.

As far as I was concerned, I did my duty in reporting something I felt was out of character for someone with a security clearance. Sgt. Manley was now someone else's issue to deal with, though I didn't have a warm fuzzy about it being resolved. My immediate job right now was to finish clearing, and I hoped to do that with a vengeance.

CHAPTER 16

Redeployment to CONUS - Freedom Birds

I don't think I've ever cleared a military post faster than I did Camp Victory. I did it in just two days. The sun, moon and stars all lined up as well as the schedule of classes, briefings and assessments. I should also give credit to divine intervention and daily rosaries, too. By late Tuesday, June 30, my clearing papers had signatures, stamps and checkmarks in all the right boxes. I had my get-out-of-Dodge letter of release from the CENTCOM AOR memo for the airport and was mentally ready to depart. All I needed was a ride to BIAP to get on the Freedom Bird.

Wednesday, July 1, 2009, was my D-Day, as in departure from Iraq. Cmdr. Schroeder offered his NTV and PO Sanchez to drive me to BIAP, and I gratefully accepted. I spent the morning saying goodbye to friends I'd met, and avoiding the idiots and assholes I wished I hadn't.

Unfortunately, Capt. Mike Corso was in the Green Zone and unavailable to see in person, but I did talk with him on the phone. "How'd you work this out, Matt?" he asked with a hint of jealousy.

I remarked with hope, "Mike, if an old retiree can get downsized outta here, you can too."

"Yeah, OK, but Rangers Lead the Way. That's our job," he joked.

"You'll get there, my friend," I said.

"I hope so because I don't want to die of non-combat boredom," Mike said.

"You won't. Just think of this assignment as a LRRP[121] with an unknown ENDEX,"[122] I offered. "Just rely on those old rusty Ranger techniques."

"OK, bro. Happy trails and stay in touch," Mike said as we ended the call.

PO Sanchez came by my CHU in the early afternoon, and helped me lug my duffle bags from there and across the ditch bridge to his NTV parked on the frontage road. Thank God he did, because the heat was pushing over 110 degrees. I drove him back to work, where he left me the keys to the vehicle. We made plans to get together for pizza after he got off work before heading to BIAP.

PO Sanchez dropped me off at BIAP with plenty of time to spare. My protective angels were still on duty, having cleared my path right up to the counter. I spoke to the Air Force sergeant manning the check-in counter. "Good evening, Sergeant. I'm Captain Matt Jerome for your flight to Kuwait."

"I need your release documents, sir, and how many bags?"

"Three bags, Sergeant," I replied and handed over my letter.

The sergeant looked at his computer screen and started typing. When he was finished, he handed me three Air Mobility Command baggage claim tickets and said, "Sir, here's an example for filling out the baggage claims," as he pointed to a poster. "Please fill these out with your destination, KEZ on top, followed by your flight number, Moose 79-8 and from SDA. These show your bags are going from Baghdad International Airport to Ali Al Salem in Kuwait. You can then place one on each bag and place the bags on that cart over there."

---

121   LRRP: Long Range Reconnaissance Patrol (pronounced "LURP")
122   ENDEX: End of Exercise

"Will do and thank you," I replied.

The Air Force sergeant advised, "Sir, you'll also need to wear your body armor and helmet during the loading. Right now, we're still on track for wheels up at 2100 hours. Boarding call and loading should begin sometime after 2000 hours. We'll give you a fifteen-minute warning so you can put on your gear."

"Roger that, Sergeant," I said, and then placed my bags on the cart. Now unencumbered by the extra weight, I found a place to sit in the waiting area designated for flight Moose 79-8. All was right with the world.

True to their word, the Air Force gave a fifteen-minute warning. When it came time to exit the building for the aircraft, I hung back so I could be one of the last to get on the plane. It worked; I got to sit on a sidewall seat of the aircraft and not in the center pallet seats.

The center pallet seats had better cushions and might have been a little more comfortable if it weren't for wearing all your gear with no legroom. The sidewall seat allowed me to stretch out and get a bit of a snooze. The C-17 took off from BIAP on time and arrived at Ali Al Salem just over two hours later.

Upon exiting the comfortably air-conditioned C-17 at Ali Al Salem Air Base just after 2200 hours, we were greeted with stifling heat and more humidity than what we experienced in Baghdad. This slapped many of us back to reality. As the Air Force unloaded our baggage pallet, we wandered over to the lodging trailer.

"Does anyone know what the temp is here? This is more humid compared to Baghdad," someone asked from behind me.

"I checked before we left BIAP," someone else answered. "It was one hundred and two degrees and forty percent humidity at eight o'clock. It's gotta be somewhere near that. Forty percent humidity is about twice as much as it was in Baghdad. It's because we're a little closer to the gulf."

"Good evening, sir," the civilian at tent two said as he pushed a map in front of me and circled a couple of locations. "You are here and the bags from your aircraft will be right behind this tent. You need to go to tent three and check in with DCS[123] at the Outbound Desk for your manifested flight. After that you can retrieve your bags and flag down a Gator[124] to move them for you."

He then pointed to a row of tents on the map. "Feel free to find a bunk in any of these tents here. You can check in anytime with the Theater Gateway in tent one for your aircraft scheduling. If you're leaving on the next Freedom Flight this Saturday, July 4, that's pretty much an all-day event from early in the morning. The schedule for that will be posted inside the covered area here." He pointed to a place on the map outside tent three. "Got any questions, sir?"

---

123   DCS: Departure Control System
124   Gator: John Deere Gator (small ATV with a bed box for moving baggage)

"No. You've summed it up quite nicely. Thank you," I said and moved out.

I did exactly as instructed and confirmed my place on the July 4 Freedom Flight in tent three. I walked back and grabbed my bags and then placed them on an empty Gator with a driver. Another soldier did the same, and the three of us lit out for some bunk time in Tent City.

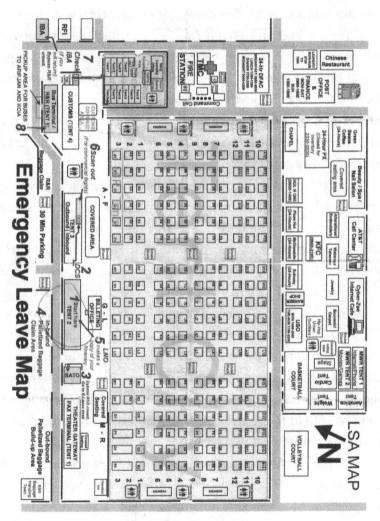

Figure 18: Ali Al Salem Air Base (LSA Map)

I had all day Thursday and Friday to do nothing while I waited for the manifest call on July 4. I got to sleep in on Thursday morning, but wasn't so lucky when a squad of Marines descended on my tent Thursday evening. They were all incoming replacements and fired up to get to wherever they were headed. *Oh well, I'll be outta here soon enough.*

That Thursday night in the tent, I had an interesting chat with another augmentee headed home from Basra. He related his story.

"Yeah, I had an assignment. As a civilian deputy sheriff, I volunteered for a position helping to guard prisoners. I thought I might be headed to Abu Ghraib or some other prisoner detention facility. When I checked in with the unit LNO at the Gateway, he said I was now needed down in Basra. The Brits had just pulled out of Basra and it was left to us to manage after their departure. I did cleanup duties down there."

I related my story about having three different jobs in my first forty-eight hours in-country. He then told me, "I had a fellow augmentee working for me in Basra who was supposed to be assisting with fire department training or some such. He did cleanup with me instead."

We wondered how many augmentees were basically reassigned as cannon fodder and placed wherever a warm body was needed.

"You know," I said to my new tent buddy, "the ideal situation is to place someone with the correct rank, the correct branch and the correct specialty within that branch to a specific duty assignment. I mean, that's what WIAS was supposed to do for the Army. Find the round peg to fit the round hole that you have in your organization. However, sometimes you can only get someone with the right branch, but not the specialty. That would be less than ideal, but certainly doable. The worst-case scenario is when you can only fill the position with someone holding the right rank, but who doesn't have the branch or specialty skills needed for the assignment. In other words, they need a warm body, *any* warm body to do the job.

That's what's happened in quite a few places, I've seen. They got square pegs and pounded them into their round holes."

On Friday morning after breakfast I wandered over to the MWR tents on the south side of the life support area (LSA) to see what kind of trouble I could get into. It wasn't a long walk, but it was a hot one as the temperature was already above 105 degrees with humidity. One of the Marines in my tent had warned everyone the night before.

"Tomorrow, guys, it's supposed to get to 115 degrees or worse. Wear your PT clothes." I was glad I took his advice.

Inside the MWR tents I saw about a dozen La-Z-Boy chairs set up with people watching a movie. What really intrigued me, though, were all the soldiers playing first-person-shooter (FPS) video games on Xbox consoles. *Call of Duty* seemed to be the game of choice. Did these guys not get enough adrenaline rush from the gallons of Red Bull they drank, the Red Man[125] they chewed, or the outside-the-wire patrols evading IED strikes? *It's a different generation for sure,* I thought.

I awoke early Saturday morning and cornered a Gator to move my bags down to the covered area behind tent three. The Air Force held a manifest formation for my Freedom Flight at 0600 to give everyone instructions for the day. An Air Force sergeant said, "If you haven't already done so, we need your baggage stacked over there." He pointed to an area on the side of the formation. "It'll be secured there until you return from breakfast. The next formation will be here at 0800 hours when you'll be turned over to the Navy Customs unit for processing.

"Since this is a commercial flight out of KWI,[126] we need a senior officer to serve as aircraft commander for the flight," the Air Force sergeant said casually.

I started thinking, *Doesn't the Air Force have a manifest for this flight that would tell them who the senior officer is?* I looked around

125   Red Man: Red Man chewing tobacco
126   KWI: Kuwait International Airport

and noticed several majors and a couple of lieutenant colonels standing in our formation, but all we heard were crickets.

The Air Force sergeant was a little more emphatic. "OK, I can't release you until we have an aircraft commander." There was still silence and no one was moving from the majors and lieutenant colonels in the formation.

About fifteen seconds had ticked off when the sergeant finally announced, "Look, any captain or above can be the aircraft commander."

I decided to jump on it. "I'll do it, Sergeant, since you can't find any suitable field-grade officer to step up for the job." I got a few looks from the assembled majors and lieutenant colonels.

The sergeant waved me over as he released the formation. "OK, see y'all back here at 0800 hours. Thank you, sir, I appreciate you taking this on," the sergeant said, somewhat relieved. "We used to automatically assign this duty to the most senior officer on the manifest, but because it's a civilian charter flight, we used to get some complaints. Why, I don't know, because it's not that big a deal. Needless to say, thank you."

"What do you need me to do?" I asked.

"The job is strictly accountability. Keep copies of the manifest with you to give to officials if requested. I'll give you some copies of the manifest when you get settled in the Navy's holding tents after you clear Customs. So, count the noses and herd the cats as needed from point A to point B. Obviously, if something happens, you'll be in charge at the scene. You have the authority to appoint an assistant. There's an Army first sergeant on this flight who should do well in that regard."

By 0800 hours the 109 people on my manifest were standing in formation back in the covered area behind tent three. A Navy senior chief addressed the formation.

"Good morning. I'm Senior Chief Anderson of the US Navy Customs Unit. We will be processing you and all your bags via tent four over there to your right. When I release you, you'll pick up all your bags and go to the covered area in front of the tent. You'll stage there as we bring you inside the Customs tent. I need the aircraft commander to come forward please."

I walked out of formation. "That's me, Senior Chief. What do you need me to do?"

The senior chief looked me over and then looked beyond me at the formation. He appeared confused.

"Sir, how'd you get stuck with the AC[127] duties? I see at least a half dozen or so senior officers in your flight."

I answered the senior chief with a wink. "I think they found out I'm a Mustang officer, so none of them stepped forward." I smiled.

The senior chief gave me a knowing smile and asked, "You were an NCO before?"

"Yup. I made it to E-7 before I went to the officer dark-side," I said.

The senior chief smiled again. "Well, sir, we will take care of your flight. Once your people get settled under the covered area with their bags, we'll take over and bring them inside to the conveyor belt metal detectors. Once the bags go through the detectors, they will bring their bags to a Customs officer at a sorting table. The Customs officer will ask questions and may or may not physically search the bag. The sorting tables are large enough for the bags to get dumped. After the bags have been checked, the Customs officer will tag the bags. The cleared bags can then be taken over to the back of the luggage truck for loading. If you'll provide me with a five-man crew for loading the truck, I will get them through Customs first."

"I can do that, Senior Chief. I've got a first sergeant as my deputy. He's already anticipated the need for a loading crew and identified volunteers. I think he's had a few deployments through here under his belt," I said.

"That's excellent, sir. Let's get this show on the road then."

127   AC: Aircraft commander

He addressed the formation. "OK. I understand you've already identified a baggage loading crew."

My first sergeant yelled out from the front of the formation, "Got it covered, Senior Chief. Where do you want us?"

"Hi, First Sergeant. Yeah. I need a minimum of five people to get their bags now and go to the metal detectors first. Once they're through, we'll start inspecting your main body."

"Roger that, Senior Chief," my deputy said. "Loading crew, grab your bags and follow me."

Seven soldiers left the formation, picked up their bags, and headed over to tent four along with the first sergeant.

The senior chief said to me, "Sir, I need you to get your bags and go through the metal detector right after the baggage crew."

"Will do," I replied and was off.

While the nine of us hobbled over to tent four with our bags and gear, the senior chief was briefing the rest of the formation on the Customs process inside the tent.

Being the AC or on the baggage loading crew had its privileges. The Navy Customs officers at the sorting tables mostly talked with us about contraband and asked probing questions.

My Customs inspector asked me to open one of my bags, and he pulled out my woobie, which was on top. He started to unfold it, stopped, and then gave it to me to put back in my bag. "You're clear, sir," the inspector said as he placed *cleared* Customs tags on my bag handles. "You can take those over to the baggage truck. Once you drop your bags, take your carry-on bags with you through the exit. Walk down the fenced path to the carry-on baggage metal detector. You'll get more instructions there."

Before I finished and walked out, I noticed three of the field-grade officers starting to dump their bags on sorting tables. I suspected this might be treatment reserved for officers or maybe just for the field grades. I didn't know and I didn't care. In either case, I was now quite happy that I had stepped forward to be the AC.

I walked to another smaller tent where I noticed a few discarded contraband items dumped near the entrance. There in plain view was a smoke grenade, an empty thirty-round M-16 magazine, a bayonet and a large pocketknife. Obviously, these were in someone's carry-on bag, and when they realized these bags would go through a metal detector and a search it was time to get rid of them.

I spoke to the chief inside the carry-on baggage tent. "Chief, you've got some contraband on the ground outside the entrance."

He looked at me and said, "Yes, sir. I suspected as much. We'll get to it after your manifest comes through. That stuff is from an earlier outbound flight, and we'll just get it all when we're done. The path is considered an amnesty area if they drop it before coming in here. However, if we find it inside this tent, there's hell to pay."

The chief was finished with my carry-on bags and said, "You're clear, sir. You can go relax in one of the tents through there. It's supposed to get to one hundred and twenty degrees or more today, so stay cool."

My first sergeant directed everyone to the same tent for accountability. We had over 100 people inside this Temper[128] tent while the temperature outside approached 117 degrees with nearly 40 percent humidity. Even with the higher humidity, the sweat evaporated instantly, leaving salt stains on clothes over time. Although our tent was air-conditioned, the air inside the tent never dropped below ninety-five degrees. OK. Arizona didn't get this bad, and besides, in Arizona it's a dry heat unless it's during the monsoon season of June through September.

Sometime after lunch, we did a headcount and discovered a few people missing. They couldn't have gone far, so we started checking the other tents. A couple of the lieutenant colonel doctors had decided it was cooler in a different tent. We were still missing one staff sergeant. Could not find her anywhere in the restricted tent area.

---

128   TEMPER: Tent, Extendable Modular Personnel (Temper)

I found the Air Force representative. "Sarge, I'm missing someone from the manifest." I gave him her name.

He looked at me, puzzled. "I assume you've checked all the tents, sir."

"That we did," I said.

"I'll have to check this out up front, sir. I'll get back to you," he replied and promptly left via a locked gate.

The Air Force sergeant returned about forty-five minutes later and found me trying to stay cool inside our tent. "Sir, I found your missing person. She's not missing really, but was pulled from your flight at the last minute."

"Pulled from the flight, but not the manifest you gave me before lunch," I said with a bit of sarcasm.

"Yes, sir. Sorry about that. No one told me either," the sergeant added sheepishly.

"Thank you for tracking that down. I'll inform my first sergeant," I said.

"Hey, Top. Have I got a story for you."

A few hours later, the Navy formed us up and marched the group to a locked exit gate. On the other side of the gate were three buses and our locked baggage truck.

The first sergeant and I posted ourselves at the gate to count noses and names. Another Navy chief unlocked the gate and started toward the closest bus. "You can send them through, Captain," he said. We loaded the buses and headed out for the hour-long ride to KWI and our Freedom Flight.

The buses drove us right up to the aircraft. Top immediately got his baggage crew off the bus to start loading the bags aboard the aircraft. While we assembled the rest of the main body in a formation, a group of four men in uniform—three Army lieutenant colonels and one Air Force sergeant—exited a nearby vehicle and approached me.

"Are you the aircraft commander for this flight, sir?" the Air Force sergeant asked.

"Yes, I am. Good evening, sir," I said to the senior officer walking toward me.

"We don't want to be a bother, Captain, but we've been added to your flight at the last minute," one of the lieutenant colonels said. "We have no checked baggage."

"That's not a problem, sir," I replied. "Once the bags get loaded, we'll be boarding the enlisted members first and then the officers. If you can just add your names to my manifest, since I'll need them for accountability."

"That's perfectly fine with us. We just need to get back to CONUS," the lieutenant colonel said as he took my copy of the manifest and motioned for the others to step back to the car so they could write in their names.

I looked at the Air Force sergeant. "I assume you already have their names for your official manifest?"

"Yes, sir, I do," the staff sergeant said as he followed the others back to the car.

I motioned for my first sergeant to come over, and I told him, "Hey, Top, change three to Plan B. We now have three more PAX[129] on the manifest with no checked bags. It's those colonels over there. By the way, when you've got the bags loaded, your crew boards first, followed by the other enlisted, and then the officers will board last. I hope our other field-grade officers get shitty seats. You and I need seats together up near the front of the plane. I'll be the last person to board, counting all the little ducks who board before me."

Our Freedom Flight left on time headed for Shannon, Ireland. After the requisite refueling and potty breaks, we left Shannon headed almost due west. We ultimately landed briefly at McGuire Air Force Base in New Jersey to drop off about half of the plane, including the three lieutenant colonels we picked up at KWI. We

129   PAX: Passengers

took off again, headed to our last stop—at Lawson Army Airfield, Fort Benning.

The cheer went up in the aircraft cabin when we finally touched down at Benning. Although everyone was whupped by the amount of time in the air, you could hardly tell it from their attitude.

I made sure everyone left the plane, which wasn't very hard to do, and I checked the cabin for anything left behind as the last person out the door and down the stairs.

We arrived at the Benning airfield on Sunday morning, July 5, primarily so that we could go immediately to CIF to turn in clothes, equipment and weapons. When we got to the CIF, the facility manager said to our assembled formation, "We have some very good news for y'all today. All weapons can be turned in first . . . without being cleaned. We have a volunteer group that wants to do that for you. Once your weapon is signed in, you can then proceed to the other CIF stations to do your turn-in."

Being able to turn in dirty weapons got a big cheer, too.

When all was said and done, I got away from CIF owing only $30 because they would not accept a commercial duffle bag for my turn-in. Oh well. I got off cheap.

I decided I would not live in the overcrowded barracks of the CRC. I phoned a nearby friend in Columbus. "Hiya, Mark. I'm back from Iraq and need to get a rental car. So, I need a favor."

"Sure, Matt, and welcome back," Mark said.

"While I was deployed, I got an alert from USAA about my credit card. It was my only credit card and USAA canceled it. I could really use a ride to the rental car place, but I also need a credit card to get the car. I tried to use my wife's card, but they won't do it without her being present. She's in South Carolina right now. I just need your card to get the rental. When I turn the car in, I'll use her card to pay for it."

Mark, a retired first sergeant and military policeman with several deployments himself, understood completely. "You must be at CRC right now?" he asked.

"You got it," I said excitedly. "I'm going to ditch this place for a hotel, too. Monday is a training holiday because of the Fourth, so I'm going to sleep in a comfortable bed for a change and not come back till Tuesday!"

"No problem, man. I can be there in forty minutes and we can catch up on the way to the rental car," Mark said.

I spent the next two glorious nights at a local motel sleeping on a king-size bed with clean sheets and a bathroom. *God is good, all the time!*

I arrived at Building 4628, Redeployment, Company E at CRC on Tuesday morning to begin the final stretch of out-processing from the Army. The training schedule showed we would be done by Friday.

God's scheduling angels were at it again on my behalf. I'd be able to leave Fort Benning, Georgia, and drive to Columbia, South Carolina, on Friday, July 10. I would meet up with Sara and Christine, and then we would all drive over to surprise Lea at her family event the night before graduation.

Hardly ever before had a plan come together so smoothly when it involved the Army. It was almost uncanny that just about every time I needed something to go according to plan and schedule this past six weeks, it did.

My good friend told me, "Matt, it's no coincidence that things are coming together. It's a God wink just to let you know He's personally involved." I'd never heard of a God wink before, but it sounded appropriate.

The week of out-processing was filled with more God winks. Because I had a rental car, I asked if anyone needed a ride to South Carolina on Friday. A fellow officer said, "Hell yeah!" He even split the cost of the car and the fuel, and helped drive.

Besides a couple of classes at the Company E building, we traveled to other places to out-process. We visited the SRP building for a medical review and another PDHA evaluation with a health care professional. They also took care of making sure our personnel records were up to date for service time and the issuance of a DD-Form 214 discharge document.

A trip over to the finance office provided us the opportunity to sit, prepare and submit for travel pay. It wouldn't be much money, since quarters and meals were provided. Still, I could go buy a Happy Meal at McDonald's with my travel pay.

I got a really nice God wink at my visit to the travel office to arrange a flight home. I have to admit they were very accommodating with my wanting to fly home from Columbia instead of Atlanta. When I told the travel lady my plans for surprising my daughter at her Basic Training graduation on July 11, she worked her magic. She couldn't get me on the same flight as my wife and other daughter, but that was OK. We were all going home close together.

By 9 a.m. on Friday, July 10, my car rental buddy and I were off. When we crossed over into South Carolina, my friend drove the rest of the way to his house. We arrived just after 1 p.m.; I dropped him off and then drove another hour until I got to Sara's hotel in Columbia. She opened the door to her room, and we embraced tightly.

"God, you feel good," I whispered in her ear as we held each other for all we were worth.

Christine stood nearby just a little embarrassed at us. "Hey, get a room. Oh, that's right, you already have one," she said. We laughed.

Christine continued. "I hate to break this up, but we need to get ready to go to Lea's family event."

"OK, OK," I said. "How much does Lea know?"

Christine replied. "She just thinks Mom's coming. She doesn't know about you or me. This is going to be a total surprise. We really need to get going soon."

We grabbed the directions to the event and left the hotel. It took us about a half hour to get there and get parked. The parking lot for the family event was filled and we could see Lea's class in formation.

We walked across the parking lot towards the formation as the soldiers were dismissed. It didn't take long for us to find Lea; at five foot nine inches tall she was much taller than most of her classmates.

"Hey! What are you all doin'? I wasn't expecting all of you," Lea said as she hugged us in succession—Mom, Christine and then me.

"How did you get here?" Lea asked me. "I thought you were in Baghdad."

I told her, "They violated my contract. I told them they didn't have the woodshop I was promised, so they had to send me home."

We all had a good laugh over that.

"Seriously, though, they really didn't need me. Obama started turning over everything to the Iraqis and we're leaving the cities, so I asked to come home. I only had four different jobs while I was there. I think KP[130] was next on the list. Also, I kind of screwed up my other hip in training and it's not getting any better. I was kind of hobbling around. I'm sure it'll need to be fixed, too."

"Oh, that sucks. I hate to say it, but let's get something to eat. I'm starving!" Lea said. "The company has a buffet set up inside."

"Spoken like a true Basic trainee who has been starved for almost three months and given only five minutes to eat," I said.

The next day, we watched Lea march with her Basic Training company during graduation ceremonies. Next stop for her, Fort Sam, Houston, Texas.

"I love it when a plan comes together," I said to Sara and Christine. "Six weeks ago, I would not have given any odds of me being here today. God works in strange ways."

My left hip only got worse after I got back from Iraq. My orthopedic surgeon, who cleared me to go back on active duty in 2008, could not believe what he saw. He said to me, "What did you do over there? When I checked you out last year, you had some osteoarthritis, but

---

130   KP: Kitchen Patrol

I never thought you'd have this kind of deterioration. We are going to need to do another hip resurfacing. Are you up for it?"

"Let's schedule it," I said.

This time around, the surgeon decided to irradiate my hip before surgery to prevent the growth of post-surgical spurs. "Whatever," I told him.

While recovering from surgery and doing not much more than physical therapy, I had a lot of time to surf the net. That's when I found the *Iraq War Logs*.

I told Sara, "Honey you've got to hear this. WikiLeaks just published to the internet some classified material from the time I was working in Iraq. They're calling it the *Iraq War Logs*. I checked their website and looked at some of these documents. They published the same secret SIGACTs that I used in preparing my presentations. To say I'm stunned would be an understatement. I mean, this is really an OMG and WTF moment."

I kept on. "I spent a couple of hours going through these logs because I just couldn't believe it. How in the hell did this happen? You know I told you about that Sergeant Manley guy and how he said he was concerned about possible war atrocities?"

Sara looked stunned. "Yes, I remember something about him. You said he didn't act like someone with a security clearance." She looked over my shoulder at the computer monitor.

"Yeah. He's the one. I wonder if he's involved. I dropped a dime on him to counter-intelligence when I cleared Victory, but have no idea what or if they did anything with it. This is really FUBAR stuff, honey. I was just getting to the point where I had put a lot of those memories away, and now this announcement just brings all that shit to the front burner. Manley just seemed a little too concerned about what he read. That is the wrong way to look at classified material. Do not make judgments about the content unless it's your job to make a judgment. Plus, he talked about it to others like me; another wrong answer. Well. Whoever did this will get caught. Chief Smallwood told me that the digital classified documents system keeps excellent records.

"Tell me, honey," I asked, "should I call the FBI or the Army Criminal Investigation Command and talk to them? You know, Henry used to work for CID when he was up in Sacramento. Maybe I'll ask him."

"If you want my advice, you already told the authorities back in Baghdad," Sara said. "You've done your duty, you've come home injured, you're recovering and you should concentrate on yourself right now. You don't need the stress that might come with this. They will get whoever it is, you said."

"Honey, guess what? The Army just arrested Sgt. Barry Manley on May 27, 2010, on various charges surrounding those *Iraq War Logs* published by WikiLeaks," I said almost triumphantly. "I had a feeling something wasn't right with him."

Old soldiers never die. They just go back to retired status.

AUTHOR'S CLOSING NOTE

More than 450 US military personnel were killed in action in Iraq during 2009. That ominous number escalated from month to month after President Obama's announcement in April 2009 during his visit to Baghdad that the US would start turning over everything to the Iraqis. The casualties increased even as we implemented the president's decision to withdraw our forces from Iraqi cities. It wasn't until December 2009 that there was a significant drop in casualties.

A very poignant memory and lesson for me occurred with the April 10 SVBIED attack on the 1-67 Armor convoy—the attack that killed five soldiers. I was relatively new in the job and did my best to help create the presentation for that attack. I did the detailed research, analysis, and documentation, but I didn't keep the details far enough away from me. I should have known better because the mind, your imagination and the memories can become quite real. I wasn't prepared for the intensely personal hero salute of those soldiers after knowing the intimate minutiae of the attack wherein they all perished. I tried to do better, but it was difficult while having to document attacks with nearly a KIA each day.

Another vivid and long-lasting memory surrounds the fratricide incident at the Camp Liberty Combat Stress Clinic on April 11, 2009, in which five military personnel were murdered by one of our own soldiers. That soldier was serving on his third deployment to Iraq and the fifth deployment while in service. I had my own appointment with a CSC that day when this incident occurred, and I remember clearly trying to call my clinic, only to be blocked. After finally getting through to someone, I learned something very bad had happened.

My faith in the military's health care system was badly shaken after I was overprescribed an anti-inflammatory medicine for my damaged hip. I heard other stories of polypharmacy[131] prescriptions being easily written and dispensed for anxiety, depression, sleep disorders and other ailments; and I heard about the killings at the CSC. *Just give them some more pills and keep them on duty.* Did the military's mental health safety net have some holes in it?

As reported in the *Fort Hood Herald*, August 29, 2012, by Elliott Blair Smith of Bloomberg News, "The military and the nation were not prepared for the mental-health needs from being in combat for more than a decade," said retired colonel Elspeth Ritchie, the top psychiatric official in the Army's Office of the Surgeon General from 2005 to 2010, in an interview. "We now confront ourselves with a mental-health crisis that is a legacy of war."

This legacy remains as our country deals with a suicide rate of twenty to twenty-two veterans each day. As reported on the *Stars and Stripes* website, in an article by Nikki Wentling, published on June 20, 2018, the "VA has now revealed the average daily number of veteran suicides has always included deaths of active-duty service members and members of the National Guard and Reserve, not just veterans."

The other item which struck me upside the head while serving in Iraq was the proliferation of non-military contractors and sub-contractors in all manner of both logistical support as well as combat and security operations, a topic for another book. It struck me that the business of war was actually a business. Scary. Go research President Eisenhower's warning about the military-industrial complex.

In my opinion, the real-life situation involving Sgt. Bradley Manning and his theft of classified information that he uploaded to WikiLeaks should not have been possible. It should never have

---

131   Polypharmacy: The concurrent prescription and use of multiple medications by a patient

happened. The Army arrested him *only* after someone outside the military alerted them. He was caught because he had disclosed to others what he had done.

I believe there was a failure of leadership and supervision of Sgt. Manning's activities. It appears no one ever verified his "need to know" before he accessed those files to view and copy. Perhaps a supervisor figured, "He's got a top-secret clearance. He knows the rules." Manning also showed some signs of instability that a leader should have picked up.

During Manning's court-martial, the court learned there was nothing to stop Manning or other intelligence analysts from installing software for high-speed download of classified information. There was little oversight on installing programs on workstations with access to classified materials.

Additionally, a lax working atmosphere allowed analysts like Manning to listen to music or watch movies from classified storage drives or personal computers while on duty. As reported by Reuters, July 8, 2013, one of Manning's supervisors, a Capt. David Lim, said he encouraged analysts to read State Department cables and other classified materials to avoid "tunnel vision." This appears to be a total violation of the "need to know" requirement for access to classified materials.

This lackadaisical approach to accessing and handling classified information set the stage for Manning to copy these files and expose them. It looks like his command did not take the job of information security and classified information handling very seriously. *Familiarity breeds contempt* seems like an apt definition of what happened. If they had established a work environment steeped in the seriousness of the duties and commensurate with safeguarding national security interests, maybe Manning would have thought twice before committing his crimes.

The website WikiLeaks in early 2010 started publishing over 400,000 classified files known as the *Iraq War Logs*, which the site obtained from Manning, a US Army intelligence analyst who served in Iraq during 2009–2010. Unrelated to the WikiLeaks exposure of classified information, the United Kingdom arrested WikiLeaks founder, Julian Assange, in April 2019 and removed him from the Ecuador embassy in London.

Classified battlefield reports known as SIGACTs comprise the bulk of the *Iraq War Logs* Sgt. Manning provided to WikiLeaks. These same SIGACTs formed the foundation of classified PowerPoint presentations that I created during my deployment to Baghdad at the same time Sgt. Manning served in Iraq. This public exposure of sensitive secret information of which I had intimate knowledge shook my confidence in an institution, the US Army, in which I had served honorably and retired.

My friend RMC(SS)[132] Roger Lynch, USN (Ret), served multiple deployments to Vietnam piloting river boats in the Mekong Delta. He was in the shit a lot. During my Operation Iraqi Freedom (OIF) deployment in 2009, I, on the other hand, read, analyzed, sorted, cataloged, and presented the shit later found in those stolen Iraq SIGACTs.

The disturbing security compromise by someone with a top-secret clearance calls into question the training, values and indoctrination the Army provided Manning as an intelligence analyst. One would also wonder how the intensely thorough FBI background investigation which granted that high-level clearance missed obvious character and integrity flaws.

We later learned it wasn't all Manning. Leadership attitudes about security classification and safeguarding files appeared nonchalant and cavalier in Manning's unit. Manning's court-martial heard evidence of the failure of leadership to supervise and manage the intelligence analysts. Manning boldly accessed these documents over several months and downloaded them to an SD card with little concern about being caught. The failure of leadership and lax

132 RMC(SS): Radioman Senior Chief Petty Officer

work environment in Manning's intelligence unit in Iraq created an atmosphere of familiarity where he could pursue this treasonous activity with near impunity.

It should be noted that the military only became aware of Manning's activities after a civilian hacker brought him to the Army's attention. With all the money being spent on civilian contractors and security experts in Iraq, how did this compromise slip through the cracks?

During my deployment as a retiree recalled to active duty, I too witnessed similar attitudes in the JOC work environment. I served with members of the other branches of service, and I can say the work environment was far from collegial or security conscious in my opinion. In the book, I downplay the lack of a mutually respectful and highly competitive work atmosphere as it would overshadow the rest of the story. At times I observed downright demeaning and unprofessional interactions between so-called leaders and subordinates. The Operations sergeant major in the JOC even remarked to me one day, "The JOC can be a meat grinder at times."

Loyalty and camaraderie were hard to find with the disparate services and turnover of transient people from the JOC. Even a warning sign posted on the wall inside the JOC seemed to set the stage for this atmosphere. The sign read something like, "There is no drinking, food or fun in the JOC." Consequently, people focused on work, keeping their heads down, avoiding contact, and then getting out.

As an augmentee in a mixed-service workforce, I resembled a worker brought in to help with the Christmas workload crunch—someone to be used and abused without exception or recourse, then let go when the "season" was over. My analogy in the book describing the rowing of a galley ship like slaves, a la *Ben Hur,* reflects my and others' attitude toward the job.

The WikiLeaks publication of the *Iraq War Logs* bothered me, but confirmed my suspicions of the work environment I experienced which took too much for granted—security, knowledge, experience, trust and loyalty. An assumption existed that if someone worked in the JOC, that person must have been cleared to do so and knew the security rules.

In this book, I highlight shortcomings of leadership, attitude and management via my own deployment experiences, events and situations. These have been dramatized for effect and understandability. To tie in with the current 2019 event involving WikiLeaks and the Julian Assange arrest, I also describe how the stealing of the Iraq SIGACTs *may have* occurred and should have been discovered.

For those who may have served with Multinational Corps-Iraq (MNC-I)—chairborne Rangers, backseat advisers and weekend wannabe soldiers—who might launch into nitpicking the details in this book of how something was done or not done, happened or didn't happen, just don't even go there.

Except for the real KIAs mentioned in the book, the characters, their names and positions are all fictional composites created for dramatic ambiance. Any resemblance to actual people living or dead is purely coincidental. When possible and necessary, I relate some events as I experienced and remember, being sure not to compromise any classified information.

The president of the United States signed Executive Order 13912 on March 27, 2020, authorizing a "Partial Mobilization" for up to one million military reserve personnel to active duty in response to the COVID-19 virus. The last executive order for a reserve call-up occurred *after 9/11* and authorized a "Presidential Reserve Call-Up" for a maximum of 200,000 personnel.

A week prior to the president's executive order, the Army's deputy chief of staff, G-1 (Personnel) LTG Thomas C. Seamands at the Army Human Resources Command (HRC), sent out a message to retirees seeking members willing to assist with the Army's COVID-19 response. The general highlighted the need for health care specialties. Accordingly, I submitted my name as willing to help with a local assignment at Fort Huachuca or Davis-Monthan Air Force Base.

On April 17, 2020, I received a phone call from a major at the HRC who asked if I would volunteer for another retiree recall in my medical service corps specialty. I told him I might be able if the assignment were local, but he informed me it would be at Fort Dix. New Jersey, so I had to respectfully decline.

My interaction with HRC for a possible second retiree recall prompts more questions as to the state of Army personnel readiness. There is nothing special about me or my previous military or civilian health care career. I possess no special certifications or skills that should be difficult to find elsewhere on active duty. In fact, I've been retired from the civilian side of health care since 2004 and retired from the Army twenty-four years ago. I last wore a uniform during my retiree recall in 2009. It's incomprehensible that the Army could not find a medical service corps officer to fill the Fort Dix assignment. Instead, they reach out to a sixty-four-year-old retiree and are willing to relocate him and his family to a duty assignment 2,400 miles away on the other side of the country. Seriously?

I hope you enjoyed the book well enough to post a positive review on Amazon and/or Goodreads.

ACKNOWLEDGMENTS

Marc Marcantonio, LTC, USA, Retired – For nearly forty years of mentoring and providing a source of strength, honesty, friendship, intellect and steadfast support . . . not to mention some great fishing expeditions over the years, and a box of much-needed cigars when I was deployed to Iraq.

Henry Sanchez, 1SG, USA, Retired – For nearly forty years as my friend, brother-in-arms, and for the care packages when I was deployed!

Roger Lynch – For your Vietnam service and encouragement to write this book and stick with it.

Joseph Sorrentino, Retired Judicial Officer – For providing your advice and feedback during the drafting of the manuscript.

GLOSSARY OF ACRONYMS, SLANG, AND TERMS

Term	Explanation or Definition
AAR	After-Action-Report or After-Action Review
AC	Aircraft Commander
ACU	Army Combat Uniform
ANC	Army Nurse Corps officer
AOC	Area of Concentration
AOR	Area of Responsibility
APFT	Advanced Physical Fitness Test
ARPC	Army Reserve Personnel Command
ASVAB	Armed Services Vocational Aptitude Battery test to determine training suitability.
BDA	Battle Damage Assessment
BIAP	Baghdad International Airport
Boonie Hat	Formally designated as "Hat, Sun, Hot Weather"
Buehring	A US military base in Kuwait known as Camp Buehring
C-1	Assistant Chief of Staff for Personnel at a Combined Service HQ
CAC	The military ID card is called a Common Access Card
CAS CUBE	Acronym pronunciation for Combined Arms Services Staff School or CAS3
CAS3	Combined Arms Services and Staff School (pronounced "Cass Cube")
CC	Carbon Copy (an email feature to provide a copy to an additional recipient)
CCIR	Commander's Critical Information Requirements

CENTCOM	Central Command
CF	Copy Furnished
CHOPS	Chief of Operations
CHU	Containerized Housing Unit
CI	Counter-Intelligence
CIF	Consolidated Issue Facility for uniforms, equipment, etc.
CIWS	Close-In Weapon System (pronounced "Sea Whiz")
Class IV	Military supply class designation for construction materials, including installed equipment and all fortification and barrier Materials
COB	Close of Business
COIN	Counter Insurgency
Combined Arms Services and Staff School	Also known as CAS3 (pronounced "CAS CUBE")
Company Grade Officer	Army Officer Pay Grades O-1 thru O-3 (Second Lieutenant thru Captain)
COP	Combat Outpost
Copysette manifold	A two-part, lightweight paper that resembled 'onion-skin' with an attached piece of carbon paper. After typing, the attached carbon part of the copysette pages could be pulled out all at once.
CPU	Central Processing Unit
CPX	Command Post Exercise
C-RAM	Counter-Rocket, Artillery Mortar defense system
C-ration TP	A small folded-up packet of toilet paper found in the accessory condiments packet.

CRC	CONUS Replacement Center where individuals report for training and equipping prior to deployment as a replacement
Crop-Dusting	The subtle art of passing gas while walking
CSI	Crime Scene Investigation
CTT/WTT	Common Task Training/Warrior Task Training
CV	Curriculum Vitae
DCHOPS	Deputy Chief of Operations
DCS	Departure Control System
DFAC	Dining Facility (pronounced "Dee Fac")
Di di mau	Vietnamese for "Go quickly" (pronounced "Dee Dee mau")
Distro	Slang for distribution list
DPTMS	Directorate for Plans, Training, Mobilization and Security
DSN	Defense Switched Network telephone or data communications number
ENDEX	End of Exercise
EOD	Explosive Ordnance Disposal
EPSQ	Electronic Personnel Security Questionnaire
Erste und schnell	German for "first and fast"
EW	Electronic Warfare
EWO	Electronic Warfare Officer
FAC	Forward Air Controller who manages airspace and aircraft operating in a given area
Field Grade Officer	Army Officer Pay Grades O-4 thru O-6 (Major thru Colonel)
FNG	Fuckin' New Guy
FOB	Forward Operating Base

FORSCOM	United States Forces Command (pronounced "Force Com")
FPS	First-Person Shooter (video games with a behind-the-gun first-person perspective)
Front Leaning Rest	Push-up position
FUBAR	Fucked Up Beyond All Recognition
Gator	John Deere Gator (small ATV with a bed box for moving baggage)
GB	Gigabyte
GITMO	Slang for Guantanamo Bay Naval Base (pronounced "Git Mo")
Green Zone	The most common name for the International Zone of Baghdad.
HMMWV	High Mobility Multipurpose Wheeled Vehicle, Humvee, or HUMMER
HUMMER	Aka HUMVEE
IBA	Individual Body Armor system
IED	Improvised Explosive Device
IMA	Individual Mobilization Augmentee
INFOSEC	Information Security
Intel	Intelligence
IOTV	Improved Outer Tactical Vest which replaced Individual Body Armor (IBA)
IRR	Individual Ready Reserve
ISF	Iraqi Security Forces
ISR	Intelligence, Surveillance, Reconnaissance
J-2	Directorate for Intelligence, J-2 (aka Joint Staff Intelligence)
JOC	Joint Operations Center
JTF-GITMO	Joint Task Force Guantanamo
JWICS	Joint Worldwide Intelligence Communications System (pronounced "Jay Wix")

KIA	Killed in Action
Klick	Military slang term for a kilometer
KP	Kitchen Patrol
KWI	Kuwait International Airport
LD	Line of Departure is a point on the battlefield where forces cross/leave friendly lines into a possible Line of Contact with the enemy.
LNO	Liaison Officer
LRRP	Long-Range Reconnaissance Patrol (pronounced "Lurp")
LSA	Life Support Area (area of a military post or base camp that provides food, lodging, recreation and other activities)
MASH	Mobile Army Surgical Hospital
McChord	McChord Air Force Base
Medical Service Corps	aka MSC. A branch designation of the Army Medical Department for health care administrators
MND-Baghdad	Multinational Division-Baghdad
MND-C	Multinational Division-Center
MND-N	Multinational Division-North
MND-S	Multinational Division-South
MND-SE	Multinational Division-Southeast
MND-W	Multinational Division-West
MNF-I	Multinational Force-Iraq (Coalition Forces)
MOBIC	Meloxicam, a nonsteroidal anti-inflammatory drug
MOS	Military Occupational Specialty
MP	Military Police
MRAP	Mine-Resistant Ambush Protected Vehicle (pronounced "Em Rap")
MRE	Meals, Ready to Eat

MSC	Medical Service Corps
MSO	Military Service Obligation
MWR	Morale, Welfare and Recreation
NCOIC	Non-Commissioned Officer in Charge
New York	A US military base in Kuwait known as Camp New York
NIPRNet	Non-classified Internet Protocol Router Network (a computer network for storing and accessing non-classified information)
NOMEX	A flame-retardant material popularly used to make clothing for pilots and air crews
NTV	Non-tactical vehicle. Usually a Toyota or Mitsubishi SUV
OAC	Officer Advanced Course
OBC	Officer Basic Course
OCONUS	Outside Continental United States (pronounced "Oh Cone Us")
OCS	Officer Candidate School
OD	Olive drab colored
OEF	Operation Enduring Freedom (Afghanistan)
OIC	Officer in Charge
OIF	Operation Iraqi Freedom
OJT	On-the-Job Training
OPS	Operations
OPSEC	Operations Security
OPTEMPO	Operations Tempo
PAD	Patient Administration Division
PAX	Passengers
PC	Patrol Cap (similar to a baseball cap)
PCS	Permanent Change of Station (relocation status of a duty assignment)

PDHA	Post-Deployment Health Assessment
PKM	A 7.62mm general purpose machine gun made by the USSR
POI	Point of Impact: where a munition lands (pronounced "Pee Oh Eye")
Polypharmacy	The concurrent use of multiple medications by a patient
POO	Point of Origin: where a munition is launched from, i.e. a rocket or artillery fire (pronounced "Pooh")
PowerPoint	Microsoft Office PowerPoint presentation software
PowerPoint Ranger	Slang term for people whose sole duty is to create graphic presentations or briefings using Microsoft's PowerPoint program
PRC	Presidential Reserve Call-Up order
PSD	Personal Security Detachment
R&R	Rest & Recuperation
Red Man	Red Man chewing tobacco
RFI	Rapid Fielding Initiative, a program designed to put the newest military gear directly into the hands of those deploying overseas
Rhino	An armored bus for transportation to the Green Zone (the most common name for the International Zone of Baghdad)
RIF	Reduction in Force
RMC(SS)	Radioman Senior Chief Petty Officer
ROE	Rules of Engagement
SAPI	Acronym for Small Arms Protective Inserts made of a ceramic trauma plate (pronounces "Sap E")

SCIF	Sensitive Compartmentalized Information Facility (a classified information facility pronounced "Skiff")
SDNCO	Staff Duty Non-Commissioned Officer
SecDef	Secretary of Defense
SERE	Survival, Evasion, Resistance and Escape
SF-86	Standard Form 86, a security clearance questionnaire for beginning a security clearance investigation
SIGACT	Acronym for "Significant Activity," a standard battlefield report (pronounced "Sig Act")
SIPRNet	Secret Internet Protocol Router Network (a computer network for storing and accessing "secret" classified information)
Smadge	Slang nickname for Sergeant Major
SOFA	Status of Forces Agreement
SOP	Standard Operating Procedure
Spec Four	US Army rank of Specialist 4 in pay grade E-4
Spidey-Sense	Spider-Man's super power
SQL	Structured Query Language is a standard database language
SRP	Soldier Readiness Processing (a system to ensure members meet medical and administrative standards before deployment overseas to combat zones)
STB	Special Troops Battalion is an organization for managing and accounting of members in Corps-level headquarters units
SVBIED	Suicide Vehicle-Borne Improvised Explosive Device (pronounced "Ess Vee Bid")
SVIED	Suicide Vest Improvised Explosive Device (pronounced "Ess Vid")

SWAG	Acronym for a "Scientific (or Silly) Wild-Ass Guess"
SWEG	Acronym for a "Silly Wild Educated Guess"
TBI	Traumatic Brain Injury
TEMPER	Tent, Extendable Modular Personnel (Temper)
Terp	Slang nickname for an interpreter
TIC	Troops in Contact report
TMC	Troop Medical Clinic (aka medical dispensary)
TMI	Too Much Information
TO&E	Table of Organization and Equipment
TOC	Tactical Operations Center usually at brigade and lower levels
TS/SCI	Top Secret/Sensitive Compartmented Information
TTPs	Tactics, Techniques and Procedures
T-wall	Concrete blast wall shaped like an upside-down T
USAR	United States Army Reserve
VA	Department of Veterans Affairs (Federal)
V-Device	V-Device on military awards denotes "For Valor"
WIA	Wounded in Action
WIAS	Worldwide Individual Augmentee System (pronounced "Why As")
Woobie	Camouflaged poncho liner

CPSIA information can be obtained
at www.ICGtesting.com
Printed in the USA
FSHW011521161020
74818FS